WATERS OF DESTRUCTION

WATERS OF
DESTRUCTION

Leslie Karst

**SEVERN
HOUSE**

First world edition published in Great Britain and the USA in 2025
by Severn House, an imprint of Canongate Books Ltd,
14 High Street, Edinburgh EH1 1TE.

severnhouse.com

Cover and jacket design by Piers Tilbury.

British Library Cataloguing-in-Publication Data
A CIP catalogue record for this title is available from the British Library.

ISBN-13: 978-1-4483-1218-4 (cased)
ISBN-13: 978-1-4483-1219-1 (e-book)

MIX
Paper | Supporting
responsible forestry
FSC
www.fsc.org   FSC® C013056

Typeset by Palimpsest Book Production Ltd.,
Falkirk, Stirlingshire, Scotland.
Printed and bound in Great Britain by
TJ Books, Padstow, Cornwall.

Praise for the Orchid Isle mysteries

"A series that will go on my must read list!"
New York Times bestselling author Deborah Crombie

"An entertaining cozy series launch. Karst rewards armchair travelers without ignoring the thorny politics of Hawaiian tourism, and firmly grounds the core mystery in Valerie's emotional struggles. Readers will be hungry for the sequel"
Publishers Weekly

"Part murder mystery, part vividly evocative,
colorful sketch of Hawaii . . . Armchair travelers
and mystery aficionados alike will find it entertaining"
Booklist

"A gorgeous yet deadly setting, a tenacious amateur sleuth,
and a real head-scratcher of a mystery. Will leave readers
longing for their next trip to the Orchid Isle"
New York Times bestselling author Jenn McKinlay

"As mysterious as a Hilo rain, fragrant as lychee, melodious as
Hawaiian pidgin, and tasty as loco moco, Leslie Karst's
Molten Death transports the reader to the best that the Big
Island can offer. You won't want to leave!"
USA Today bestselling author Naomi Hirahara

"With its compelling characters and engaging look at the
culture and customs of the Big Island of Hawai'i, *Molten
Death* is a delightfully immersive whodunnit. Fans of
well-plotted, suspenseful mysteries with a foodie
element will eat this one up!"
New York Times bestselling author Kate Carlisle

To my readers: without you, there'd be no reason to write.

A note about Hawaiian grammar and language: I have used the spelling and punctuation routinely employed currently in the Hawaiian Islands. The *'okina*, or glottal stop ['], as in the word 'Hawai'i,' is similar to the break between the syllables in 'uh-oh.' A macron (*kahakō* in Hawaiian) over a vowel [ā] makes it slightly longer than other vowels. Note also that an internal 'w' is sometimes pronounced as a 'v'; thus 'Hawai'i' is often pronounced 'Hah-*vai*-ee' by locals.

A glossary of Hawaiian and Pidgin English (the creole spoken by many Hawaiian locals) words and phrases is included at the end of the book.

ONE

'There he is again!' Grabbing the sleeve of her wife's hibiscus-print shirt, Valerie Corbin inclined her head toward a man on the far side of the carport. He was easy to spot: tall and beefy with long red hair pulled back into a ponytail. As they watched, he picked through the items in a large wooden crate and extricated a cast iron skillet. Perfectly seasoned, by the look of its shiny black finish.

'Dang,' said Kristen, shoulders slumping. 'We could totally use that pan.'

The two women had just arrived at the third of eight houses they'd mapped out for their Sunday-morning garage sale expedition, and this was the third time the red-headed man had beat them to their destination. At each location, he'd managed to cherry-pick all the best items – expensive cookware, silk aloha shirts, and carved wooden end tables – before they'd even had the chance to scope out the offerings.

'And look – he's got a vintage copy of *The Joy of Cooking* under his arm. I would have absolutely snagged that if I'd seen it first.' Letting out a growl of frustration, Valerie studied the newspaper on which she'd circled all the locations they'd scoped out for today's shopping spree. Each listing had a number scrawled next to it, based on her study of the Hilo map as to the most efficient route they should take to hit all the houses without having to backtrack.

'I say we hustle on over to the next place on the list,' she said, shoving the page back into her shorts pocket. 'He clearly mapped out the houses in the same order we did, so maybe we can get ahead of him if we skip this one.'

'Good idea,' Kristen said. She started back down the driveway, only to be immediately called back.

'Wait.' Valerie had stopped in front of a wooden chest with ornate dragons carved on its drawers. 'Check this out. It'd go perfectly with the other one Sachiko gave us. You think it'd fit in the car?'

Kristen eyeballed the piece of furniture, then unhooked a tape measure from her belt and stretched it across the chest. 'Yeah, it should go in the trunk, no problem,' she said, letting the tape snap back into place. 'But if we take the time to buy it and then load it in, he'll only get ahead of us again.' She jabbed a thumb at their competition, who was now waiting behind another patron to pay for his finds.

'Yeah . . .' Valerie let out a slow breath. 'But I really like it,' she said, tracing her fingers over the stylized dragon carvings. 'And forty bucks is a great deal. How about we just skip over the next house on the list and go immediately to number five?'

'Sure. That works.'

Once the pony-tailed man had made his purchases – he'd also discovered some framed vintage Hawaiian sheet music Valerie would have loved for their bathroom wall – they stepped up to the card table the homeowners had set up in their carport. A tiny, gray-haired woman and a pre-teen who looked to be her grand-daughter sat on folding chairs behind the table, which held a metal money box and a plate of Spam musubi wrapped in plastic.

Valerie's stomach began to rumble at the sight of the local Big Island treat: a layer of seasoned sushi rice topped with a slice of fried, glazed Spam and encircled by a strip of toasted seaweed. They'd rushed out of the house that morning at six a.m. with no breakfast first. 'How much for the musubi?' she asked.

'Two dollah,' the girl replied with a toothy grin. 'I wen' make 'em myself.'

'Well, then, I'd best take two. And we're going to buy that chest of drawers over there, as well.'

The grandmother sat forward, taking an interest in the conversation for the first time. 'That belonged to my mother,' she said, her eyes betraying a certain sadness. 'She brought it over from Nagasaki when she came here to marry my father. But now we're moving into a much smaller place, so we have to downsize. I hope you'll take good care of it.'

'I promise you we will,' said Valerie. 'We've just moved here from California and are looking to furnish our new house with things that are a part of this beautiful island.' She glanced back at the chest. 'And that piece truly is – even if it did originally come from Japan.'

The woman smiled. 'As did so very many of the families who have now made Hilo their home.'

After returning home with their garage sale finds and rustling up a late breakfast of fresh papaya and French toast made with Portuguese sweet bread, Valerie and Kristen set out for a walk. It had been raining hard during the past week – a total of eleven inches over the last three days, according to the water gauge Kristen had set up in their back yard – and they were anxious to continue their exploration of their new neighborhood.

Today's agenda was Reed's Island, a narrow spit of land formed where the Wailuku River divides into two channels (one current, one ancient) for about half a mile before reuniting just above its terminus at the Hilo Bayfront.

Accompanying them on their walk was the latest addition to the family, a mixed-breed named Pua – a 'poi dog,' the gal at the shelter had called her.

'She kind of reminds me of a flower, in a way,' Kristen observed as the scraggly white dog stopped to sniff at the base of a lava rock wall, 'so I guess her name fits.'

'You think? How so?'

'Well, to look at her, she seems like she might be pretty delicate, with those thin legs and her narrow, dainty face. But once you get to know her, you realize how tough and resilient she really is. You know, like flowers – they can hold up in a strong wind, even though they might look completely fragile.'

'Waxing quite poetic today, aren't we?' said Valerie with a laugh. 'But okay, sure. I can go with that. You're a resilient little flower, aren't ya, Pua?'

The dog looked up at her name with a wag of the tail, then trotted along as they continued on their walk. The quiet residential area was made up of both modern constructions and stately Victorian-era homes, and since the road dead-ended near the top of the narrow island, car traffic was minimal as they made their way downhill toward the town center.

'So, you glad we did it?' Kristen asked after a bit. 'Made the big move from L.A. to Hilo?'

'Yeah, I think so.'

'You think so? You mean you're having second thoughts?'

Valerie gazed up at an enormous tree whose branches arched over the road. The fractals formed by the lacy dark green leaves against the blue, blue tropical sky were mesmerizing. All of the plants here were astounding, for that matter. The sheer fecundity of the place – from tiny ferns to mammoth mango trees – was so unlike the desert clime she'd been accustomed to in Southern California.

'Earth to Val.'

'Oh, sorry.' She blinked a few times, then glanced at her wife. 'No, I'm not having second thoughts. I truly love it here. It's so . . . *different* from L.A. In a good way. And now that we're here, I'm positive it was the right decision to get myself away from, you know . . . Charlie.'

Kristen took Valerie's hand and gave it a squeeze. She did know. Charlie was Valerie's brother, who'd been killed in a car crash in Santa Monica the previous March. A crash which Valerie had survived. And the guilt that went with being the survivor – even though it was Charlie who'd been driving – was triggered far less often when she was physically removed from where it had happened and from all the places that constantly reminded her of her younger brother.

They made their slow way down the street, waiting patiently as Pua investigated all the fascinating smells along the way. 'And how about you?' Valerie asked. 'You glad to be here?'

'Absolutely. I'm thrilled to leave behind the smog, the traffic, all the people. Okay, not all the people,' Kristen amended. 'I do miss our friends.'

'Yeah, me too.'

'But we'll make new ones. We've got Isaac and Sachiko, for starters.'

Valerie chuckled. 'Starter friends. I like that. Just like sour-dough bread.'

'And I've been thinking of ways I might meet more people,' Kristen went on. 'Like maybe volunteering at some place that builds houses for folks. It'd be a good way to put my carpentry skills to work at the same time as helping others, and maybe making some new friends along the way. You think they have Habitat for Humanity here on the Big Island?'

Valerie shrugged. 'Who knows. But I bet you could "go on line" to find out,' as my dad used to say.' She looked back up at the sky, now framed by the wispy fronds of several tall, elegant palm trees. 'I wonder what I could do to meet some people,' she murmured. *And for that matter*, she continued on in her head, *I wonder what I should do with my* life, *now that I'm no longer working . . .*

Her musings were interrupted when Kristen came to a sudden halt in the middle of the road. 'Oh, wow. Look at that,' she said, staring up the steep driveway to their left. A thick coating of red dirt spilled down the asphalt onto the street, and chunks of rock and other debris littered both sides of the drive, as if they'd been shoveled out of the way.

'And check out *that* side,' Valerie said, pointing to her right. Cut into the hillside was a wide channel extending all the way down to a wood-frame house on stilts just above the river below. The home was still standing, but a reddish-brown stain reached halfway up the building's supports. The carport next to the house had not been so lucky, as the erosion had taken out half of the structure, depositing an enormous pile of mud and rocks in its wake.

Kristen swiveled around to face the uphill house once more. 'Looks like a massive flood poured over the top of that driveway and down across the island. The banks of the river on that side must have overflowed big time. Dang.' Hands on her hips, she let out a low whistle. 'I bet it was that powerful tropical storm that happened right before we got back here – the one everyone keeps talking about. Wasn't it in late August that Lane came through?'

Valerie nodded, her eyes stuck on the swath of destruction caused by the raging water. 'I'm sure glad we didn't buy a house in this neighborhood,' she said.

The next evening, Isaac and Sachiko came over to get their first look at Valerie and Kristen's new home – and to enjoy some refreshing cocktails in the process. They'd started the tour with the bedrooms and bathrooms and were now standing in the 1930s-era kitchen, admiring the built-in cupboards and yellow-and-green tiled counters.

Sachiko opened one of the glass-fronted cupboard doors and removed a large white ceramic bowl decorated with blue fish.

'My mom has a set just like this,' she said. 'She uses them for saimin and ramen soup. Where'd you find them?'

'At a garage sale last weekend. And check it out; we scored this at the same house.' Valerie walked over to a brown stoneware bowl sitting at the far end of the counter. Its interior had lines scratched into the clay that looked as if they'd been made by a comb or similar tool. 'I have no idea what it's for, but I thought it was really beautiful.'

'Nice,' Sachiko said. 'What a great find. It's a suribachi – kind of like a mortar, for grinding things like sesame seeds and herbs. My mom used to have one of these, too, but I don't think she's used it in ages. Did it come with the pestle?'

Valerie shook her head. 'Huh-uh. But that's okay. I think I'm just gonna use it for display, or to put fruit in.'

'Maybe we should start going to some garage sales, babe,' Sachiko said to Isaac. 'You know, now that we're living in the same house, we could pick out some new kitchenware together.'

'Like these?' he replied, pointing to six Martini glasses lined up on one of the shelves.

Kristen laughed. 'I thought you'd like those, brah. But you know, the thing about going to garage sales here? It's not just about all the cool stuff we've been able to buy. Getting the chance to visit so many people's homes all around Hilo has been amazing. Seeing how they live, getting to know what the community is really like, up close and personal. It's been such a great introduction to the town.'

'Not to mention the fact that having to navigate to *find* all the places has been a great way to learn our way around.' Valerie replaced the white-and-blue fish bowl and closed the cupboard door. 'Hilo has such a confusing layout. And all those one-way streets downtown don't help. I'm always getting totally lost.'

'I keep telling her it's 'cause of it being built around a bay,' said Kristen. 'So you have to think of the town as a triangle, with the main streets being the hypotenuse, connecting the north with the south.'

Isaac nodded agreement. 'And of course having all those ancient lava flows blocking your way in lots of places doesn't help, either.' He clapped his hands. 'Okay, so let's hurry up and see the basement so we can get to the drinks portion of the evening!'

The house tour completed, Kristen, Isaac, and Sachiko headed out to the lānai while Valerie got busy in the kitchen shaking up their reward. As she prepared the drinks, she listened in on the conversation outside the open door.

'Well, congratulations,' said Isaac, settling into one of the director's chairs they'd purchased the previous week at Target. 'It's a great house. And these plantation-style homes are getting harder and harder to find. Seems like dey either let 'um go till they need to be knocked down, or they end up doing a big ol' remodel to add a second story or some modern TV and game room, ruining the original aesthetic. What year did you say it was built?'

'In 1937,' said Kristen. 'All pre-war materials, and it looks like the framing is old-growth redwood. Nice and solid.' She patted the wall next to her chair like one would a prized racehorse.

'Good at keeping the termites away, as well,' Sachiko added.

Kristen smiled. 'Indeed. And I'm guessing that since it's lasted this long, the house should hold up well in the next tropical storm that happens along. I didn't spot any water damage when I inspected the basement and crawl space, and the roof seems to be securely attached. Ah, look,' she said as Valerie appeared at the door. An attentive Pua followed closely behind, her sharp nose pointed in the direction of the large tray in Valerie's hands. 'The drinks and pūpūs have arrived!'

Jumping up, Kristen took two of the cocktail glasses and handed them to their guests, then placed the bowl of Maui onion chips on the wicker table between the couples. 'Thanks, hon,' she said, taking a glass for herself.

'Did you tell them about the flood damage we saw today on our walk?' Valerie asked as she sat down with her own drink.

'Oh, really?' asked Sachiko. 'Where was it?'

'Out on Reed's Island.'

Isaac shook his head. 'Ho! Dey had some fo' realz damage out dere last month during Lane. But where dis house is . . .' He waved his hand toward the back yard. 'I think it's plenty safe fo' sure – no worry, beef curry.'

Valerie and Kristen exchanged quick smiles. They'd learned that whenever Isaac got excited about something, the local Pidgin tended to come out big time in his speech.

'Though I gotta say,' he added with a grin which revealed his shiny gold tooth, 'you two do seem to bring out the disasters 'round here whenever you're on-island.'

'Hey, no fair. We hadn't even gotten here yet when Lane passed through.'

'Yeah, but you'd *decided* to move here right around then. And there's also that small matter of the volcano blowing its wad last May when you were here . . .'

'Okay,' Kristen said, holding up her hands in surrender. 'Guilty as charged.'

Sachiko raised her drink in a toast. 'Well, we're glad you decided to come. And here's to the new house. It truly is beautiful.'

The four clinked glasses, then tasted the frothy, golden-hued concoction Valerie had prepared.

'Wow, this is delicious!' Sachiko said, smacking her lips. 'What's in it?'

'Bourbon shaken with a simple syrup made from honey, ginger, and lemon. Oh, and a spritz of seltzer and some muddled basil, as well.'

'Nice combo – very creative. I might have to try it out at the Gecko. That is, if you wouldn't mind us stealing your idea . . .' Sachiko managed the front of the house at the Speckled Gecko, a restaurant down on the Hilo Bayfront that served an eclectic mixture of Asian, Hawaiian, and Caribbean cuisine.

'Heavens, no. I'd be honored.'

Kristen leaned forward to snag a handful of potato chips. 'Valerie was a bartender back in L.A.,' she said. 'So she's got lots of fancy drinks up her sleeve.'

'Oh, right,' said Isaac. 'I remember you telling us about dat when you were here last spring. At your brother's place, right?'

'Uh-huh. Though I wouldn't say I was actually a "bartender." He'd been teaching me the ropes at his place, Chez Charles, before he died, but I still have a ton to learn.'

'Well, if this is any judge of your mixologist abilities, I'd say you're pretty darn good.' Sachiko took another sip of the drink and swished it around in her mouth. 'Very good, indeed.'

'My grandparents owned a restaurant in the south of France,' Valerie said, taking some chips for herself. 'And before I retired, I worked in the food biz, too, as a caterer for movie and TV productions. So I guess you could say it's in my DNA.'

Sachiko turned toward Valerie, a serious look now in her eyes. 'Have you ever worked with a POS?'

'Huh? I mean, sure, I had to learn the point-of-sale system at Chez Charles. It's really simple, actually. But . . . why do you ask?' Valerie glanced from Sachiko to Kristen, then back again at Sachiko.

'It's just that one of our bartenders, Hank, seems to have gone AWOL.' Sachiko let out a snort. 'He didn't show up for work last week and hasn't had the decency to let me know what's going on. No notice that he was quitting, no after-the-fact apology, no nothing. He isn't even answering my texts, and as far as I'm concerned, he's done. Even if he were to show up at work again, I'd point him to the door.'

Valerie was fairly certain she knew where this was going, but let Sachiko continue without interruption. Partly because she wasn't sure how she was going to respond.

'So . . . well, I was wondering if maybe – you know, since you have experience behind a bar – you might be willing to help out at the Gecko for a few days. Just until we find someone permanent, that is. 'Cause I know you're probably super busy getting settled into your new home and your new town an' all . . .'

Sachiko was being so very cautious and diffident that Valerie couldn't help but burst out laughing. 'It's okay, really,' she said. 'Once again, I'm honored. And you know, to tell the truth, I'm kind of tempted to take you up on it. Kristen and I were just talking this afternoon about ways we might get out into the community to meet more people and—'

'And tending bar will sure get ya meeting 'um,' Isaac interrupted with a slap to his knee. 'Though not necessarily da ones ya might wanna meet. Ha!' At a sharp glance from his girlfriend, however, he flashed her a weak smile. 'Sorry, babe. I'll just shut up now.'

Sachiko swatted Isaac lightly on the arm, then focused back on Valerie. 'You were saying?'

'Just that I've been thinking over the past few days about what I might do to occupy myself, now that I'm retired and living here in a brand-new community. I've always been so busy in my life up till now that it feels really odd to be at loose ends like this. So maybe working at the restaurant would be a good idea. I've kind of missed tending bar at Charlie's place.'

A sudden tightness clamped hold of Valerie's chest at the thought of her younger brother holding court with the customers at his popular French-style bistro in Venice Beach. A brother now forever absent from her life.

Shaking it off, she turned to face her wife. 'If you wouldn't mind me being gone a few nights a week, that is.'

'Not at all. Gives me time to watch more episodes of *The Bachelor* while you're gone.'

'Yuck,' said Valerie. 'That decides it. So when would you want me to start?'

Sachiko cleared her throat. 'Uh . . . tomorrow?'

TWO

Valerie glanced again at Kristen, who merely shrugged. 'It's up to you, hon.'

'Okay,' said Valerie, letting out a stream of breath. 'I'm in. But just don't expect me to flip Martini glasses in the air or do any of those fancy tricks like Tom Cruise in *Cocktail*, okay?'

'I promise. We in fact discourage the throwing about of liquids and glassware at the Speckled Gecko, so you should be fine.' Sachiko reached over to pat Valerie on the hand. 'You're gonna be great. And most of our customers order old-school drinks like Margaritas and Mai Tais, in any case. Or beer. Nothing too complicated, I assure you.'

'Well, then, I might just have to shake things up a bit – pun intended.'

'And that is exactly why I asked you on board,' said Sachiko with a grin.

The issue now settled, Valerie leaned back in her chair and sipped from her cocktail. She'd have to come up with a name for the concoction if she were to serve it down at the Gecko. *A Golden Girl?* No, that name was already taken, she was pretty sure. *An Island Sour?* Yes, that worked.

'So what do you think happened to this bartender guy?' she asked. 'What'd you say his name was? Frank?'

'Hank,' said Sachiko. 'And I have no idea. The last time any of us saw him was a week ago – last Monday, during this restaurant retreat we had up at Boiling Pots.'

'We went there last spring,' said Kristen in response to Valerie's questioning look. 'Remember the place on the river with those picturesque waterfalls and pools of water? But I don't remember it being the sort of place you'd want to hang out at for any length of time,' she added, turning back to Sachiko. 'Isn't it just a lookout?'

'No, there's a big grassy area there, and picnic tables and bathrooms, so it's the perfect place for a group to eat and play

Frisbee and stuff. We have our annual get-together there every fall.'

Valerie contemplated the icy contents of her glass. 'So this Hank guy who disappeared – did he seem upset at the retreat? Or have a big fight with someone and storm off in a huff or something?'

'Not that I know of. Did you see anything like that, babe?'

'Nope,' answered Isaac. 'He seemed fine last time I saw him. I just figured he'd left early to go do something else.'

'Ah, so he left the party early,' said Valerie.

Sachiko spread her hands, palms up. 'Maybe. All I know is that it was when we were all packing up the food to go home that we first noticed Hank wasn't there anymore. Kai – he's our busser – he said he thought maybe he'd had a hot date or something, but I don't think he really knew anything.'

'And then he didn't show up for work the next day . . .' Kristen prompted Sachiko.

'The night after that, actually. He doesn't work Tuesdays, so last Wednesday is when he was a no-show. But I'd still like you to come in tomorrow,' she said, turning to Valerie, 'even though it was Hank's night off, so I can show you the ropes before you fly solo on Wednesday.'

'No problem. Good idea, actually.'

Isaac drank the rest of his cocktail and set the glass down with a *clunk*. 'It's 'cause he was a malihini, I bet.'

'Now, we don't know that,' Sachiko said, annoyance creeping into her voice. 'Hank had a solid resume, and I got a really good hit off him during his interview. And he ended up being a great bartender for six months, which is a pretty long time in this biz. Besides, it's not as if it's all that easy finding experienced locals to work at the restaurant, so what am I supposed to do?'

It seemed clear that this was a running issue with the two of them. 'Uh, what's a . . . malihini?' asked Valerie.

'A newbie,' said Isaac. 'Someone from the Mainland, usually. And the problem is, most of the people who move here don't understand what it's really like. They're all, "Oh, tropical paradise! I can surf and hang out at the beach and drink Mai Tais all day long!" And then when it turns out their life is just as real here as it was back in Oklahoma or Boston or wherever they came from, with bills to pay and jobs to work – but now with black mold on their walls and centipedes and way more expensive utilities and groceries – they can't handle it and hurry back home after just a couple months, their tail between their legs.' He shook his head. 'I keep telling Sachiko not to hire 'em.'

Valerie felt her face flushing red. 'So . . . why would you want to hire me, then? 'Cause I'm certainly a malihini, too.'

'Well, you two did just buy a house here,' Isaac answered with a reassuring smile. 'So I'd say you're a safe bet to stick around for at least a while.'

The sound of splashing water and clinking glass carried across the Speckled Gecko as Sachiko led Valerie through the restaurant's lānai the next afternoon. It being not quite four o'clock, the outdoor eating area was empty save for several people finishing up a late lunch in the far corner. A squat man of about fifty with a friar's circle of short, receding hair stood behind the bar pulling cocktail glasses from the dishwasher rack and lining them up on an overhead shelf.

'Hey, Jun,' Sachiko said, 'I want to introduce you to Valerie, who's going to step in for Hank till we can find someone permanent to take his place. I was hoping you could show her around tonight so she can take Hank's shift tomorrow night.'

Jun reached across the bar to shake hands with Valerie. 'Howzit. And sure, dat'll be fine. If it gets busy tonight, it'll be great having someone else here. You got bartending experience, yah?'

'Uh, yeah. Back in Los Angeles, at a bistro in Venice Beach.'

'Oooo, zo fancy,' the bartender said with an exaggerated French accent. 'You gonna find the clientele here a bit more lowbrow than what you used to, but if you can pull a beer and shake up a Margarita, you'll do fine.'

Sachiko left them to it and headed off to see about prepping the indoors for the dinner service.

'C'mon around and I'll give you a tour of da joint,' said Jun, waving Valerie behind the carved wood bar.

She glanced at the well drink bottles underneath the bar top, then turned to examine the higher-end liquor on the shelf the customers stared at as they sat atop their stools. 'Not all that different from where I worked before, actually. Though we sold quite a few bottles of wine in addition to cocktails – reds, especially. I'm guessing that's probably not the case here, given the weather.'

'True, dat. Though we do sell lots of whites by the glass.' Jun opened the wine fridge behind the bar, and Valerie peered in at the bottles of Chardonnay, Riesling, and rosé chilling inside. 'Here, I'll show you the pre-mixes we use for cocktails,' he said, closing the door.

A half hour later, four of the six barstools were occupied, but since Jun had everything well under control, he suggested Valerie go check out the other areas of the restaurant. 'We serve food to people sitting at the bar, so it'd be good for you to meet the kitchen and waitstaff before it gets too busy.'

'Okay.' Wandering across the outdoor eating area, she stopped to admire the dolphin fountain and planter boxes filled with tropical flowers that reminded her of something from a *Star Trek* set: spiky hot-pink ginger the color of her late grandmother's lipstick, red-and-yellow heliconia dangling from six-foot-tall stalks, and shiny green philodendron leaves the size of an elephant's ear.

A woman stood in the corner of the lānai folding napkins and stacking them in a wooden box. She turned at Valerie's approach. 'Hi. I'm Annie. Are you the one who'll be filling in for Hank?'

'Uh-huh. At least for a few days, anyway. We'll see how it goes.'

'Well, glad to meet you,' she said, pushing a strand of blond hair behind her ear. 'It's good of you to step in on such short notice. After he left us all in the lurch like that.'

'Yeah, well, Sachiko's a friend of mine, so I figured it was the least I could do to help her out. Besides, I'm new to the island, so I'm actually happy to have something useful to do with my time.'

'So you retired here or something?' Annie asked. 'I mean, not that you look . . .' The flush that spread across her pale cheeks was impossible to miss.

'Old?' Valerie laughed, reaching out to give her a maternal pat on the shoulder. 'It's okay. I *am* old. More than double your age, I'd bet. Just turned sixty last spring and proud of it. And yes, you're right: my wife and I moved here from Los Angeles after we retired. But there's life in the old girl yet,' she said, flexing her arm. 'I can do fifty push-ups and craft a very mean Negroni – not, however, at the same time.'

'Good to know, on both counts.' Annie's facial color was now returning to normal. 'Here, let me introduce you to some of the other people here.' She led Valerie indoors to the pass window, through which she could see a tall man bending over a long table running down the center of the kitchen and an even taller woman standing at the hot line stove.

'Hey, Nalani,' Annie called out, and the woman looked up from stirring something in a large pot. Her dark hair was tucked under a baseball cap bearing the restaurant logo – a green gecko with bright red-and-yellow dots. 'This is Valerie, Hank's replacement.'

'Oh, hi,' she said, turning off the flame under the pot. 'Sachiko told me you'd be coming in tonight. Thanks so much for saving our ass. I owe you, girl.'

'Nalani's the owner and head chef here,' Annie said to Valerie, 'and was none too pleased when Hank was a no-show last week.'

'An understatement, I'd say,' the man at the table said over his shoulder. He lifted the two dishes he'd been plating up – fish tacos and some kind of jerk meat, Valerie guessed from the looks of it – and set them on the pass, then slapped the old-school bell that sat atop the counter. 'Order up!'

'And that's Matt,' said Annie.

The line cook nodded a hello, then quickly turned his attention to wiping down the chrome table with a side towel.

'He's kind of shy,' Annie explained in a low voice as they made their way back outdoors. 'But super sweet. And Nalani's nice too, but a little more . . .'

'Not shy?'

Annie chuckled. 'Yeah, that works. Oh, and here's our other server for tonight,' she said as a slender man with dark shoulder-length hair and a full beard to match dashed past them toward the kitchen. 'Hey, Seth, come meet our new bartender when you have a sec,' she called out as he reemerged bearing the tacos and the meat dish Matt had just plated up.

'Sure thing.' He served the couple sitting in the corner their dinner, then returned to where the two women stood. 'Howdy. I'm Seth. Great to have you on board.'

'Seth's from California, too,' Annie said to Valerie, then turned back to the waiter. 'San Diego, right?'

'Right,' he answered. 'Though I moved around a lot growing up. Navy brat, ya know?'

'I do know,' said Valerie. 'A friend of mine whose dad was in the Army ended up going to six different schools by the time she graduated high school.'

'Guess I'm lucky then. I only went to four.'

Sachiko led a cluster of customers past as they were talking, seating them at a table and handing them menus. 'Oh, good,' she said, walking back across the room. 'I'm glad to see you're meeting the other staff, Valerie. And let me know if you need anything. Though I think you'll be in good hands, working with Jun. He's been here since the restaurant opened back in the nineties and is a veritable fount of knowledge.'

'Everyone's been great so far, actually,' said Valerie. 'And thanks.'

'Okay, well, gotta run.' Sachiko glanced inside toward the front door. 'I'm on hostess duty tonight.'

'And I have to go, too,' said Annie. 'That's my foursome that just got seated.'

Valerie turned to Seth, once the two other women were gone. 'I don't want to keep you from your job,' she said, nodding toward his table.

'I think they're fine for a bit. It's best not to bug customers too much, is my feeling, unless you can see they're actually looking around for someone to help them.' He glanced at the clock above where Jun stood pulling a pint of pale ale. It was set fifteen minutes early, Valerie noticed. A common practice in bars, where it often took some doing to get your customers out once closing time came along. 'We've got a few minutes till five, when the rush should start up,' Seth said. 'You have any questions I can answer in the meantime?'

'You could go through the menu with me so I can explain dishes to anyone who wants to order at the bar.'

'Good idea.' The two took a seat at an empty table, and Seth proceeded to explain the pūpūs, mains dishes, and desserts to Valerie, describing any that she wasn't familiar with in more detail.

'What's a medianoche?' she asked, pointing to the menu. 'I mean, I know it means midnight in Spanish, but . . .'

'Oh, man, that's da bomb. It's basically a Cuban sandwich – you know, with ham, roast pork, Swiss cheese, and pickles – but made with Hawaiian sweet bread. I guess it's called that 'cause it's the perfect thing to eat when you get home late from a night on the town.'

'And the pastele? That sounds like a Mexican dessert, but it's in the entrée section.'

'Pah-tel-eh,' Seth corrected her. 'The s is silent. And it's a savory dish – originally from Puerto Rico I think is what Sachiko told me – but I know it's considered to be a local Hawaiian food. I never heard of 'em before I moved here, either, but they're kind of like tamales. You use mashed plantains instead of corn masa, wrap 'em in banana leaves, and boil them in water. Ours here are super good – we stuff them with the same kālua pork we serve as part of our plate lunch.'

Valerie closed the menu. 'Oh, boy,' she said, 'I can tell I am *so* going to gain weight working here. I don't know how you keep your boyish figure.'

'It's not easy,' he agreed, patting his stomach – which was indeed quite svelte. 'But waiting tables is a bit of a workout, so that helps. And I gave up drinking a while back, which probably helps even more. Though I gotta say, I do sometimes get a fierce sweet tooth now that I'm off alcohol.'

'Right, I've heard that's often the case. I guess 'cause your body craves the sugar it used to get from the liquor.'

Seth nodded. 'As well as the dopamine that your brain used to release when you drank. Sugar gives you that, too. I've been learning all about how cravings work in AA.'

'So, it's not hard waiting tables here, where you have to serve cocktails to all the customers? I mean, if it's not rude my asking . . .'

'No, it's fine,' he said with a wave of the hand. 'And yeah, it was hard at first, but I'm okay now. Lots of AA folks are in food service, actually. Probably because it was working at restaurants that got them drinking to begin with,' he added with a short laugh. But then his mouth tightened as he glanced over at the bar. 'Hank's in our AA group, too.'

Valerie frowned. 'I thought that kind of thing was supposed
to be—'

'Secret?' Seth finished for her. 'Yeah, it generally is. They are,
after all, called Alcoholics *Anonymous*. But Hank has always
been totally out about it with everyone here at the Gecko – just
like I am. So I think it's okay, you know, since you're now
working here, too. But the reason I bring it up is 'cause, well,
I'm a little concerned about the guy. It's just not like him to all
of a sudden drop out of sight like that. So I worry that . . .'

'He fell off the wagon?'

A barely perceptible nod was his only response.

Valerie chewed her lip. 'Have you talked to Sachiko and Nalani
about your concerns?'

'Yeah, and they agree I may be right. But what can they do?
Or anyone, for that matter? I mean, I did go by his house, but
either he wasn't there or he refused to answer. So . . .' Seth
scratched idly at a tattoo of a bird – a robin, by the looks of its
red breast – on his forearm.

Seeing her eyeing it, he gave a sheepish grin. 'Yeah, I know
it's not like a lot of the tats guys have with sharks and knives
and stuff. My Navy dad gave me a lot of grief for getting it – he
called it a "girl's" tattoo.' Seth let out a sigh that spoke volumes
about his relationship with his father. 'But what can I say – I'm
really into birds. And I'm not a big fan of knives. Or sharks,' he
added with a laugh. Then, at the sight of Sachiko seating another
table in his section, the server rose from his chair. 'I better get
to work, but it's been good talking to you. Let me know if you
need anything tonight, okay?'

'Thanks. I will.' She watched him greet the new customers
with a bright smile, then swiveled in her chair to track Sachiko
as she headed back to the hostess stand.

*Now, why hadn't she mentioned Hank's being a recovering
alcoholic when she'd told them the night before about his going
AWOL? And why had she expressed only anger about her bartender's absence – and no worry?*

THREE

The Hilo farmers market has its two biggest days on Wednesday and Saturday, with the produce and other food stands occupying the market's usual spot on the corner of Kamehameha Avenue and Mamo Street, and a separate area set up across the street for craft and gift vendors. So the place was bustling the next morning when Valerie, Kristen, and Pua walked downtown in search of vegetables for a stir-fry and a few of the buttery avocados grown locally down in Puna.

The vendor they'd nicknamed 'the bossy lady' when they'd first visited the town the previous spring was in fine form, calling out to them before they'd even reached her booth at the edge of the market.

'You wan' banana?' she said, holding up a bunch of still-green apple bananas for their inspection.

'No, thanks. But I will take some eggplant and bok choy. Here,' Valerie said, handing Kristen the leash. 'You hold onto Pua while I shop.' She passed the woman four dollars, then slid the produce into her canvas bag. 'And I'm gonna get the avos from that guy over there. His are always the best deal.'

It had rained hard the night before, a common occurrence in Hilo, and Valerie had to dodge numerous puddles that had formed on the concrete walkway. She selected and paid for three large Sharwil avocados – one ripe, two hard – then turned her attention to a table covered with papayas. 'Wow, three for a dollar. Maybe we should get some,' she called out to Kristen, who was waiting on the sidewalk behind the stall.

'As you know, I'm not a huge papaya fan, but hey, if you want to carry them all the way back uphill, it's fine with me. Here, give me the stuff you've got.'

Valerie slipped between two vendors to hand over the canvas bag of veggies, then pawed through the mound of fruit, searching for the three largest ones. Pleased with herself, she slung the papaya bag over her shoulder and returned to where Kristen stood with the dog. 'Wanna check out the craft area? Pua should be allowed in there, and we could look for some decorations for the living room.'

'Sure. Though I woulda suggested we wait till afterwards to buy the produce if I'd known we were doing that, too. But, hey, I'll just consider it an upper body workout.'

A stream of traffic was moving slowly up Mamo Street, everyone looking for that elusive Wednesday-morning parking space, but they were finally able to dart between the cars and make it to the other half of the market. All kinds of wares were being hawked: Rastafarian T-shirts, wood sculptures of whales and sea turtles, fish hook necklaces carved from bone, wheel-thrown bowls and coffee mugs, and myriad items woven from hala leaves and coconut fronds.

Kristen stopped at a table displaying watercolors of various tropical scenes. 'Oooh, I like this one,' she said, pointing to a painting of a black sand beach. Rows of coconut palms marched down almost to the water, and several surfers were catching waves in the aqua-blue water of a crescent-shaped bay. 'Did you paint this?' she asked the gray-haired woman behind the table.

'I did. It's from a photo I took of the old Kaimū Beach before the lava took it back in 1990.'

'Well, it's beautiful. How much do you want for it?'

'That one's thirty-five dollars.'

Valerie came up behind Kristen to peer down at the painting, then smiled. 'Ha. I know why you like it. She's a surfer,' she said to the artist. 'But it truly is a lovely piece. I think you should buy it, hon.'

The woman placed the painting between two pieces of mat-board, then wrapped it in brown paper and taped it shut. 'I'm so glad you bought this one,' she said, the lines around her eyes deepening with her smile. 'It's one of my favorites, and it's nice knowing it will have a good home.'

Pua was pulling impatiently at her leash, so they let her lead the way down the aisle, past racks of floral-print lavalavas and aloha shirts. The dog made a beeline for a pile of spilled fried rice and immediately scarfed down as much as she could inhale before being stopped by her human handler.

'No, not for dogs,' Kristen said, tugging her away from the delectable mess. 'Though I have to say, it does look pretty tasty. I guess I must be hungry. Whatd'ya say we head home for some lunch?'

But Valerie wasn't listening. 'Look,' she hissed, nudging Kristen with her shoulder. 'There he is again!'

It was the red-headed garage sale guy, seated behind a table stacked with some familiar items: framed sheet music of 1940s' Hawaiian crooners, a well-seasoned cast iron skillet, and a set of different-colored glass mixing bowls were among the items he had on offer.

'Oh!' Valerie approached the table and ran her fingers down the row of books nestled between a pair of monkey-shaped bookends. Pulling one out, she displayed its blue-and-white cover to Kristen: *The Joy of Cooking*.

'How much for this?' she asked the man.

He looked up from the copy of *The Atlantic* magazine he'd been flipping though. 'I can let that go for ten bucks, since it's in pretty bad shape,' he said, then squinted through his horn-rimmed glasses. 'Didn't I see you two last weekend at a garage sale?'

'Yeah, more than one, in fact,' said Kristen. 'And at each house, you managed to snag all the good stuff before us. Like that pan over there.'

'And this cookbook,' added Valerie. 'We clearly have the same highly refined taste, but you're just a lot better at this garage sale-ing thing than us.'

Setting down the magazine, he leaned forward. 'It's all in the eye,' he said, pointing at his glasses. 'Ya gotta scan everything quickly as soon as you walk into the place, and also learn to see at a glance what's worth looking at – whether the shirts are silk or cotton, whether the dishware is 1950s Japanese or modern Target-ware. I do this for a living, so I have to be quick in order to get to as many houses as possible each weekend.'

'Well, I guess I'm glad it's you who beat us out for everything, 'cause I at least can have a second shot at it.' Valerie tapped her finger on the cookbook. 'For a price. So how much for the cast iron skillet?'

'Tell you what,' he said, sitting back in his chair and folding his hands together, prayer-like. 'I was going to charge twenty bucks for the skillet, but I'll give you both items for twenty-five.'

'And how much did you pay for them at the garage sale?' asked Kristen with a wry smile.

'Ah, now that's a proprietary secret,' he replied with a grin of his own.

'Okay, deal.' Valerie extracted her wallet to pay the man. 'And we'll likely be back, since we just moved on-island and are looking to stock our house with kitchenware.'

'Well, I'm here every Wednesday and Saturday. My name's Jake, by the way.'

'And I'm Valerie and this is Kristen. See ya again soon.'

After rearranging all their purchases, they slung their fabric bags over their shoulders and headed back to their new home. Halfway up the hill, Valerie stopped and set down her purchases. 'Man. It's a lot hotter on the way back,' she said, wiping the sweat from her forehead.

'Yeah, and being later in the day doesn't help,' said Kristen, releasing her bags as well. 'Not to mention being loaded down with cast iron skillets, books, and papayas.'

'So true.'

The sound of a loud motor caused them both to turn. Away in the distance to their right, an orange helicopter was hovering in the sky, the sound of its rotors reverberating off the walls of the apartment buildings along Haili Street.

'Must be a group of tourists,' said Valerie. 'But I wonder what they're looking at.'

'It seems to be over the river, so maybe a waterfall?' Kristen shielded her eyes with her hand, squinting in the bright sunlight. 'But it's way too far downriver to be Rainbow Falls, so who knows . . .'

The two of them stared for another minute at the helicopter, now making its way slowly toward the ocean, then picked up their bags and continued on their way up the street.

By five thirty that night, all six stools at the Speckled Gecko were occupied, with additional patrons standing about the bar area – some having a drink as they waited for a table, others hoping to snag a barstool once it was vacated.

Valerie was busy, but it was nothing she couldn't handle. The Chez Charles bar had sat twelve, with far more tables to service than the Gecko, so she'd become adept at cranking out cocktails at a furious pace. Plus, as Sachiko had warned, the drinks she'd been asked to prepare so far had been boringly predictable: gin and tonics, Mai Tais, Margaritas, and the like.

As she shook up her third Cosmopolitan of the evening, Valerie considered what cocktail special she might be able to offer that night, based on the ingredients on hand. Not the Island Sour she'd made the other night for Sachiko and Isaac. Although the kitchen no doubt stocked honey, ginger, and basil, there was no time to make the ginger syrup now that the evening rush had begun. She'd have to wait till another night and do the prep in advance.

Ah, she thought, her eyes scanning the soda guns behind the bar. *I know*.

'Can I interest you in tonight's special?' Valerie said brightly to the next customer who bellied up to the bar. 'It's called the TTT, for "Tasty Tequila Tonic," and is made with Herradura Blanco tequila, tonic water, and a splash of Rose's lime juice, with a salt rim. Very refreshing, and it goes great with the fish tacos.'

'Sure, that sounds good,' he replied.

The woman next to him nodded. 'Make it two.'

Okay, I can do this.

Valerie sold twelve of her drink specials that night, and as she filled the dish rack with dirty glasses after closing, she mused on other concoctions she might serve in the future. A plethora of options were available which would complement the restaurant's varied menu of sushi, lomi lomi salmon, noodle bowls, chopped salads, grilled fish, teriyaki and jerk chicken, pulled pork . . . It would be a fun task to come up with ideas.

Once all the garnishes and mixers had been stowed away; the bottles, wells, sinks, and counters wiped down; and the used bar towels tossed into the laundry bag, she shut off the lights over the bar and headed indoors to the front of the restaurant. Annie, Seth, and Nalani were seated at a table near the pass, bottles before them.

'Take a load off,' called out the owner/head chef. 'And help yourself to an adult beverage, if ya want.'

Valerie selected a can of Volcano Red Ale from the beer fridge in the wait station and joined the three others at their table.

'So, how'd it go tonight?' Seth asked her.

'Not bad. Though there was one guy who didn't take kindly to my cutting him off when he started getting kinda belligerent after his fourth drink.'

Annie shook her head. 'That would be Brad, I bet. A big guy with an even bigger gut who drinks Seven and Sevens?'

'Yep, that's the one. I think he must have been testing out the newbie bartender,' said Valerie, pointing a thumb toward her chest, 'but he settled down once his pals told him to knock it off.'

'Well, I had no complaints on my end,' said Annie. 'All the drink orders came up promptly and the customers seemed quite happy with the cocktails. So, cheers.' She raised her beer in salute, then took a long pull off the bottle.

Sachiko and the busser, Kai, now pulled up chairs and joined in congratulating Valerie on her first night riding solo. 'Good job,' said Sachiko, slapping Valerie on the shoulder. 'We did a ton of covers tonight for a Wednesday, and everyone says all the bar orders went super smooth. And that special you came up with? I hear it was a big hit.'

'Yeah, people did seem to like it. But I also think just having a "special" drink, no matter what it is, gets people excited. You know, something new – and temporary – that won't be around the next time they come.'

'Good point. I don't know why we never had drink specials before. I guess it's 'cause Jun's always been pretty old-school about running the bar.' Sachiko glanced at Nalani, then back to Valerie. 'So, any chance you'd be willing to keep working through this weekend? And hopefully I'll have something figured out by next week . . .'

Valerie beamed. 'Sure. Happy to. Though it'd be great if I could have tomorrow off. You know, a chance to spend some time with the wife?'

'Absolutely. And I hear ya. We're of course not married, but I still need to spend at least one night a week with Isaac or he gets all pouty on me.'

'Yep, same with George,' said Nalani with a snort.

'And Jimmy, too.' Valerie looked up at the new voice to see Matt standing behind her. 'He gets on my case if I don't spend at least two nights a week with him,' the line cook said, tugging off his white jacket and tossing it over the back of a chair.

The talk moved on to local gossip. Seth had heard from a waiter at another restaurant in town that its owner had apparently ditched his wife for one of his waitresses, and she'd retaliated by using several of his canoe paddles for kindling in their outdoor fire pit.

A look of horror spread across Kai's face. 'No wayz! Dass *cold*, brah.'

Seth shrugged. 'That's what I heard, anyway.'

'I take it they're expensive, the paddles?' asked Valerie.

'Not jus' that, but you get super attached to 'um. It's a special kine thing, your paddle, 'ae?' The busboy continued to shake his head in disbelief, as if it had been his own paddles that had burnt to a crisp.

'Kai's a paddler too, in case you hadn't guessed,' Annie said, doing a poor job of hiding a smile behind her bottle of Longboard Lager.

'Yeah, I figured.' Valerie tapped a finger on her can of beer, then set it on the table. 'So I have a question for you all. Walking up Haili Street this morning, my wife and I saw this orange helicopter—'

'Uh-oh,' said Nalani before Valerie could finish her sentence.

'Uh-oh?'

The others were all bobbing their heads in agreement with this sentiment.

'That's the county helicopter,' the head chef explained. 'And whenever it's out, you can bet there's some kind of trouble. Where did you see it?'

'Hovering over the river.'

'Double uh-oh.' Nalani swiveled in her seat to look up at Matt. 'Remember last time we saw it flying up and down the river? That was not good at all.'

'Oh yeah, I remember that,' he responded, finally pulling up a chair to join the large circle around the table. 'It was when some guy fell into the water trying to cross the river over the rocks above Boiling Pots and disappeared. And then a few days later, a group of tourists see his body come flying down over Rainbow Falls. How crazy would that be, to see something like that?'

The group was silent for a moment, taking in this grisly image. Sachiko, in particular, had the look of someone who'd just eaten a bad oyster.

'So . . . you think they were looking for someone today, then?' asked Valerie after a bit.

Kai nodded. 'I wouldn't doubt it. It happens more often than you'd think, people drowning in the Wailuku River. You know what that name means, yah?'

'Huh-uh, I don't.'

'It means "waters of destruction." An' da ancient Hawaiians, they knew what they were talkin' about, 'cause it's a super dangerous river. One minute it looks all peaceful and quiet and the next, *bam*!' The slapping of Kai's hand on the wooden table caused Valerie to jump. 'The water from upstream comes pouring down like an avalanche, washing away everything in its path.'

'Yeah, we saw some flood damage the other day on Reed's Island from that tropical storm that came through in August and overflowed the banks of the river.'

'But that's not all,' Kai went on, now clearly relishing his story. 'Even when da waters are calm, da Wailuku can be dangerous – which is why most locals know not to swim there. Hell, I'm a *strong* swimmer. You gotta be, to be a paddler. But you won't catch me out dere. No wayz.'

'And why's it so dangerous?' asked Valerie, playing along.

Kai's smile was grim. 'It's 'cause of the strong currents dat you can't see from above. And dey're made worse by all these underwater caves, from when Mauna Loa erupted and flowed down the gorge. So these currents, dey pull you under and then you get sucked into one of those caves . . .' He paused for dramatic effect before delivering the payoff. '. . . and get trapped inside. Sometimes for days, until it'll finally spit out the body and send it on downriver. Like dat poor guy whose body ended up going over Rainbow Falls.'

FOUR

Valerie and Kristen's morning ritual since moving into their new home consisted of taking their coffee, toast, and yogurt with sliced papaya out to the lānai, where they'd read the daily papers, calling each other's attention to whatever stories piqued their interest. They subscribed to the online version of the *Los Angeles Times* in order to keep up with the goings-on in their hometown, but Valerie's favorite part of the morning was leafing through the hardcopy edition of the local newspaper, the *Hawai'i Tribune Herald*. The news stories, profiles, political updates, sports, and food section made for a fascinating intro-duction to her newfound home. Even the food ads – perhaps those most of all – provided a peek into a culture that was still very new to a gal who'd spent most of her previous life in Southern California.

The rain had returned overnight, so while waiting for a lull in the clouds to dash out and grab the Hilo paper from its green plastic box in the front yard, Valerie contented herself with perusing the online sports page of the *L.A. Times*. 'Good, the Dodgers won yesterday,' she said, but Kristen made no sign she'd heard.

Valerie continued swiping through the website, stopping at an article about a taco festival the coming weekend in Mar Vista. After finishing the story, she leaned back in her director's chair. 'It's so weird reading about what's going on back home,' she said. 'I mean, I know it's not "home" anymore, but that only makes it weirder . . .'

Still no response from Kristen.

'Hon?' She sat forward, startling Pua, who'd been asleep on her doggie bed next to Valerie, which in turn jolted Kristen from whatever held her attention on her laptop.

'Oh, sorry. What'd you say?'

Valerie leaned over to stroke Pua's scraggly white hair. 'Never mind. It doesn't matter. So what's got you so fascinated there, anyway? Some hot movie star gossip?'

'Nothing that exciting. Just an email from someone, is all.'
'Ah.'

Valerie didn't ask who that someone was, but neither did she return to her reading, instead continuing to scratch Pua on the back as Kristen stared out at the yellow allamanda vine growing up their carport wall.

After a moment, Kristen closed her computer and set it on the coffee table. 'Really, it's no big deal. It's just that this friend of Isaac's is building a lānai at her house, but she's only got minimal carpentry experience – Diane's her name – so he thought I might be willing to help her out a bit.'

'And I take it you said yes.'

'I did.' Kristen finally met Valerie's gaze, excitement in her blue eyes. 'And I think it's the perfect thing for me right now. A way to meet new people like we were talking about, and to help someone out at the same time. And you know how I feel about enabling women to do construction and stuff like that. I think it'll be great!'

Valerie forced a light tone. 'Yeah, you're right. That's terrific, hon. So . . . when are you going to start?'

'Well, this weekend is when she's planning on doing the floor. The foundation's already finished, thank God, since that's the hardest part. I was thinking of heading over there on Saturday to see exactly where she's at.'

'Sounds like a plan. You're a good woman.'

She meant what she said. Kristen had always been generous with her time, and Valerie was well aware of her desire to teach others – especially women – their way around a power drill and circular saw. Not to mention a voltage tester and plumber's snake. She was like a missionary on a quest to ensure that women weren't dependent on men for such things as installing a new flush valve in their toilet or repairing a hole in their living room wall.

Valerie just wished this new project of hers didn't mean that now they'd barely see each other, what with her working nights at the Gecko and Kristen about to be gone during the days.

Oh, well, she thought, shaking it off. The lānai wouldn't take that long to build, and Valerie had no intention of spending the rest of her nights tending bar. This was all merely temporary.

'Hey, look.' Kristen jumped up, breaking into Valerie's musings. 'The rain stopped. I'll go get the paper.'

She returned a minute later and dropped a slightly soggy newspaper onto the table. Valerie carefully unfolded its damp pages, then frowned.

'It's not the carrier's fault,' said Kristen. 'He thoughtfully shoved it to the far back of the box. But hey, I guess there's only so much you can do in this kind of weather.'

'No, it's not that. There's a story about that helicopter we saw yesterday. Here, check it out.' She held up the front page for Kristen's inspection. 'Body Recovered from Wailuku River,' the headline read. A photo of the orange helicopter they'd seen the day before, a rope and basket dangling from its belly, accompanied the article. Valerie turned the paper back around and read the story aloud:

> Early Wednesday morning, a woman called 911 to report seeing someone floating in the water below Rainbow Falls, and rescue personnel were immediately dispatched to the scene. After a search of several hours, the body of a man was recovered. Its condition suggests it had been in the river for a period of days, likely caught up under water before finally coming free, according to a source who asked not to be named. The identity of the deceased is being withheld pending notification to the family. Anyone with information regarding this occurrence is asked to contact the Hilo Police Department.

'Whoa.' She laid the paper in her lap and looked up at Kristen. 'It's just like the stories they were telling last night at the restaurant.'

'What stories?'

Valerie recounted what Matt and Kai had said about the dangers of the Wailuku River and the past drownings that had occurred there. 'So I have to think when they say "condition" of the body, that must mean it's all scratched up from being trapped in a lava cave. *Eauuuuh.*' A quick spasm passed over her upper body at the image this brought to mind.

And then she had another gruesome thought. 'Do you suppose it could be the missing bartender from the Speckled Gecko?'

Kristen let out a long breath. 'Oh, boy,' she said. 'Here we go again.'

They decided to spend the afternoon at Richardson Beach, at the far end of Keaukaha, a community strung out along the ocean east of Hilo. In addition to its pockets of white and black sand beaches, the rocky shoreline was home to numerous historic fishponds, their cold waters fed by the streams flowing off the slopes of Mauna Loa.

Valerie's initial thought, since the sun had burst through the clouds and it now looked to be a glorious afternoon, had been that it would be fun to head down to Puna for the day. But then she remembered with a pang: the volcanic eruption the previous May had taken out not only a huge portion of the Leilani Estates subdivision, but also many of their favorite hangout spots in the south-east corner of the island. The Kapoho tide pools – crown jewel of Puna's coastal lands – as well as the warm pond just down the road, were now both blanketed in barren, black rock, in some places reaching more than a hundred feet high. Even Kristen's beloved surf break at Pohoiki, though not itself inundated by lava, had been forever altered by flows on either side of it, and was now inaccessible to all but those willing to hike across two miles of jagged rock.

So Richardson's it was.

Making their way down to the beach by the lifeguard station, Valerie and Kristen spread their towels over the coarse black sand and gazed out at the rocky reef and the ocean beyond. A few hardy souls were doing their best to snorkel in the choppy shallows, but the water that day was far better suited for surfing or boogie-boarding than swimming.

'Shoot,' said Kristen, 'I didn't think to bring my board.' Shielding her eyes, she followed a figure out in the distance sending up a spray of foam as he carved a wave, then cut back up to its lip. 'Oh, well. Next time.'

With a grunt, she lay back on her towel and pulled her baseball cap down over her face, but Valerie continued to stare out at the seascape before them. It still sometimes sent shivers of amazement through her chest that they'd done it: actually made the move from Los Angeles to Hilo – left the City of Angels, freeways, and Del Tacos for a small town best known for its tropical gardens, farmers market, and rain. On an island in the middle of the vast Pacific Ocean, twenty-five hundred miles away from the nearest In-N-Out Burger or Major League baseball team.

Notwithstanding the whitecaps being whipped up by the wind, three long outrigger canoes were making their way through the choppy water, their occupants paddling furiously out beyond the reef which protected the small cove where they sat.

'Wow, they're sure working hard,' observed Valerie, prompting Kristen to sit up.

Squinting at the trio of six-man canoes, she nodded. 'Totally. And I don't remember seeing them paddling all the way down the coast here before. I wonder how far they're gonna go before turning back.'

They watched until the paddlers were out of sight behind the rocky outcropping at the far end of the beach and then Kristen turned to Valerie. 'I think I might like that. It looks fun.'

'Yeah . . .' Valerie wasn't so sure. 'Maybe if the water were a bit calmer than today. And if we stayed inside the breakwater.' A pause, then: 'Are there sharks around here?'

At twelve fifteen the next day, Valerie's cell rang. 'Hey, Isaac,' she said after punching 'accept.' 'What's up?'

'Nothing good.' He sounded out of breath, as if he'd been working out, but Valerie knew from the time of day that he had to be calling from the high school, where he taught biology.

Setting down the knife and the jar of mayonnaise she'd just grabbed from the fridge, she pulled out a chair to sit at the kitchen table. 'What's going on?'

'Did you read about the body they fished out of the river yesterday?'

'Uh-huh . . .'

'So it turns out it was Hank. You know, da bartender guy down at the Gecko?'

So she'd been right. *Damn.* Valerie let out the breath she hadn't even realized she'd been holding.

'And, well . . .' Isaac coughed, then went on. 'The cops were at da restaurant last night, askin' all these questions about Hank.'

'Makes sense,' said Valerie. 'They'd of course want to talk to

anyone who knew the guy. Do they know what happened? How
he died?'

'Dass the thing. According to Sachiko, they wouldn't say
anything about dat and were all mysterious about da whole thing.
But they sure did wanna talk to *her*, auright.'

'To Sachiko?'

'Uh-huh. Dey spent like an hour askin' her all about Hank
– how long he'd worked there, how she met him, how da two
of 'um got along—'

'Wait,' Valerie interrupted, standing up and starting to pace
across the kitchen. 'You mean they suspect *Sachiko* of being
involved in his death?'

'Sure sounds like it,' he said. 'I guess she was one of da last
people to see da guy that day out at Boiling Pots. And, well . . .'
He trailed off.

'And what?'

'So, apparently someone at da Gecko told da cops dey seen
Hank an' Sachiko havin' a big ol' argument the night before the
restaurant retreat.'

Valerie stopped her pacing. 'Oh, boy . . .'

'Yeah,' agreed Isaac with a sigh.

Neither spoke, and Valerie imagined Isaac was wondering the
same thing as she: If Sachiko and Hank had indeed had a big
argument the night before the bartender had disappeared, why
hadn't Sachiko mentioned it when the four of them had discussed
Hank's disappearance the other night over cocktails?

Did she in fact have something to hide?

'So, here's da thing,' Isaac finally went on after once more
clearing his throat. 'I was wondering . . . and you have to promise
not to tell Sachiko I'm asking dis, 'cause she'd kill me if—I
mean . . . not kill, you know, but . . .'

Valerie came to his rescue with a short laugh. 'Don't worry,
Isaac, I know what you mean. Go on. What were you going to
ask?'

'Okay. It's this. You were so good about figuring out what
happened with that body in da lava last spring, so I was just
wondering if maybe you might be willing to, you know . . . look
into what happened with Hank. 'Cause Sachiko sure as hell had
nothin' to do with it, I can promise you dat.'

Valerie wasn't sure what to say. On the one hand, she was flattered – if being good at eavesdropping, sticking your nose into other people's business, and lying to them was something that could be considered a positive attribute. But on the other hand, that whole thing with the body she'd discovered out at the lava flow had caused her an enormous amount of heartache and stress. Not to mention loss of sleep and arguments with her wife.

'Look,' Isaac said, no doubt interpreting her silence to mean what in fact it did. 'I'm not asking you to do much. Just snoop around at da restaurant, talk to folks, since they were all at the retreat that day, too. You're good at that. And hey, it's perfect when ya think about it. Bartenders are always talkin' story to people – dass what they do. And since you're so new there, the other staff'll just think you're being friendly when you ask about their lives and all their personal stuffs.'

'I dunno, Isaac. To sneak around Sachiko like that . . .'

'It's to *help* her, so really, it's okay,' he pleaded. 'If I could do it, I would, but dere's no way dat would work, since it wouldn't make no sense for me to be hangin' out li'dat at da Gecko all da time.'

It was obvious he was getting increasingly agitated. 'Fine,' Valerie said, caving. 'I'll do some poking around at the Gecko.'

'Auright!'

'But that's *all* I'm gonna do, okay?'

'You da bomb. I owe ya, cuz – big time. But remember, you no can let Sachiko know what you're doin', yah?'

'Yeah, yeah. I get it.'

'Kay, den. Look, I gotta go. Class is starting in a few. But I'll talk to you soon.'

Valerie set her phone on the counter and turned to see Kristen standing in the doorway. 'What the hell was *that* all about?' she asked.

'Oy.' Valerie shook her head. 'That was Isaac. It turns out the body they pulled out of the river yesterday was in fact that bartender from the Speckled Gecko, and – even though the police are keeping mum about the cause of death – I gather from what Isaac just told me that they're treating it as suspicious.'

'Whoa.'

'Yeah. And, long story short, Isaac is pretty sure that Sachiko is a suspect.'

'Yikes. That's not good.'

'No, it's not.' Valerie filled Kristen in on what she'd learned from Isaac, then sat back down at the kitchen table and began stabbing at the mayonnaise in the jar with the butter knife.

'And . . .?' Kristen said, taking the chair across from her. 'I could tell from your end of the conversation that there's more.'

'There is.' She looked up and met Kristen's gaze. 'He wants me to look into it. Talk to the other staff at the Gecko who were there at the retreat the day Hank disappeared and see if I come up with anything relevant. Anything that might help prove Sachiko wasn't involved in his death. But he doesn't want Sachiko to know I'm doing it.'

'And you agreed.'

Valerie inclined her head. 'But you shoulda heard him, Kris. The guy was desperate. I didn't feel like I had much choice.'

Kristen held Valerie's eyes a moment longer, then smiled. Reaching across the table, she took her wife's hand. 'It's okay. You do seem to be pretty good at this sort of thing. I say go for it, girl.'

FIVE

Bartenders tend to be jovial types. Perky and upbeat, quick to smile, and always ready to listen to an amusing – or long and tedious – story. But it's also important that they possess a great memory and that they be organized and in fine physical shape.

Friday night at the Speckled Gecko was a prime example of all the above.

'That's two Margaritas over, one no salt; a G and T; a Stoli Martini; a Chard; and a pint of Longboard, right?'

'Right,' said Annie. 'I'll be back to pick 'em up in a jiff; got an order up.'

'No worries.' Valerie turned to grab three highball glasses from the shelf above her head, dipped one in the rimmer sponge, then in the salt, and filled all three with ice. She was pouring tequila into one of the glasses when Jun slid behind her bearing a pair of Mai Tais.

'Can you slice more limes when you got a minute?' he called out as he passed by.

'On it!' Valerie shouted back. *Not.* She still had to finish up this order and tend to the deuce who were staring her down from the far end of the bar before she could even think about slicing more fruit.

And then Seth appeared at the bar rails. 'Got a Cosmo, a Daiquiri, and two Mojitos!'

Yes, you definitely had to be at the top of your game to bartend on a weekend night at the Speckled Gecko. And it was still only six fifteen.

After the last of the night's customers – a raucous group of tourists from New Jersey – had finally been persuaded to leave the restaurant, Valerie leaned against the carved wood bar and drank down a full glass of ice-cold water.

'Busy night,' observed Jun, popping open a bottle of Stella.

'Yup.'

She'd been hoping to ask her fellow bartender about Hank during their shift tonight, but that sure hadn't happened. By the time she'd arrived at the Gecko at four o'clock, happy-hour rush was already in full swing, and the rush hadn't let up all evening.

Jun chugged half his beer, then set about emptying the garnishes in the well. Coming to stand next to him, Valerie grabbed a bar towel and wiped down the areas vacated by the inserts he was cleaning. 'So you heard about Hank, I imagine?' she said.

He shook his head. 'Just awful. What a way to go.'

'It must have been hard for you to hear the news . . . You know, you two working so closely together like you did?'

Valerie couldn't tell if his glance her way was one of irritation at her prying or merely a look of 'well, duh, of course I'm upset.'

'I'm handlin' it,' was all she got for an answer.

Okay, so he obviously wasn't one to talk about his feelings – at least not with a virtual stranger. She tried another tack, 'Were you here last night when the cops came?'

'Uh-huh. It was right in the middle of dinner, when everyone was totally in da weeds. Not that they gave a hoot about that,' he added with a snort. 'And then they wanted to talk to all of us – right *then*.' Jun ran a hand over his thinning gray hair, then grabbed a pair of empty beer bottles off the bar and carried them over to the recycling bin.

'What, they couldn't wait?' asked Valerie.

'They didn't want to. But Sachiko laid down the law and basically told 'em to get the hell out until after closing.' He chuckled at the memory, happy to talk now that it wasn't about him. 'You shoulda seen 'em back down once she switched into her angry girl mode. She can be pretty scary when she wants to.'

Scary? Sachiko? This was a side of Isaac's girlfriend Valerie had never witnessed. Peering through the double doors into the indoor dining area, she watched as the front-of-the-house manager counted the cash and closed out the register. 'That's weird,' Valerie said. 'She's always seemed so calm and . . . I dunno, mild-mannered whenever we've hung out.'

'I guess you must not have been around too many restaurant managers, den, is all I can say. Dey *all* got one scary side.' With a grunt, Jun hefted the trash bag from the bin and carried it out the back door to the recycling and garbage area behind the restaurant.

Was that true? Valerie wondered as she restocked the beer and wine supply. *Were all restaurant managers scary?* Her brother Charlie hadn't seemed so to her, but then again, he was her baby brother. *Had he been scary to the other employees at Chez Charles?*

But for that matter, was what Jun had just told her even true – that Sachiko had an 'angry girl mode'? Or was it merely the classic case of a man thinking what a woman does is 'angry,' whereas in another man it would simply be shrugged off as being 'real' or 'honest'?

The two of them finished closing down the bar, their conversation moving on to more mundane topics: the weather, their work schedules for the next few days, and the proposal to repave parts of the highway down in Puna that had been covered by the lava flow the previous May.

Then, his work done for the night, Jun checked his phone, then bid Valerie farewell and headed out the back door, not bothering to say goodbye to anyone else.

Valerie, however, still had work to do.

Wandering into the dining room, she found Seth setting tables and Annie folding napkins for the next day's lunch service. 'Need help with anything?' she asked.

'Nah, we're pretty much done,' said Seth, 'but it's super sweet of you to offer.'

Annie set the last of her napkins on the top of the stack and clapped her hands. 'Well, you can help me drink some beer, if you want.'

The two of them grabbed cans from the wait station fridge and pulled out chairs at the same table as the other night. A couple minutes later, they were joined by Seth and Kai, the server wheeling a bicycle out from the storage room. He leaned it against the wall in the wait station and joined Kai at the fridge, helping himself to a ginger beer as the busser popped the cap of his Corona. Post-work drinks with the staff was clearly a well-established tradition at the Gecko.

Valerie hadn't spoken to Sachiko since her conversation with Isaac earlier in the day, but was hoping to get the chance to do so now. If nothing else, she wanted to at least gauge her reaction to all that had happened in the last twenty-four hours. Right now, Valerie could see Sachiko through the pass, talking to Nalani in the kitchen. She couldn't hear any of their conversation, but both wore serious expressions. After a minute, Sachiko shook her head, said one last thing to the restaurant owner, then emerged into the dining room.

'Hey, guys,' she said, coming to stand at their table. 'I think I'm gonna head on home. I'm pretty pooped.'

Annie looked up and patted her on the arm. 'No worries. I totally understand.'

'But everyone did great tonight. Especially given . . .' Glancing toward the back of the restaurant where the bar stood, Sachiko swallowed. 'Well, anyway, I really appreciate it. See you all tomorrow.' Then, flashing a half-hearted smile, she turned and headed for the front door.

'She seems pretty upset,' Valerie said to the group once Sachiko had gone. 'Not that she doesn't have reason to be, of course.'

Seth blew out his cheeks, his fingers tapping out a cadence on the wooden tabletop. 'The whole thing is so surreal. I mean, one day Hank's here tending bar, and then the next . . .'

'He's not,' finished Kai. He was focused on the wall across the room, eyebrows drawn close. 'It's kinda hard to even take it all in.'

Annie took a long pull from her beer, then set down the can with a *smack*. 'Yeah, and having half the Hilo police force here last night asking all these creepy questions sure didn't help any.'

'Creepy?' asked Valerie. 'What do you mean?'

'Like, did I know if anyone here at the restaurant had any kind of grudge against Hank, or did I see him arguing with anyone in the past week or so.'

'And "Who was the last person to see him that day at the retreat?"' added Seth. '"Cause I gather they found Hank's car still parked at the Boiling Pots parking lot, so they figure he must have died while still up there. They also asked me how come no one noticed that his car was still there even though he wasn't around. That's the question that got me. It's like they're trying to pin his death on one of *us*.' He looked over at Annie and Kai. 'Did they ask you guys that, too?'

'Uh-huh,' they answered in unison.

'But the park was full of people that day,' said Seth, 'so there were a bunch of cars in the lot. It's not like you're gonna notice something like that, or who left before anyone else.'

Valerie studied her fellow workers for any signs of guilt or nervousness.. But all she saw on their faces was annoyance and nods of agreement. Did none of them feel any sadness at the bartender's sudden death?

'So, *did* anyone here have a grudge against him?' she asked.

The three employees glanced at each other, but no one spoke.

Of course. I'm the outsider, so why would they trust me? She needed to be more subtle with her questioning.

'Okay, that came out wrong. Let me rephrase it. It's just that I'm curious, since I never met the guy: What was Hank like? I mean, was he friendly? Did people in general like him? Did his customers like him? 'Cause, from what you're telling me, the cops seem to think *someone* sure didn't like him.'

Annie let out a noisy breath. 'Yeah . . . well, let's just say he had a pretty high opinion of himself, which I think some people might have taken the wrong way.'

'Might have?' said Kai with a short laugh.

Valerie turned her attention to the busser, eyebrows raised in encouragement for him to elaborate. Which he did.

'So da guy, he comes in here all cocky, acting like he's this primo bartender—'

'Well, he was in fact a pretty darn good bartender,' Seth broke in. 'Not that that excuses his attitude, of course. But, as you may have noticed,' a glance Valerie's way, 'Jun's getting a little long in the tooth, as they say, so he was lucky to have Hank helping out.'

'True,' agreed Kai with a nod. 'But what about his temper? That sure didn't help Jun any.'

Seth waved his hand dismissively. 'Yeah, he did sometimes lose his cool and yell at us, but it's not like he was some kind of Gordon Ramsay celebrity chef character, kicking holes in cabinets and throwing dishes at people. As far as I'm concerned, he wasn't all that different from a whole lotta guys I've worked with at restaurants.'

'So is it true,' asked Valerie, leaning forward, 'that Hank and Sachiko had a big fight here the night before the retreat?'

More glances between the other three at the table, though thankfully no one asked where she'd heard this piece of information.

'I wouldn't call it a "big" fight,' said Annie after a bit. 'But yeah, they definitely had words.'

Seth sat back in his chair with a frown. 'Which I'm sure is why the cops spent so much time talking to her last night. And why she wasn't in much of a mood to hang out and be social just now.'

'Could you hear what the argument was about?'

All three shook their heads. 'They were in the office with the door closed,' said Annie. She swiveled in her chair to face Seth. 'But if I had to guess, I'd say it was about that customer he got into it with the night before. Don't ya think?'

'Maybe,' said Seth noncommittally.

'What happened with the customer?' asked Valerie.

Annie took a sip of beer before replying. 'Hank apparently wasn't too pleased about the guy criticizing the drink he'd made for him. What was it? A Gimlet . . . or Tom Collins? Jun would remember, 'cause he's the one who had to cool Hank down. Anyway, I'm thinking that when Sachiko heard about it – 'cause she wasn't there the night it happened – she must have called him into the office to talk about it, which is what we all heard.'

'Heard what?' The four of them looked up to see Nalani striding across the dining room.

'Uh . . . we were just talking about poor Hank,' said Annie.

'Uh-huh.' Hands on hips, the head chef eyed the group for a moment before pulling up a chair.

Valerie cleared her throat. 'It was me asking about him, actually. I was just wondering what might have happened to him . . . how he might have died.'

'Well, one thing's for sure,' said Kai, slapping his palm on the tabletop, 'no way would Hank have gone swimming in da river that day like the cops were sayin'. He paddled with our club and woulda for sure known how strong da current was. It's been super dangerous – even more than usual – ever since Lane. Nobody went in that day.'

Matt emerged from the kitchen, wiping his hands on a side towel. 'What do you think we should do with all those pork chops we have left over from tonight's special?' he asked Nalani.

As the two discussed possibilities for a new dish the following night, Seth stood and walked over to the wait station. 'Time for me to go home and get some beauty sleep,' he said, tossing his empty bottle into the recycling bin and grabbing the handle bars of his bicycle.

'Nice wheels,' said Valerie, admiring the blue-and-gray mountain bike.

'I keep tellin' him he needs to get some *real* wheels,' said Kai with a snort, 'but dis one, he too cheap to buy a car.'

Seth shook his head. 'And as I keep telling you, there's no need to add to all the world's carbon emissions when you can get around just fine without a car. You, more than anyone, Kai, should care about the environment, being a paddler.'

But the busboy merely rolled his eyes in response. It seemed clear this was not the first time they'd had this discussion.

Valerie turned to Kai. 'So, which club do you paddle with?' she asked.

'Da Mahina Canoe Club. We won three races this season,' he said, flexing his bicep with a boyish grin.

'You must be a pretty tight-knit group. You know, hang out together when you're not paddling and stuff?'

'Absolutely. Dey's my homies, for sure.'

Which means they all probably knew Hank pretty well, too. 'It sounds like a great community, paddling. When my wife and I saw some guys out there today, we both commented that it looked like a lot of fun.'

She had Kai's full attention now. 'Oh, yeah, it's awesome. Nothin' like being out in da ocean, getting a good workout, communing with whales and dolphins. And da oddah paddlers, dey da best. You really should try it.'

'Maybe I will. Any chance I could come down sometime when your club is practicing to watch and meet some of the guys you paddle with? Oh, wait, are there women in the club, too?'

'Yah – we got da women an' da men, for sure. Wanna come

down tomorrow morning? We meet at seven on Saturdays at the hālau – you know, the clubhouse down at the canoe beach. It's the blue-and-green one pretty much in da middle of all da clubs.'

'Rain or shine?'

He laughed. 'Dis be Hilo, girl. We paddle unless it's like one tsunami out dere.'

SIX

Rain spattered against the kitchen window the next morning as Valerie ground beans and spooned them into the coffee maker. Punching the 'on' button, she walked to the window and peered outside. Black clouds shrouded Maunakea, but she knew that didn't mean a whole lot with regard to what the weather might be later on in town. As Kristen loved to note, 'showers on the slopes' was pretty much par for the course in east Hawai'i Island.

The screen door into the living room slammed shut, and a moment later, Kristen came into the kitchen wiping her face with her sleeve. 'It looks pretty good out over the ocean,' she said. 'Just your regulation trade wind clouds, so I think it should be fine down at the beach.'

In their short time in Hilo, they'd learned that the weather tended to come from the east, in the direction of the trade winds, and that if they spied squalls out over the ocean, it was a good bet it'd be raining at their house within fifteen to twenty minutes.

'There's a nice rainbow out front, if you want to go see.' Kristen dropped the newspaper onto the kitchen table, then held out a pink piece of paper. 'Oh, and this was stuck into the screen door.'

Valerie read the notice: 'Annual Kumiai Picnic This Saturday at Carlsmith Beach, 3 to 6 pm. Hot dogs and sodas provided, bring a side dish or dessert to share.' A note was scribbled at the bottom of the flyer: 'Sorry about the late notice, but hope you can come. Welcome to the neighborhood! your neighbor, Shirley.'

'What's a . . . koo-mee-ai, I wonder?' said Valerie, carefully sounding out the word.

'That's what they call a neighborhood association here,' Kristen replied in a breezy tone. 'It's a Japanese word that dates back to when the Japanese immigrants first came to the island to work on the sugar plantations.'

Valerie eyed her wife with a knowing smile. 'And you'd like

me to believe that was a piece of information you already possessed . . .'

'Nah,' said Kristen, returning her grin. She held out her phone. 'I had to look it up online.'

'Well, glad to know there are some things you don't know. This Shirley, here.' Valerie tapped the pink sheet. 'Isn't she the gal who lives two doors up the street? The one with all the orchids growing on that big tree fern?'

'Yeah, I think you're right.' Kristen checked the status of the coffee and, seeing it had dripped through, filled a travel mug with the brew. 'So you wanna go to the picnic? Seems like it'd be a great way to meet some more of the neighbors.'

'Sure, sounds fun. I can make my famous celery and date salad.'

Valerie helped herself to coffee, and the two of them headed outside to their car – a blue RAV4 they'd had shipped over from the Mainland. A scattering of raindrops hit the windshield as they drove down the hill toward town, but by the time they arrived at the Bayfront Park, the clouds had cleared and the sun was sparkling off all the puddles collected in the road.

'Told ya,' said Kristen as they pulled into the parking lot.

Valerie patted her on the knee. 'Yes, dear. You win the weather forecasting award for the morning.'

They drove slowly past the various canoe houses until they spotted a group of people milling about in front of one. 'This has gotta be it,' said Valerie. 'Yeah, blue and green – those were the colors Kai said. Oh, and there he is.'

Kristen parked next to a jacked-up pickup with enormous tires and a bumper sticker depicting a seated Polynesian woman in a red-and-white dress. Kai looked up as they climbed out of the car.

'You made it!'

'What, you didn't believe I'd come? Ye of little faith. And hey, you not only got me, but I brought along my wife, as well. She's actually way more interested in paddling than I am, so she wanted to come down with me to watch and meet you all.'

Valerie introduced Kai to Kristen, and he pointed to all the various paddlers present, naming them in turn. Valerie did her best to commit them to memory – Stuart, Bob, Toshi, and . . .

Mike? – but when he added the names of the six guys carting one of the long canoes down to the water, she gave up trying.

'I thought you told me there'd be women here, too,' Kristen said, looking around at all the paddlers gathered about.

Kai grinned. 'Dey'll be here, no worries. But it's an important practice today for da men. We only got a few more weeks till da queen race that finishes out the season – da Moloka'i Hoe.'

'Cool!' said Valerie. 'Where's it take place? Can we come watch?'

'Not unless you wanna fly to O'ahu. It's a long-distance race from Moloka'i to Honolulu – forty-one miles.'

'Wow.' Kristen let out a breath. 'That's a long way to paddle, dude.'

'Well, we don't all paddle da whole time. There's a team of ten of us, and we switch out paddlers e'ry half hour or so.'

Valerie glanced at Kristen, then back at Kai. 'Uh . . . how do you do that – switch paddlers mid-stream? Or, mid-ocean, rather.'

He laughed. 'It ain't easy, I no kid you. Dere's an escort boat dat follows us, and da guys, dey jump in da water and swim up to the canoe and climb in when da oddah one, he jumps out.'

'Do the women do the race, too?' asked Kristen, and Kai nodded.

'Fo' sure. Though da Mahina club women aren't doing it dis year. It's a separate race on a different date – da Na Wahine O Ke Kai – but it's da exact same route as for da men.' At the sound of a roaring engine, he looked up. 'Ho! And here's da ladies, right on cue!'

A black SUV came barreling up to where they stood, followed by an older model Honda. The driver of the SUV, a lanky gal with long black hair, jumped down and strode toward them, a polished wood canoe paddle in her hand. 'Where's Leilani?' she asked, craning her neck to see who might be there at the hālau.

'I just got a text from her a few minutes ago saying she's sick,' answered the guy Valerie thought might be named Mike.

The woman's face fell. 'Well, Sasha sure as hell better show up, then. No way can we go out with just the three of us.' Then, noticing Valerie and Kristen for the first time, she said, 'Who are you? Do you paddle?'

'Uh . . .' Valerie's eyes grew wide. 'We just came to watch, is all. I've never even been out in a canoe.'

'Hey, I'd be willing to give it a shot,' said Kristen. She turned to Valerie. 'C'mon, it can't be all that hard.'

'I don't know . . .'

The two women who'd arrived in the Honda had now joined the group. 'I just heard from Sasha,' said one. 'She's not coming, either.'

'Damn.' The dark-haired woman stared out at the ocean for a moment, then returned her gaze to Valerie and Kristen. 'You'd be doing us a huge favor. We really need to get in a practice today, and it's pretty much impossible to paddle an OC-6 with only three people.' She held out her hand. 'I'm Tala, by the way. And this is Mara and Becca.'

'Kristen.' She took Tala's hand. 'And this undecided gal here is Valerie.'

All six of them were now staring at her: Kristen, the three other women, Kai, and maybe-Mike.

After a moment, Tala frowned, then slapped both hands on her board shorts. 'Okay, look,' she said, 'how 'bout we just go for a short paddle inside the breakwater and you can see what you think. And if you hate it, we can come back and drop you off. You do know how to swim, though, right?'

'I can swim fine. I grew up near the ocean, in Southern California.' Valerie chewed her lip for a moment as the others continued to give her pleading looks, then raised her hands in defeat. 'All right, fine; I'll do it. Just don't expect too much from me, though, okay?'

'Awesome!' They all crowded around and clapped Valerie on the back. 'You're gonna love it!' said Becca.

She took in the enormous canoe before her and swallowed. *We'll see about that.*

But it turned out to be good fun after they got out into the bay – and after the not-so-fun start to the adventure.

'Oh, but you can't paddle without first proving you can climb back in again if we huli,' Tala had said as soon as they'd gotten about ten strokes away from the beach. 'It's kind of an unofficial rule. Are you two okay with a bit of a dip before we head out?'

'Uh . . . I guess so.' Valerie glanced back at Kristen, who nodded.

'Fine with me. We'll have time to dry off while we paddle.'

'Alrighty, here we go!' And then, at the count of 'three,' Tala, Becca, and Mara had all leaned to their right, causing the now off-balance canoe to capsize, sending Valerie's seat cushion – along with the paddle Becca had loaned her – floating off into the distance.

Once she'd blown the sea water from her nose and recovered from the shock of being suddenly plunged into the ocean, Valerie swam off to retrieve her cushion and paddle, then returned to the others. The four other paddlers had by then righted the canoe, and Tala and Mara had already scrambled back into the craft and were bailing the water with scoops fashioned from gallon milk jugs.

'Swim around to this side,' Tala shouted at Valerie, 'but watch out for the ama!' This, apparently, was the outrigger. 'Just hoist yourself up and swing your leg over the side.'

Kristen, bobbing in the water next to her between the ama and the canoe, grabbed hold of the side and easily lifted herself up and over, as if she were simply climbing out of a swimming pool. She was followed quickly by Becca, who took her seat in the second position.

But when Valerie attempted to do the same, she quickly realized that the other paddlers' height and long arms were an important asset which she lacked. After three tries, unable to lift her body high enough out of the water to throw her leg over the gunnel, she sank back in the water in defeat.

'I can't do it,' she croaked, hoping she didn't sound as whiny as she felt.

'Yes, you can,' encouraged Mara. 'Grab hold of the 'iako – that's the boom connecting the canoe to the ama – and use that as leverage.'

Valerie did as she was told and, after two tries, succeeded in wrapping her legs around the boom. But then there she was, hanging from the 'iako like a trussed wild pig, unsure how to maneuver from that precarious position into the canoe. Finally, after many shouts of encouragement from her fellow paddlers, she was able to work her way over to the gunnel and fling her legs over the side, then flop her body onto the floor of the canoe like a landed fish.

'Well,' she said, panting and rubbing her shin – which she'd managed to whang on the seat post in the process – 'that was about as ungraceful as could be.'

'Hey, but you did it, and that's all that matters.' Tala grinned. 'And we didn't have to help you, which is great. Anyone who can get back in by themselves – no matter how inelegantly done – can call themselves a true paddler. 'Cause you never know if there'll be anyone there to help you if you huli out in the open water.'

Great, thought Valerie, as she picked up her paddle and scrambled onto her seat.

But after that, it *was* in fact great.

Tala told Valerie and Kristen – whom they'd placed in the third and fourth positions from the front – that they should time their strokes with the person's paddle two seats ahead of them and explained that they were to switch sides paddling on the 'ho!' of 'hut, hut, *ho!*'

And then they were off. The canoe sliced through the water surprisingly quickly, and before Valerie knew it, they were halfway to the breakwater.

'You doing okay?' asked Mara from her place at the back of the canoe as steersperson, and Valerie nodded.

'Yeah, doing great!'

'All right! You're looking good, too. Though you might wanna jam your paddle farther into the water. You'll get more bang for your buck with each stroke.'

It was tiring work, but the wind and ocean spray on her face felt delicious. Valerie could see the two men's canoes from the Mahina Canoe Club far in the distance, having cleared the breakwater and now on their way down the coast in the direction of the beach they'd been at the day before. *Ah, that must be why the canoes were all the way down there*, she realized. *They're doing long-distance practices to prepare for that big race that's coming up.*

Concentrating on her strokes, she tried to keep them deep and consistent, and listened for Becca's 'hut, hut, *ho!*' in the position in front of her, so as not to knock paddles with her if she neglected to change sides at the correct time.

After about twenty minutes, Tala called a halt, and they glided to a stop. No one spoke as the canoe bobbed gently in the dark blue water. The bay was calm, and the only sound was that of water lapping against their hull. From where they floated just inside the breakwater, Valerie could see the blocky form of an enormous white cruise ship docked at the Port of Hilo.

Ahhh . . . She stretched her arms and leaned back on her seat. So peaceful. And wonderful to be so close to the natural life of the bay. Valerie had heard stories of whales surfacing close to paddlers and dolphins following canoes, but other than a scattering of birds she guessed might be some kind of tern, she'd spotted no sea life today.

'What time of year are the whales here?' she asked.

Becca dipped a hand in the water and splashed it on her face. 'It's a bit early yet, but you might see them starting to show up around now.'

Scanning the horizon for any sign of whales, Valerie considered how she might bring up the subject of Hank. That was the primary reason she'd come down to the canoe house this morning, after all. And while they were actively paddling, it was pretty much impossible to have any kind of real conversation. Now was the time, if she wanted to pick their brains about the dead bartender and paddler.

She'd just settled on saying something vague like, 'Did you hear about Hank?' when Mara called out from behind her, 'Oh, wow – check out all the fish!'

To their right, a school of some twenty silver fish with long, pointed beaks were leaping from the water.

'Cool!' said Kristen. But no sooner had she spoken than the school moved in their direction. Within seconds the fish began shooting all around them, as if a sudden squall had descended over the canoe.

'Watch out!' shouted Tala, holding up her paddle to swat one away. Valerie ducked down to protect her face as the fish whizzed past, their needle noses like a blast of tiny spears flying through the air.

A loud *thunk* caused her to look up. 'It's in the canoe!' hollered Becca, jumping up from her seat to avoid the razor-sharp beak of the fish now flopping about at her feet.

'Grab it by the tail!' yelled Tala.

Becca gave her friend a look that said, '*You* grab it by the tail.' But after a moment, she tentatively reached out a hand, then shot it forward and, in one swift motion, grabbed the end of the writhing fish and tossed it from the canoe.

They all breathed out as one. It was now quiet, the school of needle fish having returned to its normal habitat under the sea as quickly as they'd appeared.

'Whoa, that was close.' Valerie sat up straight and shook out her arms, letting go of the tension that had overtaken her during the excitement. At a low sound from behind, she swiveled around on her bench. 'Did you say something?' she asked Kristen.

'No, I think it was Mara.' The two peered back at the steersperson, then gasped when they saw her clutching her upper leg, a grimace contorting her face.

'Ohmygod, are you all right?' shouted Valerie. And then she noticed the blood dripping from beneath Mara's hand, staining the water pooled in the canoe a bright pink.

Mara met Valerie's eyes and gave an impatient shake of the head. 'Damn fish got me good. I think I might need stitches.'

SEVEN

They returned to shore as quickly as possible, with Kristen now moving back to the empty fifth seat and taking on steersperson duties as Mara held a T-shirt over her leg to stanch the bleeding. Once the canoe had been dragged far enough onto the black sand beach to not be in danger of washing away, they hurried Mara to a chair in the hālau and had a look at her leg.

'Ouch. That's quite a slice, girl.' Tala frowned, then grabbed a bottle from a cloth shopping bag on the floor of the canoe house and poured water over the wound.

Becca peered at Mara's thigh, worry on her face. 'We should get you to urgent care. Don't want to mess with getting a staph infection or some flesh-eating bacteria.'

Valerie winced. 'Eeew. Really? Flesh-eating bacteria?'

'Oh, yeah. Ya gotta be super careful around here if you get any kind of cut. You know, wash it real good with antiseptic and keep it covered up.' Becca found a clean towel and wrapped it around Mara's leg. 'There's like twenty different bacterial infections you can get with wounds in the tropics.' She held out her hand to Mara. 'C'mon, I'll drive you to the clinic.'

Once they'd helped Mara limp to Becca's car, Valerie, Kristen, and Tala walked back out to the canoe. Valerie attempted to heft the front end with a grunt. 'Not sure the three of us will be able to carry it back to the rack unless we drag it,' she said.

Tala shook her head. 'Nah, we don't wanna do that. The thing weighs more than four hundred pounds, and the hull would get all scraped up if we dragged it. But it's okay; you two can get going, if you want. I'll just wait for the guys to get back from their paddle, or maybe some others'll show up who can help me with it.'

Kristen glanced up at the sun. 'It's only what, around eight or so? I do have to get back to meet someone at ten, but we could hang out a little longer. That way, if only a few other people show up, we can still haul this thing up to the canoe house.'

'Thanks.' Tala graced her with a toothy grin. 'I appreciate it. C'mon, let's go sit down while we wait.'

After heading to their car to retrieve their bags and a pair of towels they kept in the back, Valerie and Kristen carried chairs from the hālau out into the sun next to Tala. 'Did you bring a change of clothes?' she asked them.

'Uh-uh. As you may recall, we weren't planning on going out in the water.'

'Till this mean ol' lady bossed you into joining us.' Tala's laugh was deep and melodious. 'And then after all that, the outing was cut short. Sorry about that. But hey, you interested in trying it again – when maybe we'll get in a *real* paddle? 'Cause I gotta say, you both looked pretty good out there.'

Valerie dug her toes into the warm sand and snorted. 'Right. I don't know about me looking all that good, but you seem to be a natural, Kris.'

'It's only 'cause of my long arms,' replied Kristen. 'But yeah, I'd totally be up for going out again sometime. It was super fun.'

Once again, Valerie felt the eyes of others upon her. 'Sure, I'm game,' she said. 'But maybe not for – what was the distance of that race the guys are prepping for? Forty miles?'

'No worries; we rarely paddle for more than a couple hours. And we wouldn't subject you to anything even that long your first time out. We practice sprints, too. This Tuesday morning at eight is our next meeting, if you want to come down. We're always looking for new blood.'

'Well, you certainly got some of that today,' said Valerie. 'Blood, that is.'

'Ha!' Tala slapped her knee. 'Not exactly what I had in mind.'

They stared out at the water, watching a trio of red-and-white canoes make their way around the end of the breakwater and then turn for shore. Not the Mahina canoes, Valerie noted, which were painted the same blue and green as the hālau.

'So, you heard about Hank, I imagine?' she said after a while.

Tala turned to face her. 'Hank, the paddler? No, should I have heard something about him? What happened?'

Oh, boy. So I have to be the one to give her the bad news?

'Uh, well, he's dead. They pulled his body out of the Wailuku River the other day. You hadn't even heard he'd gone missing?'

Valerie glanced at Kristen, who inclined her head ever so slightly to indicate she knew what Valerie was doing.

Tala frowned but said nothing in reply. Then, after a bit, 'How do you know . . .' She continued to hold Valerie's gaze, confusion in her eyes.

'It was on the front page of the paper the other day, which is why I thought you would have heard. I'm really sorry to be the bearer of the bad news.'

'No, I mean how do you know he paddled with us? Didn't you say you just moved to town? So how would you even know that?' The confused look had now morphed into what seemed like suspicion: *Who was this island newbie bringing bad juju to their canoe club?*

'Oh.' Valerie shook her head. 'It's only because I work at the Speckled Gecko where he and Kai both work . . . worked.' A pause. 'Anyhow, Kai's the one who invited me down here this morning to watch your practice.'

'Ah, got it.' This appeared to satisfy her. She shook out her arms, then leaned back in her plastic chair. 'Dang. That is so friggin' weird. Do they know what happened to him?'

Valerie shrugged, unwilling to divulge at this time what little she knew about Hank's demise. 'All I've heard is that he hadn't been seen for almost a week before they found his body in the river.'

'Ugh. Not a nice way to go.'

'So, were you two close?' asked Valerie, eager to get as much information out of Tala as possible before the paddlers in the three canoes arrived to help them carry the canoe off the beach.

'Not really.' Tala took a sip of water. She certainly didn't seem terribly upset by the death of her fellow paddler, which was interesting information in and of itself. 'We mostly practice in teams of either all men or all women since there aren't that many mixed races, and you mostly get to know the people you actually paddle with the best. I mean, we do all socialize together some-times – go out for breakfast after practice or hang out at each other's houses at parties and stuff. But Hank . . .'

'I take it you two never really hit it off?'

Tala leaned over to scratch a spot on her lower calf, just above a geometric pattern tattooed around her ankle. 'Yeah . . . you could say that,' she answered slowly. 'I mean, I don't want to speak ill of the dead or anything, but—'

'But you're gonna, nevertheless,' interjected Kristen with a wry smile. At the tensing of Tala's body, however, she held up her hands. 'Oh, god, don't worry. We never even met the guy. Though from what little I do know, he was definitely not on many people's most popular list. So, what were you going to say?'

When Tala didn't immediately answer, Valerie's brain ran through a series of internal curses, and she did her best not to shoot dirty looks at her wife for causing the interruption. But after a moment, the paddler thankfully went on.

'It's just that he had kind of a high opinion of himself, is all.'

Valerie nodded encouragingly. 'So I've heard.'

'But he was a great paddler – super strong and competitive as hell. So the guys put up with it. Though Craig sure won't shed too many tears at his loss.' She put a hand to her mouth, then shook her head. 'Sorry, I shouldn't have said that. The poor guy is dead, after all.'

'No, it's okay. Really.' Valerie glanced at Kristen, who was now keeping quiet after her previous misstep. 'I'm sure it's cathartic for you to talk about it.'

'Yeah, maybe. 'Cause it sure is bizarre, having someone you know – even if you weren't particularly close – all of a sudden just be . . . gone.' Tala scooped up a ball of sand and clenched it in her hand, then let it fall through her fingers.

The red-and-white canoes were now nearing shore, and Valerie was willing Tala to finish telling them about Craig and Hank before they made it to the beach.

'So, Craig had some kind of issue with Hank?' she prompted.

Tala's eyes tracked the canoes as she answered. 'You know about that long-distance race coming up?'

'Yeah, the Moloka'i . . . something?'

'Hoe. Right. Well, Hank and Craig were both vying for the role of starting stroker. It's a huge honor, since the stroker is the one who sets the pace and is usually the strongest paddler on the team.'

'But wait.' Kristen finally reentered the conversation. 'I thought the paddlers switched out during that race, you know, took turns paddling and then resting in the escort boat.'

Tala nodded. 'True, but even on a long, open ocean race like that where you switch out strokers a bunch of times during the race – way more often than for the other positions, actually, because of how grueling it is – it's still a big deal to be the *starting* stroker. 'Cause that's who gets all the glory, by being the one who goes in first and who gets to paddle out of the harbor with everyone watching, rather than sitting in the escort boat waiting to go in later as a second-string paddler. It's kind of like a ball player who gets to be the starter as opposed to someone they bring in later off the bench.'

Tala turned to face Valerie with a grin. 'Plus, the strokers are pretty much always the paddlers with the biggest egos. And yes, I know this well since I, too, am the stroker for the women's team. But frankly – and I doubt this will come as much of a surprise to you – the guys are generally way more invested in who gets picked as starting stroker on a long race than the women.'

Kristen laughed. 'No, not much of a surprise.'

'Not only that,' Tala went on, 'but Craig and Hank have been super competitive all summer about which of them will be picked as the A-team stroker for the regatta season next year – you know, the short sprint races they hold in the bay?'

'And now that role – as well as starter for the Moloka'i race – will for sure go to Craig,' said Valerie.

The first of the red-and-white canoes had now made landfall. 'Yup,' Tala responded, then stood and headed down to the shore.

Valerie's shift at the Speckled Gecko that evening didn't start till five, but since Kristen would be gone all afternoon working on the lānai-building project with Isaac's friend, she decided to head down there early. Kristen had taken the Toyota, so Valerie was planning on taking an Uber to work. But then, glancing out the kitchen window and seeing the dark clouds over the ocean were still quite a ways off, she opted to walk to the restaurant instead.

As she strolled down their street, past white wood-frame homes topped with a mix of green, white, and red metal roofs, she considered what drink special she might offer that evening. *Perhaps something with gin and lemongrass . . .* But no, that would require at least a day's preparation, as the aromatic herb would require steeping in either the gin or a simple syrup.

And the Island Sour idea she'd come up with also required advance muddling of the ginger and honey. But since she'd be early today, those were two tasks she could complete for later on in the week.

Maybe something simple like a passion fruit Martini for this evening. Or rather, a 'liliko'i' Martini – that's what they call it here. Better yet, liliko'i with a hint of cayenne pepper.

Yes. She liked that.

Pleased with her cocktail plans, Valerie allowed her thoughts to turn to her investigation. She was hoping to finally get the chance to talk to Sachiko tonight, and was also eager to catch Kai before the dinner rush began and ask him about what Tala had said that morning about Hank and Craig.

But when she came through the Gecko's front door, she saw a young man in a white apron she didn't recognize clearing the dishes from a large table. 'Kai's got the night off,' Seth told her when she asked about the busser.

Oh, well. She'd have to wait till tomorrow to see if he had any insights about the two paddlers' relationship. *Had it extended beyond simple competitiveness?*

Stymied on that front, Valerie headed for the restaurant office in search of Sachiko. Although Isaac had sworn her to secrecy regarding her snooping around, that didn't preclude Valerie from merely talking to his girlfriend about Hank. In fact, she reasoned, it would be far more odd if she *didn't* seem curious about the dead bartender, wouldn't it?

'Knock, knock.' Valerie tapped lightly on the open door, and Sachiko looked up from the paperwork spread out across the wooden desk. Worry lines creased her forehead.

'Oh, hi. You're here early. Everything all right?'

'Yeah, I just thought I might get a head start prepping for some drink specials for later on in the week. That is, as long as you don't think Jun will mind . . .'

Sachiko laughed, smoothing the lines from her face. 'I doubt it. He's been here way too long to get his feathers ruffled by something like that. Jun's not a drink special kinda guy, but I'm sure he'll be fine with you doing the extra work to maybe garner some extra bar tips for the both of you. So how's it going at the bar, anyway?' The frown was now back. 'I'm sorry I haven't been better about checking in with you before, but . . .'

'Oh, lord, you so shouldn't have to worry about me,' said Valerie with a wave of the hand. 'The better question is, how are *you* doing? 'Cause it's certainly been an incredibly stressful week for everyone here. I mean, not only losing Hank like that, but then having the police come and ask a bunch of questions . . .?'

She let that last sentence hang, hoping Sachiko would jump in and provide some details about what exactly they'd asked about – or better yet, about the argument she'd apparently had with Hank the night before the picnic at Boiling Pots. But instead, she merely turned to stare blankly at the poster on the wall advertising the previous year's Merrie Monarch hula festival.

After a moment, Sachiko leaned forward in her swivel chair and appeared to reach out for something, then set her palm atop the old-school blotter paper on the desk. 'Yeah . . .' she said, making a ball with her fist and then relaxing it again, 'it's been a pretty lousy week, all right. But hey, at least we have a fab new bartender,' she added with a forced-but-perky smile. 'Thank goodness for small favors.' Gathering the papers before her into a pile, she tapped them on the wooden desk to even the pages, then pushed back her chair. 'Well, I guess I should go see about tonight's reservations.'

Valerie could take a hint. 'Right.' She returned Sachiko's smile and headed for the kitchen, intending to rustle up some lemongrass, ginger, and honey for her simple syrup infusions. In the wait station, she ran into Seth, who was sliding sheets printed with the evening's dinner specials into the plastic inserts of a stack of menus.

'Hey, Valerie,' he said as she passed by. 'Howzit?'

'Not bad. Though my arms are a bit sore from paddling this morning.'

'Ah, so Kai convinced you to go out with them, did he? He's been trying to get me paddling ever since I started work here, but I keep telling him I'm not much of a water person.' The server chuckled. 'He doesn't like to take no for an answer, though.'

'It was actually the women who did the convincing. They were two short for their canoe, so my wife and I agreed to try it out.

Pretty fun, actually. Until one of the paddlers got her leg sliced by a needle fish, that is.'

Seth blanched. 'Ugh. Now that's an unpleasant image. See why I don't like the ocean? But I hope she's okay.'

'I'm sure she had to have stitches, but the wound didn't look super bad. Though they were talking about things like flesh-eating bacteria and . . .' She stopped when she noticed his face turn an even paler shade than before. 'Oh, sorry.'

He smiled weakly. 'I'm just a little squeamish, is all. Not so good with hearing about blood and gore. You should see me when I have to get a shot.'

'I'm guessing it wasn't easy to hear what happened to Hank, then,' said Valerie, grabbing the opportunity to steer the conversation toward the dead bartender.

'No, it was horrible. But it was the news of his death more than how it happened that really got me.'

'Oh, so the cops told you how he died?'

'Huh-uh. They were mum about that. But the fact that he was fished out of the river like he was? Eauugh.' Seth shuddered. 'It can't have been pretty.'

Valerie couldn't disagree with this. 'No, I suppose not.' She watched for a moment as he continued to stuff the inserts. 'But I get what you say – that just hearing that he was gone was so hard for you. 'Cause it seems like you and Hank were pretty close, at least from what you told me the other day. And how you were defending him last night when they were all going on about his temper.'

He stared at the card stock sheet in his hand, mouth tight, then shoved it roughly into the plastic. 'It's just that I hate it when people don't understand how hard it can be – you know, recovery. And how a guy can get kinda snarky and bitter sometimes when he's going through all that.' When Seth finally turned to look at Valerie, she couldn't tell if his eyes were angry or sad.

Maybe both.

'So, anyway,' he went on, exhaling loudly, 'I just think they need to cut him a little slack, is all. Especially now that he's gone.'

EIGHT

At the sound of an unfamiliar engine the next morning, Pua roused from her post-breakfast nap and let out a high-pitched bark. 'Hush,' said Valerie, reaching down to smooth the bristles that had sprung up along the dog's spine. 'It's just Isaac and Mom.'

A moment later, they heard the car doors slam, followed by voices coming down the driveway. Pua jumped up from her spot in the sun and trotted over to greet the pair as they came through the gate into the back yard, now satisfied that they were neither ax murderers nor a strange poodle having the audacity to wander into her territory.

'How was surfing?' asked Valerie.

'Okay.' Kristen laid her board on the grass, turned on the hose, and began to spray it down. 'Pretty sloppy, but there were a few good sets.'

Isaac made himself comfortable on the floor of the lānai next to Pua, who had returned to her spot in the sun. 'And hey,' he said, 'any day surfing is better than any day working, yah?'

'You forget that I'm retired, dude. So every day can be a surfing day for me.'

'She one mean old sistah, dat one.' Running his fingers through his wet, shaggy hair, Isaac lay back on the woven lauhala mat and threw an arm over his eyes to block the bright, tropical sun.

'No comment,' replied Valerie. 'But hey, would the young working stiff care for some coffee?'

'That might take some of the sting out of the bad case of Sunday-itis you two be bringin' on me right about now,' he said. 'But at least tomorrow won't be so bad. It's midterms, so I get to read magazines most of the day – in between checking to make sure da kids aren't looking at each other's answers, that is.'

Valerie went to fetch the coffee, and Isaac sat back up to accept his mug with a toothy grin. 'Ah . . . You are now wholly forgiven.'

He took a cautious first sip, then looked up, his expression now serious. 'So . . . any news . . .?' A quick glance toward Kristen, who'd now stowed her clean surfboard in the garage and was heading back to the lānai.

'She knows all about it,' said Valerie. 'No secrets between these old married broads.'

Kristen came to stand next to her wife and wrapped an arm about her waist. 'Yep, I do indeed know – and am here to help as well, if you'd like.'

'Thanks. That's sweet.' Isaac's usually cherubic face was droopy as his eyes searched Valerie's, awaiting the response to his question.

'Okay. I haven't found out a whole lot, but here's what I do know.' She ticked off the items with her fingers. 'One. Hank and one of his fellow paddlers apparently had a serious competition going on between them, which might not have been all that friendly.'

Isaac shrugged. 'I can't see that being a reason to kill da guy.'

'No, maybe not. But it is something. And I have yet to learn any of the details of their relationship. For all we know, there could be more to it than just the paddling.'

'What if Hank was having an affair with the other guy's wife?' Kristen put in, causing Isaac to snort.

'An' what if he was an undercover CIA agent, killed by a Russian spy?' he replied. 'What ifs ain't gonna do nothin' for us.'

'Okay, how 'bout this? Number two, the general feeling down at the Gecko is that Hank was a real know-it-all, and he apparently had a bad temper, to boot. It's obvious he wasn't too well liked by the restaurant staff.'

This seemed to please Isaac, whose sagging face perked up a bit. 'I like that,' he said, but then frowned. 'But wait. Sachiko is one of the staff, too . . .'

'True, but she wasn't there for the conversation I'm talking about, so we don't know she thought that about Hank, as well.' Valerie caught a quick shift of Isaac's eyes. 'Or *did* she?'

He didn't respond. Which was a response itself, as far as she was concerned.

'Great. Okay, answer me this, Isaac. What do you know about an altercation Hank got into with one of his customers a couple nights before the retreat?'

'Uh . . .'

'Did Sachiko tell you about it? And that she apparently called Hank into the office the next night to chew him out about what happened?' Still no answer from Isaac. 'And that this was the very night before the retreat? It had to have been the argument the cops were so interested in.'

He was shaking his head. 'I don't know anything about dat. But if he did get into it with a customer, she woulda had to talk to him about it – you no can do something li'dat if you're an employee. But if it's true, it does explain why the cops are so interested in her.' He tapped a fingernail on his coffee cup, then stopped. 'What if that customer had something to do with his death? You need to figure out who he is.'

'I'll ask Jun, don't you worry. But speaking of Jun, there's something else I need to ask you.'

Isaac put his head in his hands, and his voice came out small and muffled. 'What?'

'He told me that Sachiko can get scary – that was the word Jun used, "scary." So what's that about? She's always seemed super cool and collected whenever I've been around her. And certainly never scary. Is she different at work? Does she have an angry side I don't know about?'

A moan was all that came out of Isaac, causing Pua to come over and try to lick his face through his hands.

Valerie plopped down into one of the director's chairs. 'Look, Isaac. I get that this is really difficult for you, and that hearing things about Sachiko that might look bad for her makes it even worse. But I can't help you if I don't know all the facts – the complete truth about what's going on.'

'I know.' He reached out to stroke Pua's fur, providing her an opening to give him a full-on face washing with her small pink tongue. 'And to answer your question, yeah, she can get kinda intense on occasion. She likes to keep everything in her life in control and can have a hard time when things go wrong that she can't personally do anything about. So if she's super stressed about something she really cares about and then someone else screws up, making it worse, she can be pretty . . .'

'Scary?'

'Uh-huh.'

Kristen settled into the other director's chair. 'And I'm guessing,' she said, 'that being the front-of-the-house manager at a busy restaurant with a high turnover of untrained staff isn't all that conducive to keeping her stress level at bay.'

'Not much.' Isaac sipped his coffee, then lay back down on the wood decking. 'And neither is being involved with a guy who's not always so great about being on time or remembering to do things he promised he would. So, yeah, I've seen the scary Sachiko, too.'

Okay, not good. Valerie returned Isaac's smile, even though he wasn't looking her way and she didn't feel very smiley at the moment. Then again, neither was he, no doubt. It was merely an automatic response on both of their parts. She couldn't imagine that Sachiko had anything to do with Hank's death, but this new information was definitely troubling. If the police believed that Hank was killed by someone else – as opposed to merely falling into the river by accident – then she made for an easy suspect.

'So how's Sachiko doing, anyway?' asked Valerie. ''Cause she seemed kind of listless last night at work. Not that it's not to be expected, of course, given all she's going through.'

Isaac sat up again and wrapped his arms around his knees. 'Yeah, she's taking the whole thing pretty hard. And, well, there's one more thing you don't know that's got her even more depressed.'

'Oh?' said Valerie and Kristen in unison.

'I'm not supposed to tell anyone, but . . .' He swallowed, then cleared his throat. 'So she has this little wooden carving that's really special to her – a fox with a scroll in its mouth that hangs from a string.'

Kristen nodded. 'Yeah, I think I've seen her with it. It's reddish brown and kind of roundish, right?'

'Uh-huh. It belonged to her grandfather and has some kind of Japanese name I can't remember. Anyway, she really loves that thing and carries it around in her pocket as, like, a good luck charm or something.'

Valerie and Kristen waited as he took a moment before going on.

'Well,' he finally said, 'apparently, when they fished Hank out of da river, that little fox was in his pocket.'

That afternoon, Valerie and Kristen drove down to the kumiai picnic at Carlsmith Beach – called 'Four Mile' by locals, because of its spot along the Keaukaha coastline. Soon after they greeted the other early arrivals gathered around the tables and barbecue pit, however, they were tempted into the inviting aqua ocean just beyond the state park's covered pavilion.

The ocean here was protected by a reef, and it seemed almost like a swimming pool to Valerie as they walked down the path to the water – an impression made even stronger by the presence of a stainless steel ladder aiding one's entry from the spit of black lava rock into the sea.

The two of them kicked off their rubber slippahs and sank into the clear, refreshing water. Almost immediately, Valerie shrieked in delight. 'Ooooh . . . there's a turtle!' she called out.

'Don't touch it!' Kristen splashed away backwards to get out of the way of the large, dark shell that floated between the two of them.

Valerie shrieked again, but this time less in delight than fear, as the creature swam toward her, its large jaws snapping at her submerged hands. 'Kinda hard not to touch it when it's the one trying to touch you,' she said, yanking her arms from the water.

'Well, do your best to avoid it,' replied Kristen. 'It's illegal to touch them.'

A laugh from behind made Kristen turn. 'Yeah, she might have to arrest you,' said a pale young man in bright blue-and-pink swim trunks, elbowing the woman next to him in the ribs.

'That joke gets old fast, Steve.' She shot her companion a quick side-eye, then turned to the others with an embarrassed smile. 'Hi, I'm Amy, and this smart aleck here is my next-door neighbor.'

Ah, thought Valerie, who'd assumed the two were a couple. But then she noticed how Amy was sizing up her and Kristen – a look she recognized well. *Were* they *a couple?* was what Amy was clearly wondering.

'And I think you must be my neighbors, as well,' Amy went on, 'since I saw you two earlier over at the pavilion with the kumiai group.'

Yep, definitely checking us out.

'Oh, hi, good to meet you,' said Valerie. 'And yeah, we just moved here from California, so it's our first time at one of these events. I'm Valerie, and this is my wife, Kristen.'

A slight flicker of a smile from Amy at the word 'wife.'

The four shook hands.

'So I take it you're a cop?' asked Kristen.

'Yup. Though I'm kinda under cover right at the moment,' she said with a grin, indicating her black-and-white polka-dot bikini.

The turtle was now nosing around Amy's legs, and she gave its shell a gentle shove with her hip. 'People feed them here, is the problem, so they get aggressive. Best not to reach your hands out, lest they go for your fingers, which can be quite painful. And I speak from experience.'

'Oh, should I be doing a citizen's arrest, then – for past misconduct?' asked Steve, prompting a swat to his shoulder by the bikini-clad cop.

The four of them paddled about in the calm blue water, making idle small talk about Hilo and the Big Island, until Valerie declared, 'Well, I don't know about anyone else, but I'm ready for some of those hot dogs,' and started back toward shore. The others followed after her and, once toweled off, they returned to the picnic pavilion. Amy and Steve introduced them around to the others at the picnic, and then Valerie made a beeline for the table, now loaded down with an array of enticing dishes the kumiai members had brought.

Shirley, the neighbor who'd slipped the picnic invitation into their screen door the day before, was scooping sticky rice onto her plate. 'So, how are you two settling in?' she asked. 'I see you planted a hāpu'u fern in your front yard. It's lovely.'

Valerie nodded. 'Yeah, our friend Isaac gave that to us as a housewarming gift. He dug it up from a friend's yard in Volcano Village. I hope it likes this lowland climate okay. Though the ones in your yard seem pretty happy – as well as those gorgeous orchids you have growing on their trunks.'

'Yes, there's a reason they call this the Orchid Isle,' Shirley said with a grin. 'They just adore this climate. Oh, this salad looks yummy,' she added, helping herself to the contents of a large wooden bowl.

'It is, indeed,' said Amy, who'd beat them to the table and had already forked some of the salad into her mouth. 'And such an unexpected combination of ingredients: celery, dates, nuts, and cheese? Weird but delicious. Do you know who brought it?'

Kristen pointed a finger at her wife. 'Val did; it's one of her potluck standbys and always a crowd favorite.'

'Would you be willing to share the recipe?' asked Amy. 'I'm supposed to come up with a dish for my mom's birthday party later this week, and this would be perfect.'

'Sure, no problem. Happy to share it.'

Valerie, Kristen, Amy, and Steve took their plates over to the lawn and sat down to eat. 'So, did you two move here for work?' asked Steve after swallowing a bite of three-bean salad.

Kristen shook her head. 'Uh-uh, we both just retired.'

'Lucky you,' said Amy. 'I've still got a ways to go before I get there. So what did you do for work?'

'I was a union carpenter, and Val was a caterer for the film and TV industry.'

'Hence the expert salad-making chops,' Amy said with a nod toward her plate.

Valerie gave a reverential bow of the head. 'Yep. Salads are big with the figure-conscious actor crowd. So how about you, Steve? What's your gig?'

'I'm an MFT – a marriage and family therapist, here in Hilo.'

'He's good, too,' said Amy. 'He was really helpful with my sister when she was dealing with a messy divorce.'

'So did you grow up here?' Kristen asked Amy.

'Not in Hilo, but up in Waimea. I moved down here after I finished my field training and got assigned to Hilo five years back.'

'You like it?'

Amy laughed. 'The job or Hilo?'

'Both, I guess.'

'Well, living in Hilo has been a bit of a change from where I grew up – and not just 'cause of all the rain. It's a lot bigger and not as wealthy – or haole – as Waimea, so the culture is pretty different. But I do love it here, especially the neighborhood where we all live.'

Valerie was nodding. 'I totally agree. The culture here is completely different from L.A., too, but in a good way. It's so much more relaxed and easy-going.'

'The aloha spirit,' said Steve with a grin. 'It's alive and well. Though I know that of course in your job, Amy, you do see the darker side of life around here.'

'What's your position with the police department?' asked Kristen.

'I'm still just a patrol cop, but I'm hoping to move up into investigation one of these days. I'm studying for the test to become a detective.'

Valerie's ears perked up at this. 'So, speaking of investigation, did you hear about that man whose body they found in the river last week?'

'Sure, it's been all over the news.'

'Okay, I mean not just hear about *him*, but I was wondering if you maybe heard anything about what might have *happened* to the guy. You know, since you're a cop an' all . . .'

Amy shook her head. 'I doubt I know much more than what you read in the paper. As I said, I'm just a lowly beat cop, so I'm not privy to investigations like that. But what I can tell you is that this isn't the first time they've pulled a body out of that river. People think it looks all calm and peaceful and decide to go for a swim, not realizing how dangerous it really is.'

'Yeah, so I've heard.' Valerie gazed out at the people splashing about in the turquoise water just beyond where they were seated, then turned back to Amy. 'That guy they pulled from the water – Hank . . . I don't know his last name. Well, he was a bartender at the place I'm now working, the Speckled Gecko.'

'Marino is his last name,' said Amy. 'I do know that much. Or it was . . .' She trailed off.

Seeing the concern in Amy's eyes, Valerie shook her head. 'No, we weren't friends or anything. I never even met the guy. But the others at the Gecko are obviously pretty upset. And concerned about what happened, since the questions the cops have been asking suggest they think his death wasn't an accident.'

'Ah . . .' It was Amy's turn to gaze out at the blue ocean. And Valerie couldn't help but notice that the look of concern had now transformed into a deep frown.

NINE

Sunday was a walk in the park compared to Valerie's previous two nights at the Gecko. Come six o'clock – at which time the previous evening the bar had been three-deep with thirsty customers staring down Valerie with the same look Pua gave her when it was time for her dinner – there were only four people seated at the stools, one of them Kristen.

Valerie slid thin lemon slices onto the rims of two highball glasses and carried the drinks to the end of the bar, then came to stand before her wife.

'I like watching you work,' Kristen said. 'You're very good at it.' She nodded toward the couple who'd just gotten their drinks. 'So what's that cocktail? One of your specials?'

'Uh-huh. I'm calling it a "Hawai'i Island Iced Tea," a blend of Knob Creek rye, turmeric-ginger-infused black tea, and a splash of simple syrup made with locally sourced honey.'

'Nice presentation – both the drink and the explanation. I may have to get one of those after I finish this boring Mai Tai.' Kristen lifted the fruit-laden toothpick from her cocktail and nibbled at a chunk of pineapple.

Seeing Annie approach the server area of the bar, Valerie headed over to take her table's order. As she set about making the drinks, Kristen watched her wife work, mixing up a pair of Margaritas; grinding mint, lime, and sugar for a Mojito; then shaking up a frothy Grey Goose Martini.

'You truly are good,' she said when Valerie returned. 'I guess I never really watched you bartend at Chez Charles. Or at least I never paid that much attention when I did watch.'

'Thanks.' Valerie filled a tumbler from the soda gun and took a long drink of water. 'I do enjoy it. It's a satisfying blend of chaos and order.' Setting down the glass, she leaned forward and said in a low voice, 'So, what do you think about me doing it on a more permanent basis?'

'Working here at the Gecko?' Kristen chewed her lip as she

swiveled around in her chair, taking in the splashing dolphin fountain; the planter boxes a riot of yellow, pink, and green; the wood-carved bar; and finally her wife's face, flushed with excitement. 'Yeah,' she said with a nod, returning Valerie's smile. 'I think that's an excellent idea. As long as it's not every night of the week. I would still like to see you on occasion.'

'Agreed. No way would I be full-time. I'm thinking only three nights a week, max, with maybe a lunch shift once in a while if I'm needed. I still want to be able to enjoy our own cocktail hours together on our own lānai.'

'Sounds good.' Kristen raised her glass in salute, then drained it. 'And now I'd like one of those Hawai'i Island Iced Teas, if you please.'

Jun arrived for his shift at seven, though it was clear to both Valerie and the head bartender that he wasn't much needed that night. Although the six stools were occupied, the patrons all had fresh drinks, and the dining room bar orders had now dwindled to a trickle.

Downtown Hilo rolls up its sidewalks pretty darn early, especially on a Sunday night.

'I could restock the mixers, if you'd like,' Valerie said once they'd put away the glasses from the last dishwasher load.

'How 'bout you wipe down the backbar bottles instead? Been long time and dey all be kinda pilau. Dirty,' he added at her questioning look.

'Oh, got it. Sure thing.' She grabbed several bar towels and began the laborious process of removing each bottle, cleaning underneath it and wiping off its dust, then returning it to its place on the shelf.

In between making drink orders, Jun loaded the undercounter dishwasher with the rarely used glasses hanging from the rack – red wine, snifters, and flutes, mostly – which had also gotten grimy over the weeks or months since they'd last been washed.

By a quarter past nine, all the stools had been vacated and the bar area was empty of customers. *Time to pick Jun's brain.*

'So,' Valerie said, 'I was wondering if you remember that argument Hank got into with a customer a couple days before he went missing.'

The bartender closed the wine fridge he'd been stocking and turned to face her. 'Yah . . .?'

'Uh, well, can you tell me what it was about? And who the customer he argued with was?'

Jun continued to stare at her, his mouth pursed like that of Valerie's French grande-mère back in Marseilles when she was displeased. 'Is dis just idle curiosity,' he said after a moment, 'or you got a reason for asking 'bout all dat?'

Should she tell him the truth? That Isaac had asked her to go behind Sachiko's back and try to figure out how Hank had died, since he was worried that the cops suspected his girlfriend of murder?

Not.

'I'm just curious, is all. Especially about who it was Hank argued with, so I can know to be careful around him . . . or her. Was it that big guy with the big gut who drinks Seven and Sevens by any chance? 'Cause he got kind of belligerent last week after one too many . . .'

'Brad?' Jun said, then shook his head. 'Nah, it wasn't him. It was a guy I never seen before – some local brah who was clearly pissed off at Hank before he even made 'um dat drink.'

'What was he pissed off about, do you know?'

Jun shrugged. 'Dey had some words right when he come into da bar, but I no can tell you what dey said.' Picking up a wet bar towel, he wrung it out over the sink, then glanced quickly at Valerie. 'But I do got an idea.'

'Oh, yeah?'

'I'm tinkin' it had to do with a woman,' he said, twisting the rag even more. His jaw, Valerie noticed, was tight, and she could see a vein pulsating on his neck.

Could it be that this was personal to Jun, and not merely idle gossip about a fellow employee's dalliance with a customer's girlfriend or wife?

'Uh, is that something Hank did often?' she asked. 'Hit on women?'

A snort was his response. 'Just ask Annie.'

'Okay . . .'

Now she was truly confused. Were Annie and Jun involved? Or was she merely another woman Hank had hit on, in addition

to someone Jun had a personal attachment to? But these didn't
seem like questions Jun would be all that eager to answer right
at that moment.

'So, did you tell any of this to the police when they were
here?'

Another snort. 'No wayz I'm gettin' mixed up in whatevah
Hank had goin' on in his life, an' if Annie wants to talk about
all dat to da cops, dere's nothin' stoppin' her.' He pulled out his
phone and looked at the screen. 'Any chance you willing to close
up? 'Cause I'd love to cut out early if I could . . .'

'Sure. No problem.'

Now, what could that possibly have been all about?

After closing up the bar that night, Valerie was about to head
straight home without joining the other staff for their nightly
beer, but spying Sachiko in her office, she stopped and tapped
at the door.

'Hey,' she said when Sachiko looked up from her laptop at
the sound. 'I didn't think you were working tonight.'

'I hadn't planned on it, but I've gotta figure out this scheduling,
and it's easier if I do it here rather than at home.'

Valerie smiled. 'Yeah, I imagine Isaac can be a bit of a distrac-
tion when you're trying to concentrate. But I may have some
news that'll make that scheduling a little easier.'

'Oh, yeah?'

Valerie stepped into the room and leaned against the ancient
wooden filing cabinet next to the desk. 'I've decided that I'd like
to continue bartending here at the Gecko on a more permanent
basis – if you want me, that is.'

'Ohmygod, that's wonderful news! Of course I want you!'
Sachiko jumped up and came around to give Valerie a hug, then
shook out her arms with a great show of released tension. 'I
didn't want to say anything – you know, make you feel pressured
– but I've been having a heck of a time finding anyone even
remotely qualified to tend bar here. They're all either completely
inexperienced or look like they haven't had a shower or combed
their hair in at least two months.'

'Well, I'm glad I'm a step up from that,' said Valerie with a
laugh. 'But there is a caveat: I'd like to work only Wednesday,

Friday, and Saturday nights, with an occasional lunch shift if you need me. I am, after all, supposed to now be retired.'

'No problem; I can totally work with that. Jun wants five full days, so he can do lunch and dinner every day but Wednesday – if you could take Wednesday lunches, that is . . .'

'Sure, I guess I could do that. Though I better check with Kristen before anything's set in stone.'

Sachiko nodded. 'And Seth can step in as a sub if ever needed. He's got a little bartending experience.'

'Sounds good. So, can I ask you something about Hank?'

'Uh . . . sure . . .' said Sachiko. But the quick frown suggested she wasn't all that pleased about where the conversation was now headed.

'It's actually about Jun, too, since he's the one who brought it up.' A lie, granted, but only a small one. 'He was talking about how Hank was a bit of a ladies' man, and—'

'A bit?' The frown had now been replaced by a rolling of the eyes.

Good. She was clearly happy to talk about this aspect of her former bartender.

'Yeah, well, okay. So maybe he implied it was a little more than a bit. He said Hank had been hitting on Annie, for one.'

'Really? Dang. That's news to me. If it's true, I sure wish she'd told me. I could have had a word with him about it . . .' Sachiko trailed off, and Valerie wondered if she was thinking of the words she *did* have with Hank shortly before his death.

'But here's the thing: I also got the impression from what Jun said that there was something going on between Hank and someone Jun was involved with, as well. Is Jun married?'

'He is.' Valerie could see the wheels turning in Sachiko's head as she stared blankly at a spot above Valerie's head, considering this new information. 'What exactly did he say?'

'Well, it was more his body language than anything else.' Valerie started to explain how Jun had seemed particularly tense when talking about Hank's propensity for hitting on the ladies, but then stopped as she realized where this story line was taking her: how she'd asked Jun about the argument Hank had gotten into with that customer – which in turn had been the catalyst for those words Sachiko had the following night with the bartender.

Which Valerie most definitely did not want her to know she'd
been asking about.

'So, anyway,' she went on, 'it just seemed like Jun's reaction
was personal, as opposed to an outside onlooker's mere annoyance
or disgust or whatever with Hank's behavior toward other
women.'

Sachiko was eyeing her differently now. Was it suspicion? Or
simply curiosity about Jun's behavior as well as Valerie's interest
in that behavior?

Worried that it might be the former, she hastened to quell any
such suspicion. 'And so I was just thinking this might all be
something you'd want to know, being Jun and Annie's supervisor,
an' all . . .'

'Right.' Sachiko shook out her arms once more, but this time
it suggested that she'd rather not, in fact, be hearing any of this.
'Look, I'll check in with Annie to see if she wants to talk about
Hank's behavior. But I'm guessing that now that he's . . . gone,
she'd probably rather just let it go. And as for Jun, well, I'm
thinking that's not really any of my business.'

It was Valerie's turn to purse her lips and frown.

'What?' said Sachiko.

'Never mind.' Valerie waved her hand. 'It's nothing.'

'Wait.' Sachiko's eyes got wide. 'You don't think that any of
this could have something to do with Hank's death?'

When Valerie simply gave a shrug for an answer, Sachiko sank
slowly back into her chair and let out a long breath. 'Shoots.
Well, I guess I don't know whether to be happy or sad about
that prospect . . .'

It rained hard for much of that night – one of those intense
tropical rains that thrashes the palm fronds, spatters against the
windows, and crashes down upon the metal roof like a thousand
percussionists pounding out a heavy metal drum solo.

Valerie loved it. Unlike in California, where a storm such as this
would cause power outages, flooding, and landslides, a rain of several
inches in Hilo merely meant that you probably wouldn't want to
mow your lawn the following day – not unless it cleared by morning,
that is, in which case the fierce afternoon sun would do its work
and it would be dry enough to mow by mid-afternoon.

And Valerie found the steady thrum of rain upon the windows and roof to be relaxing and meditative. Since moving to Hawai'i, she found she slept better than she had in years. And she certainly didn't have to worry about watering the garden or the grass.

Kristen, however, was grumbling about the weather when they turned off the lights to go to sleep, as she had plans in the morning to help her new friend Diane build her lānai. To Kristen's relief, however, the dawn broke to clear skies, with the bright sun glistening off all the raindrops clinging to the yellow hibiscus and pink plumeria in their back yard.

'I told you it would be nice today,' said Valerie as they sat sipping coffee and reading the morning papers.

'Yep,' was all the satisfaction she would get from her wife.

But that was okay. Kristen was the one who was generally 'right' about things such as this – or at least the one who liked to be right – so a simple 'yep' in this instance was satisfaction enough for Valerie.

'So what time you heading off?' she asked.

Kristen consulted her phone. 'Soon. I said I'd be there by ten, and I have to stop by HPM Building Supply to pick up a few things on my way.'

'You'll be back for dinner, right?'

'Absolutely. I'll be home by five at the latest. Wouldn't want to miss cocktail hour.'

Downing the rest of her coffee, Kristen came over to give both Valerie and Pua a kiss goodbye, then headed indoors. A couple minutes later, Valerie heard the screen door slam, followed by the starting of the car engine.

So what was on her agenda for the day? It was nice having the job at the Gecko to give her a new purpose in life, but it still left the daytimes mostly unoccupied. And until Kristen's lānai project was completed, it looked like Valerie was going be left alone quite a bit.

'How about a walk, before the rain returns?' she said, slapping her knees. Hearing these magic words, Pua jumped up from where she'd been asleep in the sun and began to bark. 'I'll take that as a yes.'

The dog followed her indoors, where her high-pitched yips increased in volume and frequency upon seeing Valerie grab the leash from its hook above the dog bowls. They made their way down the front steps, Pua leading the way, and had just started up the street when a voice called out Valerie's name from behind. Turning, she saw Amy striding toward them, a plastic-wrapped plate in her hands.

'Glad I caught you before you left,' Amy said, catching up to them, ''cause I have a welcome-to-the-neighborhood gift for you and Kristen.'

Valerie accepted the plate and examined the baked goods underneath the plastic wrap. 'Oh, wow, purple brownies – thanks! They look amazing! Are they made with those sweet potatoes I saw for sale at the farmers market?'

'Close.' Amy pulled one out and handed it to Valerie, causing Pua to sit and assume her paws up, 'please give me a treat!' position. 'They're made from ube – a purple yam from the Philippines. But it is similar to the Okinawan sweet potato you saw at the market. And these are actually more blondies than brownies, since there isn't any cocoa in them. Though they do have white chocolate chips, as you can see. Maybe I should call them "ubies" . . . or "mauvies." Nah, neither really works.'

Valerie bit into the chewy bar, then smiled. 'Who cares what they're called – they're delicious!'

'Happy to give you the recipe, if you like, in return for that salad recipe of yours. It's from my lola – my Filipina grandma. Here, I'll take them back and leave them on your porch so you don't have to carry them on your walk.'

'Care to join us?' asked Valerie. 'I was thinking of heading over to Reed's Island. That is, if you're not on your way to work or anything . . .'

'My watch doesn't start till two forty-five, so sure, why not?'

After setting the plate on the small table by the front door, the three of them set off again uphill. Pretty much all walks in Hilo, Valerie had noticed, were either uphill or down – not a whole lot of flat was to be had on an island composed entirely of volcanoes.

As they walked, Amy pointed out some of the houses on their street: Mr Ikeda's perfectly manicured garden; the place where some grad students at the university were living (their yard was overrun by weeds); a house now owned by a family of four from

Connecticut; Shirley Kahele's beautiful hāpuʻu ferns with pink and yellow orchids sprouting from their hairy trunks.

'I've only lived here five years,' Amy said, 'but even in that time there's been a lot of changes in the neighborhood. I'm told that back in the day it was mostly Japanese, but as the old folks pass away, a lot of times their kids have already left the island or just don't want to move from where they're now living, even if they're still in Hilo.' She shrugged. 'Sad, really. Though of course I wouldn't be renting my place on the street if the original family were still here.'

'We bought our house from someone named Hayashi,' said Valerie. 'And it's exactly like you said: the realtor told us it had been the owner's mom's house, but he now lives in Seattle, and no one else in the family wanted to keep the place.' She shook her head. 'I really love living here, but sometimes I kinda feel like an interloper – just another haole coming over from the Mainland and buying up the locals' land.'

'Hey.' Amy laid a hand on her shoulder. 'I didn't mean to make you feel bad by bringing this all up. I for one am glad you're in the neighborhood.'

'Thanks.' But her unease remained as they walked on, crossing Waianuenue Avenue and making their way over to Reed's Island. *Was* it wrong for her and Kristen to have come to Hawaiʻi and added to the gentrification that was already pricing so many people out of the land their families had occupied for decades – if not centuries?

But then again, the same could be said for where they'd just moved from in Mar Vista, a neighborhood in Los Angeles that had once been home to numerous Japanese – until they'd been shipped off to internment camps during World War II – as well as families from Oaxaca, Mexico. Now, although the sleepy Westside community was still home to many of Asian and Latin American descent, the skyrocketing property values in the desirable area were quickly driving out all but the very wealthy.

Valerie was startled from her musings by Amy stopping in the middle of the street and letting out a low whistle. 'Yikes. Look at that. I haven't been out here since Lane came through. Intense.'

'I know,' said Valerie. 'And imagine how intense it must have been during the storm when this slide happened. I sure wouldn't want to live in one of these houses.'

'Agreed. This close to the Wailuku River? No way. You know what the name means, right?'

'Uh-huh. And it certainly has been causing its fair share of destruction of late.'

Amy eyed her with curiosity. 'You're not just talking about Lane, are you?'

Unsure whether to broach the subject of Hank's death with the police officer, Valerie merely shrugged and continued to stare at the raw channel the angry river had cut through the property below them.

'Have you ever been up there?' Amy asked after a bit. 'Where he was last seen?'

'You mean Boiling Pots? Not since last May, when I first visited the island. So I don't really remember what it's like.'

'You wanna go there now?'

TEN

A half hour later, they climbed out of Amy's slate-gray SUV at the Boiling Pots parking lot. Passing a large grassy area where Valerie imagined the Speckled Gecko staff picnic must have been held, they walked up a concrete ramp onto the overlook and gazed down at the Wailuku River.

The pots were barely at a simmer now, and it was an idyllic scene that met their eyes: a swath of shiny-green monstera vines leading down to a flat shelf of smooth black lava rock, through which the now calm river gurgled and formed inviting pools of water. In the distance upstream, Valerie could see several water-falls, the sound of splashing water mixing with that of mynah birds squawking amidst the orange flowers of an African tulip tree.

She nodded toward a beaten, muddy path running from beneath the overlook railing – and immediately under three large signs declaring: 'Area Closed,' 'Violators May Be Prosecuted,' and 'Flash Flood' – down the steep bank to the riverbed below. 'I can see that people aren't too good about obeying the warnings.'

'Nope. And on a day like today, I can see why they'd be tempted to go for a dip. But what they don't realize is that within those serene-looking pools lie a host of treacherous currents just waiting to suck an unsuspecting swimmer into an underwater cave.'

Even though she'd heard this description before, Valerie couldn't help but shudder. The thought of being sucked into a cave, struggling to get free while unable to breathe in the black, black water was too horrifying for words.

With a shake of the head, she tried to force the grisly image from her mind. 'You think that's what happened to Hank?'

'I don't know. But even if I did, I couldn't tell you. Since it's still an unresolved case at this time, the lead detective would have my hide if I talked about it with anyone outside law enforcement.'

'Sure, I get it,' said Valerie. 'But what about me telling you things I know . . . or find out? Would that run afoul of the department rules?'

'I guess not. But I'm not so sure you trying to "find things out" is such a good idea.'

'Oh, don't worry. I just mean anything I happen to learn working at the Speckled Gecko. You know, being a bartender an' all, I might hear things folks say after a few drinks.'

'Uh-huh.'

Valerie was pretty sure Amy could see through this fudging of the truth, but nevertheless, she went on, ignoring the sage advice. 'And then if you thought it was important, you could pass whatever I told you on to the detective?'

'I suppose. If I thought it was relevant and truly important . . .'

Turning her back on the menacing river, Valerie leaned against the metal railing and stared out at the grassy area, the restrooms, and the parking lot beyond. 'Okay, so, here's the thing,' she said. 'I know the police suspect Sachiko – the dining room manager at the Gecko – of having something to do with Hank's death. But I also know there's no way she had anything to do with it.'

'And how, may I ask, do you know that?'

'Okay, so maybe "know" is a bit strong. But it's just that I've spent a lot of time with her, and I can't believe she could possibly have any anything to do with it. It's just not in her makeup.'

Amy flashed a patronizing smile. 'You never can know what someone is capable of. I get that I haven't been a cop all that long, but I've seen enough in those five years to know that people can do some pretty surprising things – things that aren't always all that pleasant.'

'Like murder?'

'Maybe. But more often sudden surges of anger that can lead to unexpected acts of violence. Violence that *could* . . .'

'. . . lead to death,' Valerie finished for her. Turning back around, she gazed again at the calm scene below as she thought about Sachiko. It was true that both Jun and Isaac had said she had a scary side that could flare up when she was stressed. But the question was, could she have become angry enough with Hank to whack him over the head with a heavy rock and then shove him into the treacherous Wailuku River?

Although she didn't *want* to believe that such a scenario could be true, Valerie knew in her heart it would be naïve to assume it was *impossible*.

'Hey, hon,' said Kristen coming into the kitchen and setting down her bucket of tools with a clatter. After leaning down to greet the barking Pua, she crossed over to give her wife a quick kiss, then grabbed a tall glass, filled it with cold water from the sink, and drank the whole thing down. 'Oof. I don't think I'm quite yet acclimated to working in the tropics.'

'Yeah, I can imagine. Just walking uphill to our house from downtown still makes me break out into a sweat like I'm reliving my days of hot flashes.'

'Oh, lord, banish the thought. I'm so glad those days are long gone.' Kristen set down her glass with a smack of the lips. 'Dang, but that Hilo water tastes good. Somebody ought to market it on the Mainland.'

'I saw in the paper that somebody is in fact trying to do so, but I guess they've run up against administrative regulations or something.' Valerie picked up the knife she'd set down when Kristen had come in and continued slicing an array of brightly colored bell peppers. 'So how was it today – other than the heat?'

'Good. We got all the posts up for the roof that needed to go in before the flooring, so next time we'll start putting in the joists.'

'And how is it working with Diane – you know, since you said she didn't have any experience with carpentry or anything?'

'Oh, she did great. I think maybe it's 'cause of what she does for a living. She's a technical writer for some Silicon Valley company – I didn't understand exactly what they do. But I'm guessing being able to translate how to do . . .'

'Tech stuff?' Valerie filled in, and Kristen laughed.

'Right. If she can explain how to do tech stuff in a way that us regular folks can understand, it probably means that she has a technical mind. Anyway, I like working with her. It's fun teaching someone who's such a quick study.'

'Yeah, I bet.' Valerie was pretty sure her wife wasn't thinking about it right then, but she couldn't help but remember the time Kristen had tried to teach her how to change a toilet handle and

had finally given up in exasperation. Although she possessed
many fine qualities, Valerie was well aware she did not have
what would be called a 'technical mind' – at least as far as
construction and mechanical operations went.

'So whatcha makin'?' Kristen asked, snagging a slice of red
pepper.

'Chicken fajitas. And check out what's for dessert.' Valerie
indicated the plate on the counter behind her, and Kristen bent
down to peer at the baked goods beneath the plastic wrap.

'Purple brownies? That's different.'

'Amy brought them as a housewarming gift. They're made
with ube, a kind of purple yam. And they're not technically
brownies, since they don't have any cocoa in them.'

'Huh. Well, they look yummy to me, cocoa or not,' said Kristen.
'You want me to make you a drink?'

'Sure. How about a Margarita, to go with tonight's culinary theme?'

'Good idea. I think I'll have one, too, before I go shower.'
Kristen set about squeezing limes, fetching two glasses and
coating their rims with salt, then filling a cocktail shaker with
ice, tequila, triple sec, and lime juice. 'So, what'd you do today
while I was sweating like a pig in the hot sun?' she asked, shaking
the metal canister and pouring the frothy liquid into their glasses.

'Amy and I went up to Boiling Pots.'

'You did?'

Valerie accepted her drink, clinked glasses with Kristen, and
took a sip. It was a refreshing mix of tart, sweet, salty, and cold.
'Mmmm, perfect,' she said. 'And yeah, we did. It was actually
her idea.' Valerie explained how they'd walked with Pua to Reed's
Island and got to talking about Tropical Storm Lane. 'And then
when I said something about how dangerous the Wailuku River
was, she gave me this knowing look and asked if I'd ever been
up to Boiling Pots.'

'She knew you were talking about Hank, then?'

'I guess. I mean, I had been talking about his death at the
picnic yesterday, so she knew that it was something that was on
my mind. Anyway, when I said I'd been to Boiling Pots last
spring but didn't really remember the place too well, she asked
if I'd like to drive up there with her right then.'

'Interesting. I wonder why.'

Valerie nodded as she swallowed a sip of Margarita. 'Yeah, me too. I can only think that maybe since she could tell it's something I'm interested in, she was just being nice?'

'Or what if she wanted to get you talking about it all in order to find out what *you* know about his death?' Kristen said. 'She is a cop, after all. So maybe she was conducting her own investigation about the case.'

'Maybe. But she's just a patrol cop, not a detective or anything, and she said she doesn't have anything to do with the case. You think she'd lie about something like that?'

'Just 'cause she's not officially on the case doesn't mean she wouldn't be interested to hear anything you might know about it.'

Valerie set down her drink, picked up her chef's knife, and sliced the root end off a yellow onion. 'It's actually funny you say that, because after she told me that even if she did know anything, she wouldn't be permitted to divulge information to me about the case, I asked if that meant I couldn't tell *her* anything I might learn.'

'And what'd she say?'

'Well, after advising me she didn't think it would be wise to go sticking my nose where it didn't belong – my words, not hers; but that was the gist of her advice – she said she supposed it would be okay for me to tell her stuff.' Valerie swung around and pointed the knife at Kristen. 'So you think it was all a ruse to get me talking about what I know?'

'Probably not, but who knows? And if so, it could be solely because of her own curiosity and nothing to do with being a cop. I mean, it is an interesting puzzle, how and why the guy died the way he did.'

'That it is.' Valerie took another drink, then recommenced slicing her onion. 'Amy did have one interesting thing to say.'

'Oh, yeah?'

'It was after I'd told her I knew the cops were looking at Sachiko as a possible suspect—'

'Suspect, you mean; no "possible" needed. By definition a "suspect" is merely "possible."'

'Whatever.' Valerie shook her head in exasperation and went on with her story. 'And I said I didn't think there was any way it could have been Sachiko.'

'Lemme guess: Amy was skeptical of your certitude.'

'Right. No surprise there, really. But it's *how* she said it that got to me.' Valerie stopped cutting and turned to face Kristen once again. 'She said: "You never know what someone is capable of."'

'So?' said Kristen. 'That seems like a pretty obvious statement.'

'Yeah, well, remember what Isaac said about how Sachiko can get really stressed when stuff goes wrong that she can't control, and that when that happens and she gets angry, she can be pretty scary. That was his word: "*scary*."'

'I don't think that means anything,' said Kristen with a snort. 'When guys act like that it's just them being "like a guy," but for women they're always described as "angry" or "scary." It's just pure garden-variety sexism.'

'Yeah, I thought the same thing, too, when I first heard it. But what about how Hank got into it with that Gecko customer and how Sachiko then gave him that dressing-down for it the very night before the staff picnic at Boiling Pots? And that little wooden fox that she loves so much that was found in Hank's pocket when they pulled him out of the river?' Valerie raised her hands in a flourish, like a prosecuting attorney who'd just dropped a vital piece of evidence before the jury.

'Jeez, girl. It almost sounds like you *want* it to be Sachiko.'

'No,' said Valerie, letting her arms fall limply to her side. 'It's the last thing I want. But it's also something I can't help worrying might be true.'

It was drizzling again the next morning, and as Valerie peered out the window to see if she could spot any blue sky to the east, Kristen came to stand next to her.

'It looks pretty gloomy out there,' Valerie said. 'You think they paddle in the rain?'

'Do polar bears go out in the snow?' answered Kristen with a laugh. 'I bet the only time they don't paddle is when there's a big-time serious storm. If they canceled every time there was a light rain like this, they'd hardly ever get to go out. I say we head on down there.'

'Okay.' Part of Valerie was bummed she didn't have an excuse to bag out this morning – the whole huli and then fish-attack experience from last time had rattled her nerves pretty bad. But at the same time she was relieved, as she really wanted the chance to meet that Craig guy and see if she could suss out his feelings regarding Hank.

At a little before eight, they pulled up in front of the Mahina Canoe Club hālau. Tala, Becca, and another woman were standing by Tala's SUV, drinking from travel mugs, but no other paddlers were in sight.

'Hey!' Tala called out as they walked up to join them. 'So glad you came! I was worried the rain might have kept you away.'

'What? A little rain in *Hilo*? No way.' Kristen glanced Valerie's way with a grin.

Tala introduced them to the third woman – Sasha, who they learned had to deal with a sick kid during the previous practice. 'Glad to be back today,' she said. 'I really need my time out on the water to keep my sanity.'

'So how's Mara?' asked Valerie. 'Did she need stitches?'

Becca nodded. 'Yeah, she did. But it looks like she'll be fine; there's no sign of infection so far. The bummer, though, is that she can't go in the ocean for another week or so, and Leilani's still sick, which means we're without a steersperson for the time being.'

'Why can't either of you do it?' Kristen asked, glancing from Becca to Sasha.

'No way.' Sasha gave an emphatic shake of the head. 'I'm just a grunt number three seater. No steering for me, thank you very much.'

'And I *could* do it, for sure,' said Becca, 'but I really want to work on my stroking and endurance.'

'Ah, got it,' said Kristen. ''Cause the steersperson has to stop paddling a lot to do the steering. Well, I guess I could give it a try. I did have a bit of practice on Saturday. But you'll have to show me the ropes.'

'Awesome!' Becca punched fists with Kristen, then started toward the hālau. 'All right then, let's jam!'

Their paddling session that morning went off without any of the drama of the previous time: no dunking in the ocean and no needle-nosed fish flying overhead. But it was certainly exhilarating, racing across the bay as they dug their paddles deep into the water, and the rain sheeting down their faces only added to the excitement.

Once past the breakwater, they headed north, up the Hāmākua Coast. Now out in the true ocean, the water was far choppier, and Kristen had her work cut out to keep the bow of the canoe pointed toward the oncoming waves, lest they be knocked over by the strong surges. It was also more difficult to make headway, as they were now going against the current, and after about a half hour the muscles in Valerie's arms started to ache from the effort she was making.

Tala must have been feeling it, too – or, more likely, she was simply taking pity on the two newbies – because just when Valerie thought her upper arms were going to explode from pain, the stoker lifted her paddle from the water and called out, 'Okay, let's stop for a bit!'

Valerie set down her paddle and shook out her arms, then wiped the water from her face. Looking up, she realized the rain had stopped, and large patches of blue had now appeared in the sky. She turned to study the coastline off to their left. 'Is that Honoli'i?'

'It is,' said Kristen, squinting in the bright sunlight. 'It's weird to see it from this angle, though. Looks like the wave action is pretty good. Maybe I should go surfing when we get home.'

'Speaking of which, we should probably head back.' Tala took a drink from the water bottle at her feet, then picked up her paddle. 'I'm guessing this is enough of a workout for you two gals, being your first real paddling session an' all. Oh, and check it out.' She pointed at two blue-and-green canoes in the distance. 'The boys are coming back in. Let's see if we can beat them to the hālau.'

With a war cry worthy of a Viking marauder, Becca lifted her paddle above her head and shook it like a spear. 'E hele kākou!'

ELEVEN

They didn't beat the men back, but they came close. As soon as the guys realized the women were trying to outpace them, they stepped on the gas and raced as if their lives depended on it. Or, at least, their egos. Which perhaps they thought even more important.

Once they'd made landfall, the paddlers all jumped out into the shallow water and grabbed hold of the canoes to keep them from drifting off again. 'Hey, Stuart, how far did you guys go?' Tala asked a lanky guy with close-cropped hair as they set about dragging the heavy craft up onto the black sand beach.

'Almost to the radio tower. Craig wanted to go all the way to Onomea Bay, but I gotta be at work by eleven.'

Ah, so that's Craig. Valerie studied the tall, muscular man Stuart had indicated, the stroker who'd been vying for position with Hank.

Craig shook his head in derision. 'I told Stuart he needs to change his work schedule if we're going to get in any real workouts before the Moloka'i race. How we supposed to ramp up for forty-one miles if we don't even do ten in practice?'

'Whatevahs,' responded Stuart. 'We can go all the way up there on Saturday if you want.'

From the amused looks on the other men's faces as they watched the exchange, Valerie guessed this wasn't the first time these two had been at odds. Or was it that the other paddlers, too, had experienced similar interactions with the strong-headed stroker?

Valerie and Kristen helped the others lift the canoes onto their racks and hose them down, then washed off the two paddles they'd been using and handed them to Tala.

'Thanks for lending these to us again,' said Kristen. 'But I'm thinking it's time we went and bought our own.' She turned to Valerie. 'Whatd'ya think, hon? You all in for this paddling thing?'

'I don't know about *all* in, but yeah, in enough to have my own paddle, I'd say. If I'm gonna keep at this, I could certainly use one with a little shorter handle.'

Tala laughed. 'Yeah, it's good to have the right size, that's for sure. So, a bunch of us are going out to breakfast now. You two wanna come along?'

'Now that's something I'm definitely all in for,' said Valerie. 'And we even brought a change of clothes this time.'

The others were already seated when Valerie and Kristen got to the Kekoa Diner, a 1970s-era place with a long counter, red faux-leather booths, and waitstaff decked out in aloha-print uniforms. On the wall behind the hostess stand hung dozens of signed, framed photographs of celebrities – some famous, others less so – many bearing accolades for the 'ono-liciousness of Kekoa's pancakes, ox tail soup, saimin, and loco moco.

Valerie was happy to see that the chair across from Craig was free. Grabbing the place next to Kai, she took her seat on the other side of the table from the stroker, letting Kristen take the one in between Tala and Becca. There were eight of them in total, including Toshi and Mike sitting at the far end of the long wooden table.

Craig was ribbing Kai about his paddling style, but it seemed from the Gecko busboy's easy manner to be good-natured banter. 'You only knocked paddles with me once today,' Craig said. 'Not bad.'

'Brah, if you'd just paddle more regular like, it'd be easier for me to call da changes,' responded Kai with a grin. 'You would totally suck as a drummer.'

The approach of the server put an end to their ripostes and made Valerie grab for her menu. Hurriedly, she scanned the six-page tome.

Breakfast or lunch? Breakfast, she decided. It was only nine thirty, after all.

Sweet or savory? Savory. She needed some protein after that workout this morning. As she was staring at the myriad offerings of omelets, benedicts, and eggs with Portuguese sausage, Spam, crab cakes, bacon, pork chop, or ham, she realized the table had grown silent and everyone was looking at her.

'Oh, sorry,' she said. 'I'll have the . . . uh . . . the pork chop and eggs! Over easy, with sourdough toast.'

'Dass a good choice,' said Kai as the waitress collected their menus. 'Da pork chops super 'ono here.'

'Ah, good to know. So, what time did you guys head out this morning? It sounds like you must have been out for a while to go – what, almost ten miles Craig said?'

'We paddled out at around seven thirty, so it took us . . .' He consulted the time on his phone. 'A little over two and a half hours, I'd say.'

'Wow,' said Valerie. 'That seems pretty fast.'

'Not really. If we'd been really racing, we coulda done it a lot faster, but—'

'But you guys were totally slacking today,' Craig cut in with a harsh laugh.

'Do you think not having Hank makes a big difference?' Valerie asked, then immediately worried this might be an insensitive question to ask about their fellow crewmember who'd just died.

'Hank?' said Craig with a snort. 'No way. He may have thought he was a big shot paddler, but no one else did.'

An uncomfortable silence settled over the table. Valerie glanced at Kai and saw he was staring down at his cup of coffee, avoiding Craig's eye. The busser's right thumb, she noticed, was tapping nervously on the table.

'Dude,' said Mike. 'A little respect for the dead, yah?'

'Whatever,' mumbled Craig. 'Sorry.'

'Not sorry,' Valerie saw Tala mouth to Becca, who nodded agreement.

As the conversation moved on to the less emotionally charged subject of the paddlers' hotel arrangements in Moloka'i and Honolulu for the upcoming race, Valerie pondered what she'd just heard – and witnessed. It seemed pretty clear there had been no love lost between Craig and Hank. But was Craig's competitiveness with regard to his fellow stroker enough for him to have actually killed the guy? And if so, why would he so blatantly show his hand like that, demonstrating for all the world the animosity he felt toward Hank?

And what did Kai's obvious discomfort about Craig's outburst mean? Was it simply the unease one would naturally feel from the insensitivity of the guy's statement? Or was it something more – something personal to Kai?

'I'm gonna walk down to the farmers market in a bit,' said Valerie as she made coffee the next morning. 'You need anything? Or wanna come along?'

Kristen glanced at the clock on the stove, then shook her head. 'No can do. I said I'd be at Diane's by ten. I didn't realize we'd slept in so late.'

'Yep. That's what staying up till midnight streaming trashy movies will do. But I gotta say, it was nice snuggling up on the couch with you, Pua, and a big bowl of buttered popcorn.'

'And getting to watch Kevin Bacon and Reba McEntire do battle with a bunch of prehistoric worm monsters didn't hurt any, either,' said Kristen with a laugh.

'So true.' Valerie finished pouring water into the coffee maker, then turned and leaned against the counter. 'But seriously, I've missed not having our evenings together over the past week.'

'Me, too, hon. I mean, I'm glad you've found this new job at the Gecko, but I'm also glad it's only gonna be three nights a week from now on.'

'And the occasional lunch.'

'Right. But it's the nights when I miss you most,' said Kristen, planting a romantic kiss on her wife's lips. 'And speaking of missing you, I better get ready to go. What time do you start work tonight?'

'Four. I'm flying solo, and I gotta have the bar all set up by five when the hordes descend. So I'm guessing I won't see you till I get home from work – or tomorrow morning, if you're already asleep.'

'Yeah, I'll probably be beat from working on the lānai and hit the hay early. But tomorrow I'm free, and you have the night off, so let's do another romantic evening in.'

'Sounds like a plan.'

Valerie took her coffee outside and settled down with the newspaper on the blue director's chair. They'd definitely need to get some actual furniture out here sometime soon, she thought as she looked about her. A comfy couch and an upholstered chair or two would transform the area into an outdoor living room.

Maybe another garage-sale day would turn up some good furniture finds.

Which reminded her: that guy Jake from the garage sales would be at the market today, and she had something to ask him. Better not dilly-dally too long, in case he went home early.

Once Kristen had left, Valerie finished her coffee, grabbed a few cloth bags, and gave Pua a goodbye dog biscuit. 'No dogs allowed in the market – sorry. But this should make up for it.' The dog seemed to agree and carried the treat to her bed where she lay down and crunched it with relish.

As she walked downhill toward Kam Avenue, Valerie gazed out at the bay, where white waves were crashing over the break-water. A barge stacked high with containers was slowly making its way toward port, riding low in the water from all the cargo being shipped into the east side of the island. It was a warm day – already into the eighties – but puffy trade wind clouds filled the horizon, their dark gray bottoms suggesting they were in for some showers later on in the afternoon.

Once at the market, she made a circuit of the fruit and vege-table stands, checking the prices of tomatoes, the size of the avocados, and the freshness of the cilantro the sellers had on display. After making her purchases – including several liliko'i and a great deal on an enormous bunch of apple bananas – she made her way across the street to where the non-food vendors plied their trade.

Jake was in the same spot he'd been the week before. 'Howzit,' he said as she walked up to his stall. 'Didn't see you garage sale-ing last week. Are you finished furnishing your new home?'

She set down her bag of produce. 'Not hardly. In fact I was just thinking today that we need to go out again to look for some furniture for our lānai. So, did you snag any great items last week?'

'Well, I did score these gems.' He held up a stack of white ceramic soup bowls decorated with multi-colored dragons and geometric designs. 'I thought you might be interested, since you're clearly a cook.'

Valerie picked one up and turned it over. A square design with Asian characters was printed on the bottom.

'That's a kanji chop mark,' said Jake. 'They're mid-century

restaurant ware, very good condition. Here, check out the phoenix and a dragon on each of them. I'll give you the set for a hundred bucks.'

She set it back down. 'No way I'm paying twenty-five dollars each for these. I've seen them at the thrift stores for half that. And I bet you only paid, what . . . about six bucks each?'

'I never reveal my sources,' he said with a grin. But she could tell she wasn't far off the mark.

'So, speaking of Asian artifacts, I was wondering if you know much about Japanese objects d'art.'

'Some. What sort of *object* are you wondering about?'

'It's a small, roundish carving of a fox made from some kind of reddish-brown wood that belongs to a friend of mine. It has a scroll in its mouth and hangs from a string, and she says it belonged to her Japanese grandfather.'

Jake was nodding as she provided the description. 'Sounds like a netsuke, these little carvings that, back in the day, Japanese men used for securing the containers they stored their personal belongings in to the sashes of their kimono. You say it's in the shape of a fox?'

'Uh-huh.'

'Then my guess is it's an Inari, the messenger for the Shinto spirit of grain – usually rice, since it's the most important grain in the Japanese culture.'

'Isn't that a kind of sushi, Inari?' asked Valerie.

'It is indeed.' Jake was clearly enjoying this, getting to play professor to Valerie's curious student. 'And it's called that because the tofu pockets that the sushi rice is stuffed into traditionally have corners that look like a fox's ears.'

'Ah. Cool.'

'Hai. Sugoi desu,' said Jake with a quick bow. Now he was just showing off.

'So are they valuable, these neh . . .'

'Netsuke. And it depends – on the quality of the carving and who made it, as well as how old the piece is. They stopped making netsuke to actually be used as fasteners back in the early twentieth century, once the Japanese had mostly adopted Western dress. After that, the ones made were largely ornamental, rather than utilitarian. So it's generally the older ones that are the most valuable. And some can be quite valuable, indeed. I once saw one carved from ivory selling for over two thousand dollars – though who knows if they actually got that price.'

'Huh. Interesting.' Valerie thanked him for the information and made her way back across the street and up toward Keawe Street. If Sachiko's carved fox was as valuable as Jake thought it might be, then could Hank have stolen it from her?

TWELVE

After what Kristen had said that morning before going off to work on Diane's lānai, Valerie was surprised to see her heading across the outdoor dining area that night at the Gecko. 'Hey, girl!' she said with a wave. 'I thought you were gonna hit the hay early.' And then she noticed there was someone else following Kristen toward the bar.

The pair took the two empty barstools, and Kristen leaned over to give Valerie a kiss on the cheek. 'Hey, hon,' she said. 'This is Diane.'

'Oh, hi! Pleased to finally meet ya.' Valerie extended a hand to shake. 'Kristen's told me a lot about you.'

'All good, I hope!'

Kristen grinned. 'But of course. And to answer your question, Val, we decided we needed some nourishment after all that hard work today, so here we are. But I'm still planning on making an early night of it. One drink and something to eat, and then this girl's off home.'

Valerie found a pair of menus from under the bar and handed them out. 'So what's your pleasure, drink-wise?'

'You got a special tonight?' asked Kristen.

'I do. It's called a Hilo Sunset, made with gin, triple sec, and freshly squeezed tangerine juice, with a splash of Campari drizzled on top.'

'Yum. I'm in.'

'Ditto,' said Diane. 'Sounds like just what the doctor ordered.'

'So how's it going with the lānai?' Valerie asked as she made their cocktails.

'Great. We got all the joists in, so we're making good headway.'

Valerie wasn't positive exactly what a joist was, but knew it had something to do with the structure of the floor. 'I bet it's exciting, seeing it all come together,' she said to Diane. 'I can't imagine living here in Hilo without an outdoor space to hang out in.'

'Totally. I'm so thankful to Kristen for coming to my rescue to help me get it finished.'

'Except for that one board I made a complete hash of today,' said Kristen with a shake of the head. '"Measure four times, cut once" should be my mantra going forward. Oy.'

'Hey, at least you didn't knock over an entire box of nails and have to crawl down in between the deck footings and spend fifteen minutes picking them all out of the dirt.'

'True, dat.' Kristen slapped Diane lightly on the shoulder, then reached for the menu. The two seemed to have become quite friendly, Valerie observed as she served them their drinks. It had only been – what – three days they'd spent together so far? And here they were already acting like best buddies.

Not that she found it too surprising. Diane seemed like a fun gal, and she knew Kristen had to be missing all her friends back in Los Angeles.

As am I, thought Valerie with a pang. *Maybe. instead of spending all my energy trying to solve Hank's murder, I should be finding some new friends of my own.*

'I think I'm gonna have the kalbi ribs,' Diane announced, bringing Valerie back to the here and now.

Kristen studied the menu offerings. 'So what makes it a "kalbi" rib rather than any other kind?'

'It's the cut of meat,' Diane answered before Valerie could say anything. 'They're beef short ribs, but cut flanken style, across the bone. And the marinade is to die for – shoyu, brown sugar, and a *ton* of garlic and ginger. They're really good here – tender inside but with a caramelized and smoky crust. So 'ono!'

'Dang, girl. You want a job working here?' said Valerie with a laugh. ''Cause I don't think I could have described it any better.'

Kristen closed her menu with a *snap*. 'Okay, you convinced me. Make it two orders of the ribs.'

'Oh, and I'm paying,' said Diane. 'No argument.'

'Hey, no argument from this end. But now I may have to get dessert, too.'

Valerie left them to their bantering and punched the food order into the POS terminal. Yes, she definitely needed to work on making some new friends here in Hilo.

Once she'd closed up the bar that night, Valerie headed for the indoor dining room where the other staff were drifting in to imbibe their after-work libations. She selected a Big Wave ale from the drink fridge and took a seat next to Kai, joining the busser, along with Nalani, Matt, Seth, and Annie at the round table.

Nalani was talking about a palm grove down in Kaimū. 'I think I've heard about that place,' said Annie. 'There's a whole bunch of coconut palms there that people planted, right?'

'Uh-huh. Back in 1990, the lava flow that took out Kalapana Village also covered over Kaimū Bay, where there'd been a beautiful black sand beach covered with coco palms coming all the way down to the surf.'

Ah, right, thought Valerie. The place in the watercolor Kristen had bought at the farmers market.

'And it was da best surf spot on da island,' put in Kai. 'Or so I heard, anyway, since I wasn't even born yet.'

Nalani nodded. 'It was a devastating loss, to have that precious spot taken by Pele – though she did add acres of new land to the island in the process. So, not too long afterwards – once the lava had cooled – people started bringing sprouted coconuts to the new land and planting them to replace those that had been lost. They'd haul water and soil down there and care for the palms until they took hold and started to grow on their own.'

'I planted one when I first moved to the island,' said Seth. 'Some guys I knew took me to this place in Kapoho where there were a ton of sprouted coconuts all over the ground, and we each took one down to Kaimū to plant. It was incredibly moving, seeing all those palm trees springing up from this barren rock – there's gotta be hundreds of them there now.'

'Wow, that sounds amazing.' Annie's eyes were shining. 'I can't believe I never heard about it before.'

'Well, if you want to see it,' said Nalani, 'I'm going down in the morning to plant a palm for Hank and you're welcome to join me. That is, if you're not working lunch tomorrow.'

'I'm not, and I'd love to come along!'

'So is that a tradition,' Valerie asked, 'planting a palm for someone who died?'

Nalani shook her head. 'Not as far as I know. But since he used to live down dere near Kaimū, I thought it'd be a nice gesture. And I've been wanting to go say hi to a friend who works at Uncle Robert's, so I figured I'd combine the two.'

Hank used to live down at Kaimū? This was the first Valerie had heard of it. 'I'm not working tomorrow either,' she said. 'Mind if I tag along, as well? I've only been down to the grove once, and helping plant a palm for Hank seems like a lovely idea.'

'Sure, the more the merrier. I gotta be here to talk to da meat delivery guy at ten – dey been shorting me on a couple items the past couple weeks – so why don't we meet here 'bout ten fifteen, and we can all ride down in my car.' Nalani glanced at the time on her phone, then shoved back her chair. 'Okay, gotta jam; da hubby awaits my arrival.'

'Me, too,' said Matt. 'Including the hubby part,' he added with a grin.

After they'd left, Kai downed his bottle and stood. 'You heading out, too?' asked Valerie.

'Nah, just getting another drink, since Sachiko and Nalani aren't here to see. When the cat's away, yah? Anyone else want another beer – or ginger beer?' he asked.

Seth and Annie shook their heads. 'I'm good.'

'And I only just started on mine,' said Valerie. 'So, do they really care if we have more than one drink after work?'

'Nah.' Kai popped the cap off his Longboard Lager. 'Long as we don't overdo it, dey're cool.'

But from the looks of the others at the table, Valerie got the feeling that maybe their bosses weren't actually too keen on the help drinking up their profits. 'Speaking of Nalani and Matt having to get home to their husbands,' she said, 'do you know if Hank had a significant other?'

'He never mentioned anyone to me,' said Seth. 'Though I do know he went through a messy divorce on the Mainland a while back – which is probably why he moved here, I'm guessing. Why do you ask?'

'Uh . . .' *Think fast, Val!* 'Well, hearing Nalani talk about planting that coco palm for him, it just got me wondering if he had any family here – or back on the Mainland. You know, who'd be mourning his loss. 'Cause I haven't heard anything about a memorial service or anything . . .'

Seth nodded. 'Ah, right. Well, from what I can tell, I doubt his ex would care much about any memorial for Hank, and he never mentioned having any kids.'

Annie was shaking her head. 'And I don't remember him ever talking about a girlfriend here on the island, either.'

'Or maybe a boyfriend?' Valerie suggested, which drew a snort from Kai.

Annie turned to face the busser. 'What, you think there's something wrong with that?' she said, shooting a glance in Valerie's direction.

'No, no, it's not that,' said Kai quickly. 'I got no problem wit' da gays. But I tink maybe Hank did.'

Valerie raised an eyebrow. 'Oh, yeah? How so?'

'It's only 'cause of some stuffs I heard him say behind Matt's back – not so nice tings about da guy.'

'Homophobic things?' asked Valerie, and Kai nodded. 'Did Matt know?'

The busser shrugged. 'I nevah wen' tell um, but someone else might-a.'

Valerie turned toward the other two at the table, her raised eyebrows asking the question.

'I never heard Hank say anything about Matt, good or bad,' said Annie.

Seth shook his head in agreement. 'Me neither. And if I had, I wouldn't have told Matt. Why make unnecessary waves?'

'Maybe it was just 'cause we paddled together that he said those things around me,' Kai said with another shrug. 'You know, macho guy talk, to try an' impress me?'

'Maybe,' Valerie said. 'Or maybe it's one of those "me thinks thou doth protest too much" situations. You know,' she added when this statement was met with blank stares from the others, 'maybe Hank acted like that in order to throw you off track and conceal something about himself.'

Kai was frowning. 'You saying you tink maybe da guy really was gay?'

'Who knows? But it's not uncommon for those who seem the most homophobic to act that way 'cause of feelings they have themselves that they're ashamed of or are trying to hide from others. Guys, especially – it can be really hard for them in our macho culture.'

'I dunno,' said Kai. 'He nevah seem māhū to me.'

From the context, Valerie took this to be the Hawaiian word for gay. And from the frown on Annie's face, she guessed she had serious doubts about Valerie's theory, as well. Which made sense, given what Valerie knew of Hank's reputation as a ladies' man – including his supposedly having hit on the server.

But what was on her mind at that moment far more than the question of *why* Hank had said those things to Matt was the fact that he'd said them. Could Hank and Matt's relationship have been such that it gave the mild-mannered cook reason to hurt Hank – or even want him dead?

THIRTEEN

'**M**orning!' The back door opened, and Pua came charging across the kitchen and straight for her water bowl. 'I guess I must have been really tired last night,' said Kristen, who hung up the leash, then headed straight for the coffee machine. 'I didn't even hear you come home.'

Valerie popped up the bread she had in the toaster and set about slathering it with butter. 'Yeah, I was afraid Pua's barking was gonna wake you, but you were dead to the world. Thanks for coming in for dinner, by the way. It was a nice surprise.'

'My pleasure – those kalbi ribs were outstanding, as was that delectable cocktail. And speaking of food,' Kristen said with a nod at the toast and pair of eggs spattering in a pan, 'what's with the big breakfast?'

'It's 'cause I'm going down to Puna this morning with some people from work and I'm not sure if I'll get the chance to grab lunch while we're out. I would have waited to see if you wanted to join me, but I gotta get out of here ASAP.' She checked her phone. 'Shoot. I only have fifteen minutes – I shoulda gotten up earlier.'

'Wait, you're going down to Puna today? I thought we were going to spend the day together.'

'I know. I'm sorry, hon. I would have told you last night if you'd been awake. It's just that Nalani – you know, the Gecko owner – is going down to plant a coco palm for Hank at that palm grove we visited with Isaac last spring, and when she said he used to live down there, near Kaimū, I realized I might be able to learn more about the guy if I tagged along.'

Kristen smiled. 'Ah. So it's some sleuthing you're after. I guess I can't keep you from that. And hey, maybe I can go over to Diane's today and do a little more work. Oh, and by the way, I invited Isaac and Sachiko to dinner tonight – I hope that's okay. It's the only day both you and her have off at the Gecko, and we haven't hung out with them in a while, so . . .'

'Sure, it's fine. Want me to pick up some poke or something at the store on my way home?'

'Nah, I was thinking of just throwing some chicken on the grill or something easy like that. Don't you worry about it.' Kristen leaned over to give Valerie a kiss on the cheek. 'Okay, I'm gonna go hop in the shower. Good luck with your investigation!'

Kristen was being awfully cheerful and understanding about all this, Valerie mused as she chowed down on her eggs and toast. Was it simply that – her wanting to be sweet to her wife? Or could it be that she was actually *happy* to have an excuse to go back to Diane's house today?

As Valerie thought about it, she realized she had no idea if the woman was single or involved, straight or gay. She'd never asked, and Kristen hadn't volunteered the information. But then, with an impatient shake of the head, Valerie downed the rest of her coffee. *Get a grip, girl. Are you really going to let yourself be jealous that your wife has found a new friend? Don't be such a loser.*

Standing up, she took her plate to the sink and washed it off. *No.* She was going to be a mature and supportive spouse, just like Kristen was being. And who knew, maybe she, too, would soon find a new friend – maybe even someone at work like Nalani, or Seth, or Annie.

An hour and a half later, Nalani pulled into the parking area down at Kaimū, next to a large wooden structure with multiple hand-painted signs advertising 'smoothies,' 'local food,' and the like. Above the entrance, between a Hawai'i state flag and one of the sovereignty movement, hung a wooden sign reading 'Uncle's 'Awa Club.' Several other cars were parked along the dead-end street, and as Nalani shut off the engine, Valerie could see a group of people emerge from the structure bearing plastic cups of bright pink and yellow beverages.

Although it had been drizzling once again when they left Hilo, the sky down here was clear and blue. Valerie climbed out of the back seat and stretched her legs, then turned to stare up at the black, lava-covered pali that climbed up toward Kīlauea volcano. The last time she'd been down here with Isaac and

Kristen the previous May, there'd been a plume of smoke rising from Pu'u 'ō'ō, but shortly after their visit, the vent had ceased its activity with the start of the new eruption that had devastated Leilani Estates and the community of Kapoho.

An eruption that, although now quiet, was still making its presence known. On the drive down, they'd crossed its path, where a thick metal sheet had been placed over the cracked highway and steam rose eerily on either side of the road, its sulfuric haze obscuring the skeletal forms of burnt trees.

Nalani was lifting plastic bottles from the trunk of her car and setting them on the ground. 'You didn't tell me this was going to be a cocktail party,' said Valerie with a chuckle as she took in the seven gin bottles. 'Or is that all for Pele?'

'Anyone who comes out with me to da grove's gotta be a sherpa,' she answered, handing Valerie two of the bottles. 'Gotta water my babies.' After Nalani had passed Annie two of the containers, she placed two more into a daypack and slung it over her shoulder. Then, picking up the last bottle and the sprouted coconut she'd brought along, she led the way out toward the ocean.

The path took them first across a large parking lot, which Nalani explained was used for the big Wednesday-night market and concerts held at Uncle Robert's 'Awa Bar. 'It's a big deal,' she said. 'Hundreds of people come to dance, eat 'ono grindz, an' socialize.'

'Who's Uncle Robert?' asked Annie.

'Robert Keli'iho'omalu. He grew up down here in Kalapana on land his family had owned for generations, and when the lava came in 1990, after it destroyed Kaimū Bay and most of the village of Kalapana, his family prayed and watched as it came for their property and then miraculously stopped – right on their front lawn. Some people say that a higher being intervened, but I like to say that his land was spared because of his aloha spirit.'

Nalani turned to look back at the large wooden structure. 'He was a special kine man, Uncle Robert, revered for his generosity in welcoming everyone to his home, regardless of where they came from. An' he had a vision for his family homestead of self-sustainability, and of spreading awareness of Hawaiian culture and the practice of mālama 'āina – care for the land.'

'Wow,' said Annie, stopping to shake a pebble from her rubber slippah. 'He sounds like an amazing guy. Does he still run the whole market and bar and everything?'

'He passed away in 2015, but his family is still carrying on with his vision. As are lots of locals down here. Check out all da oddah things besides coco palms that people have planted.' Nalani pointed out a papaya, a noni, and a kukui nut tree. 'And dere's even breadfruit out here now.'

'So, who did that?' asked Valerie, nodding toward a brightly colored scene someone had painted on a broad swath of lava rock. 'It looks like a Hawaiian crest or coat of arms.'

'I don't know, but I do know dere's uku people who claim all this new land that Pele added to the island for the Kingdom of Hawai'i.'

'Well, it's beautiful,' said Annie and started once more down the path.

They heard the sea before they saw it – the booming of powerful waves as they came crashing down upon the lava rock beach. The three of them walked out and stood gazing down at the churning surf, roiling in a fury of whitewater. Out past the waves, the ocean was a vibrant turquoise, becoming a deeper and darker blue as it stretched out toward the horizon.

'Da old Kaimū Beach was steep like dis, too,' said Nalani, 'but it was black sand – not big ol' rocks like now – and da water wasn't nearly as rough as dis. I only ever seen a couple a guys surfing here at dis new beach, and it was scary just watching 'um – no wayz would I try it.' Turning away from the water, she headed for one of the taller coconut palms to their left.

Instead of following after her, Valerie stood a moment to take it all in. There must have been hundreds of palm trees out on that desolate, new lava rock land, from tiny sprouts to more established trees, some ten to fifteen feet tall. Only a few, however, bore any coconuts, and those were small and green.

'How come so few of the trees have any fruit?' she asked as she rejoined Nalani and Annie. 'They've gotta be old enough by now to produce coconuts.'

'It's 'cause of the harsh conditions out here.' Nalani had set down her pack, along with the sprouted coconut, and was surveying the palms, hands on hips, as would a farmer taking in a grove of orange trees. 'It's pretty much a desert – hardly any rain – so da trees, dey take a lot longer to grow than up dere Hilo-side. Plus, take a look at what kind of soil dey have to grow in.' She dug into the ground and held up a handful of black sand. 'Not many nutrients; plus it doesn't hold da water. The first trees only started to have any coconuts in the past few years, and dey're about twenty-five years old now. Which is why I bring out my own water,' she said, unscrewing the cap from one of the bottles. 'And sometimes I bring out fertilizer, too. Here, you can each water one of my trees – there's six of them – and we'll keep the last bottle for Hank's new one.'

Nalani pointed out the palms in her personal 'grove,' which she, her husband, her daughter, and three family friends had planted over the years since the Kalapana lava flow. While Valerie and Annie poured the water around the bases of the six trees, Nalani dug a shallow hole in the black sand for the sprouted coconut she'd brought with her.

'Should we say a prayer or something?' asked Annie as Nalani held the coconut aloft in her hands.

She lowered the coconut. 'Was Hank religious?'

'I don't know. But it seems like we should say something.'

''Kay, you can do it, den.'

'Oh.' Annie frowned, clearly unprepared for the charge she'd brought upon herself. 'Uh, okay. So . . . we plant this coconut today in memory of Hank Marino, whose life was cut short at a young age. I'm sure he will be missed by many people, and we hope his spirit will live on in the form of this beautiful coconut palm.' She glanced from Nalani to Valerie. 'Either of you want to add anything else?'

'Nah, I'm good,' said Nalani.

Valerie shook her head. 'And I never even met the guy, so . . .'

'Okay, then. I guess you can go ahead.' Annie gestured for Nalani to set the baby tree down in the hole.

Once she'd planted the coconut, being careful not to damage the tiny roots emerging from the shell and leaving its top half above the sand, Nalani poured water around the edges. 'Sorry about da gin bottle, Hank,' she said with a wry smile. 'But den again, maybe wherever you are now, you can enjoy your gin again with no problems.'

The coconut watered, she tamped down the soil, then stood. 'Right,' she said, collecting the empty liquor bottles. 'That's it, then. Let's go get a smoothie.'

'It doesn't seem like you were super close to Hank,' Valerie said to Nalani as they started back toward the parking area. 'Either of you, for that matter,' she added with a glance back at Annie, who was lagging behind. 'So it's awful sweet of you to go to the trouble to come out here and plant a palm for the guy.'

Nalani waved a hand. 'As I said before, I wanted to come down anyway to visit a friend who works at Uncle Robert's, so no biggie. But also, even though Hank did have his issues, he didn't deserve to die like that.'

'Yeah, I heard he had a bit of a temper,' said Valerie. 'Not to mention a rather high opinion of himself, as well.'

'But you gotta balance that with da fact he was a recovering alcoholic. That can't be an easy path for anyone.'

'True. That's what Seth said, too.' Valerie knew several people who were on the wagon – her brother Charlie's business partner, for one – and was well aware that the demons that could cause someone to abuse alcohol didn't miraculously disappear simply because they stopped drinking.

'Anyway,' Nalani went on, 'it actually felt pretty good to do that for Hank – way more than I expected. I guess having someone you work with that closely die so suddenly really does a number on you.' She walked on for a moment, brow furrowed, then stopped in the middle of the path and turned to face Valerie and Annie. 'Maybe we should have some kind of more formal memorial for Hank – something everyone at the restaurant can take part in. Only if dey want to, that is. But it seems like it might be good closure for all of us. Whatd'ya think?'

'Seems like a good idea to me,' said Valerie. 'But then again, as I said before, I never even met him.'

Annie, who had been silent throughout this whole discussion, nodded. 'Yeah, I agree. I think it would be good closure for us all.'

'Good. I'll talk to Sachiko about it,' said Nalani, starting once more down the path. 'Maybe we can do it next Monday, when the restaurant's closed.'

They walked on for a few more minutes, passing a couple on

their way out to the ocean bearing lawn chairs and a cooler. Once back at the road, Nalani stowed the empty liquor bottles in the trunk, and then they walked over to Uncle Robert's.

The building was essentially an enormous wooden A-frame, open on all sides to allow the breeze to pass through the structure. Once inside, Valerie saw that there were a variety of different areas: a bar, a dance floor, a section with picnic tables, and several stalls selling food and drink.

Nalani headed straight for the smoothie stand and fist-bumped a burly guy with a top knot in his dark hair. 'I think I'm gonna get some 'awa,' said Annie. 'I could use a little boost right about now.'

Valerie followed her over to the bar. 'I've never tried it,' she said. 'What exactly is 'awa?'

'It's "kava" in English – you know, that root they grind into a powder and make into a drink? 'Awa is the Hawaiian word.'

'Ah, I've heard of that. But isn't it more of a depressant than a stimulant?'

'It's actually a little of both,' said the woman behind the counter, 'and can affect different people in different ways. For me, it makes me more focused and relaxed. But it's also good for relieving tension, and I've heard a lot of people say it has a euphoric effect on them. 'Awa has been used for centuries as a medicinal plant, and for the ancient Hawaiians it was a ceremonial drink, brought out only on special occasions. Lucky for us, now we can have it anytime we want. Care to try some?'

Valerie could tell this was not the first time the gal had given this spiel. Nevertheless, the bartender in her was curious about the beverage. And besides, she didn't have to worry about driving home. 'Sure,' she said, 'I'm game.'

'Make that two,' said Annie.

From a large wooden bowl, the woman ladled what looked like iced latte into a pair of coconut-shell cups and handed them over. 'Hmmm . . .' Valerie said, rolling the liquid around her tongue. 'Tastes very . . . earthy.'

Annie laughed. 'Yeah, it's kind of an acquired taste. But then again, so is coffee, right? So, it looks like Nalani might be a while,' she said with a nod toward the cook, who was now listening intently to whatever the guy at the smoothie shack was telling her. 'Wanna go sit till she's done?'

'Sure. And let me get these – my treat. Why don't you go over and save me a seat while I pay.'

'Hey, thanks! I can't argue with that.'

Once Annie was gone, Valerie turned to the gal at the counter. 'Do you happen to remember a guy named Hank Marino who used to live down here?'

'Hank? Sure, I remember him. He used to come here a lot, before he moved up to Hilo.'

'You mean here, the 'awa bar, or here at Uncle Robert's in general?'

'Here, the 'awa bar. He came pretty much every day for his little pick-me-up, which is how come I know him. He was even talking about getting a job at Uncle Robert's before he decided to move. But it's been a while since I've seen the guy. I guess he must hang out at the 'awa bar in Hilo these days,' she added with a laugh. 'So, are you a friend of Hank's?'

The server clearly hadn't heard about his demise. *Do I want to be the one to tell her?* Valerie thought not. 'Uh, well, he used to tend bar at the restaurant I also work at, and I heard tell he used to live near Kaimū, so I was just curious if you knew him, is all.' She looked about her, then turned back to the woman. 'It sure is beautiful down here. So much more peaceful than Hilo. I wonder why Hank moved.'

'Oh, I can answer that,' said the gal. 'It was the paddling. That was about all he talked about, once he got into it. The guy was completely obsessed. But I do gather he's actually pretty good at it – or so he said, in any case.' *Was that a rolling of the eyes?*

'Yeah, I heard about his passion for paddling. But that was the reason he moved?'

She nodded. 'It was too much of a drag, having to drive all the way up there for the early practices they do, so he decided to move to the big city.'

'Ha. Big city. Right. Though I guess compared to down here, Hilo is pretty crowded. But still, it's kind of a big deal to pull up roots and leave the place you've been for a long time.'

'Oh, I don't think Hank lived down here all that long,' the woman said. 'And it didn't seem like he had a lot of friends here – at least he never came in to the 'awa bar with anyone else. Plus, the guy seems pretty haole. I think he said he was from

Pittsburg or someplace like that. Definitely not a kamaʻāina. He's probably better off up in Hilo, actually.'

'Yeah, that makes sense.' Valerie pulled out her wallet and paid for the two drinks. 'Well, thanks for introducing me to ʻawa. Have a good day.'

'You, too. And tell Hank that Kayla says hi!'

Valerie merely responded with a nod and a smile as she turned to go. Kayla would no doubt at some point learn that Hank was in fact dead and wonder why the heck that chick who'd been asking about him hadn't had the grace to tell her. *Good thing I'm not planning on becoming a steady customer down here*, she thought as she made her way over to the picnic tables. *'Cause I'm guessing I'd be persona non grata if Kayla ever saw me again.*

'You were there a long time,' said Annie when Valerie finally joined her. 'Was there a problem with the POS or something?'

'No, but we ended up talking about Hank. I gather he was quite the regular customer at the ʻawa bar. Do you suppose that runs afoul of the rules of AA? Or maybe he wasn't yet in AA when he lived down here?'

Annie shrugged. 'Who knows?'

Valerie sipped her beverage, which she'd neglected while talking to Kayla. Its aroma was a blend of dirt and ginger, and the taste was somewhat bitter. Nevertheless, she imagined she might get used to it if she drank it with any frequency. But the numbing effect the drink was having on her mouth and tongue? Not so much.

She set the cup aside. At least she now knew she wouldn't be tempted to come back down here for more. Though Annie, she noticed, had already finished hers.

'So, I'm curious about something,' said Valerie. 'You know how Nalani was saying it can't have been easy for Hank, his being an alcoholic, and how she was willing to cut him some slack about his temper and stuff because of it?'

'Uh-huh . . .'

'Well, I've worked with some folks who had drinking problems, and it's true they're not always that easy to deal with. So I was just wondering about Seth. I mean, he *seems* like a pretty mellow guy, but I know he's AA, too, so I'm just wondering if I should,

I dunno . . . be careful how I act around him. You know, in case he has a temper, too . . .?'

Annie leaned back with a laugh and slapped her knees. 'Seth? God, no. I mean, I've seen the guy lose his cool – we all do from time to time. It's a stressful job, and customers can sometimes be total jerks. But he's not a *bit* like Hank.'

The way she spit out these last few words indicated a fair amount of hostility. Should she ask a direct question about Hank's hitting on her? No, better to take an indirect approach. 'Yeah,' said Valerie with what she hoped was a knowing look, 'I've heard he could be a bit of a masher, as my mom liked to say.'

Annie frowned. 'A masher?'

'You know, a guy who hits on women in a creepy, aggressive way?' Valerie glanced around her, as if ready to divulge a secret, then leaned forward. 'Like, I heard that he'd been coming on to Jun's wife – do you know if it's true?'

'I never heard about that, but it wouldn't surprise me in the least.'

'How so?'

'Because that's the way he was – a "masher," as you say. I kinda like that word; maybe we should bring it back.'

Annie chuckled to herself, and Valerie thought she detected a slight slurring of her words. *Guess that 'awa was pretty strong.* Another reason not to drink it.

'Anyway,' Annie went on, 'he tried it on me a couple times, but I was so not interested. *Yuck.*' She shook out her arms, as if trying to rid herself of the memory.

'So why – if you don't mind my asking – did you want to come down here today, if that's the way you feel about the guy?'

Annie stared out toward the food stand, where a line of people were waiting to order loco moco and plate lunches of lau lau and kālua pork. 'I'm not exactly sure,' she said after a bit. 'I did want to come check this place out after hearing Nalani talk about it, so when she invited me to come along, I figured I might as well. But now . . . I dunno. Maybe it wasn't such a great idea, after all.'

Valerie was about to ask her to elaborate when Annie suddenly stood. 'Looks like Nalani's done talking to her friend,' she said. 'I'm gonna hit the ladies' room before we go.'

'Good idea.' Valerie followed her to the restroom, where they were joined in line by Nalani. *Dang*, she thought as the two other women chatted about Nalani's friend. *I shoulda been quicker.* Would she be able to get Annie talking like that again, or had she now missed her chance?

FOURTEEN

Kristen wasn't there when Valerie returned home at two thirty, but a note on the kitchen table said: 'At Diane's – back by 3:00.' She'd just made herself a PB&J sandwich and had settled down at her computer to check her email when she heard a car pull into the driveway. Peering out the window, she saw Kristen pull her bucket of tools from the back seat of a bright red sedan, then wave goodbye as Diane pulled back out and headed down the street.

'Hi, honey, I'm home!' Kristen called out in her best Ricky Ricardo voice. Valerie heard the *clunk* of her work boots as she dropped them onto the front porch, then the slamming of the screen door as she came inside.

'I'm in the study!' Valerie shouted back.

After a minute her wife came into the room, having already changed from her blue jeans into a pair of khaki shorts. 'How was the excursion down to the palm grove?' she asked.

Valerie raised a finger as she swallowed her mouthful of peanut-butter-slathered bread. 'Good. And productive. I talked to a woman who knew Hank when he lived down there, and she said he used to come in where she works for a cup of kava every day.'

'Oh, yeah?' Kristen reached for the other half of the sandwich and, after waiting for an approving nod from Valerie, took a bite.

'Yeah. And she said some interesting things about the guy – that he always came in alone, for one. So she thinks he didn't have a whole lot of friends in the area. And I'm guessing it also means he wasn't romantically involved with anyone while he lived down there.'

'Or if he was involved with someone,' said Kristen, taking a seat on the armchair across from the desk, 'she wasn't into kava.'

'Or *he* wasn't,' said Valerie.

'What – you think Hank might have been gay?'

'No, not really. But I did hear last night from Kai, the Gecko

busser, that Hank was making homophobic remarks about Matt
– he's one of the cooks at the Gecko. So it's possible the guy
was a closeted queer who was needing to prove to others that
he wasn't.'

Kristen shook her head. 'Or more likely he was simply a
garden-variety straight jerk. I mean, from what you've said, the
guy was a macho braggart who liked to hit on every woman he
met.'

'True. And Annie – the Gecko server who went down there
this morning with us – she confirmed that she was one of the
women he hit on, and she seemed pretty disgusted by it.'

'Enough to whack the guy?'

'That's the sixty-four-thousand-dollar question, I guess. Or
one of the many, anyway. And then I asked her if one of the
other servers, Seth – who's also AA – had a temper like Hank,
and she said she had seen him lose his cool at work, but that he
was nothing like Hank. Nevertheless, I suppose he should be on
my list, as well, even though the guy seems totally sweet and
mellow.'

'It's a stressful job, being a waiter, so I'm guessing anyone
could lose it once in a while.'

'That's exactly what Annie said. But getting back to those
comments Hank made about Matt, if this was a running issue
between the two, maybe Matt could have just had enough of it
all at that restaurant retreat and been the one to whack the guy.'

'Were people drinking alcohol at the retreat?' asked Kristen.

'Probably. I know most of them are drinkers, anyway. Though
Hank was supposedly AA – as is Seth. Oh, which reminds me:
Do you know if 'awa – kava – is off-limits for people in AA?'

'Well, it is a mind-altering drug, so I suppose it depends on
why you're using it. If it's just another way to manage whatever
demons drove you to drink in the first place, then I'm guessing
it wouldn't be such a great idea.'

'Hmmm . . .' Valerie stared out the window at a white egret
that had landed on their front yard and was pecking at bugs in
the grass. 'Because I'm thinking, since Hank was clearly really
into 'awa, then maybe that makes it more likely he would relapse
with alcohol, too.' She turned to face Kristen. 'I need to find out
if he seemed drunk at the retreat.'

'So what were the other things you learned about Hank from the kava gal?'

'Oh, right. She also told me that he'd been asking about getting a job at Uncle Robert's, but then decided to move from Kalapana up to Hilo to make it easier to get to the Bayfront for paddling. Which shows how much he was into the sport – you know, to leave his newly adopted community because of it.'

'Or maybe he moved for an entirely different reason, and that's just what he told her.'

Valerie grinned. 'Ha! You're getting as suspicious of people as I am, my dear. I gotta say I kinda like this sleuthy Kristen. Oh, and there's something else, too. So after Annie told me how Hank had been hitting on her and how grossed out she was by it, I asked why, then, did she go down to the palm grove to plant a palm for the guy?'

'And?'

'She said that she'd been wanting to visit the palm grove for a while, so when Nalani was talking about going down there this morning and invited her along, she figured, why not?'

Kristen frowned. 'So how is that relevant to anything?'

'It's what she said next that was weird – something like, "But now I'm wondering if it was such a good idea to come." What do you suppose she meant by that?'

'Hey, I wasn't there, so I have no idea. But didn't you ask her what she meant?'

'I was about to, but then all of a sudden she stood up and said she had to go pee, and then Nalani joined us and the moment was gone.' Valerie thought a moment, watching the egret as it flapped its long wings and took to the air clumsily, landing on the neighbor's roof. 'I can't help but wonder if maybe she's feeling guilty about Hank in some way . . .'

It was Kristen's turn to smile. 'In some murderous way, you mean?'

Valerie laughed. 'Yeah, maybe. But then again, she did drink that big cup of kava pretty quickly. I didn't like the way it made my mouth numb, so I only had a few sips, but maybe it had an effect on Annie. Depressants can make you kind of morose, so it could have just been that – the whole planting of the palm for a guy who died in such a creepy way was making her sad or

upset or whatever. She did fall asleep in the back seat for a lot
of the drive back up to Hilo.'

'There ya go.' Kristen slapped her knees and stood up. 'Okay,
well, I better get cooking for tonight.'

'I brought a hostess gift,' said Sachiko as she stepped into the
living room with Isaac at a little past five. Kneeling down to give
Pua the love her furiously wagging tail made clear she was
craving, she handed the package to Valerie and accepted an
enthusiastic greeting from the excited dog.

Valerie opened the box to peek inside. 'Oh, wow – mochi!
Yum!'

'It's from Two Ladies Kitchen.' Sachiko stood back up and
wiped her face with her shirt sleeve. 'The pink are chi chi – milk
flavored; the yellow are liliko'i; the green are tsunami mochi,
filled with sweet bean paste; and the pastries are manjū, filled
with sweet potato paste.'

'Domo arigato,' said Valerie with a bow. 'And now I'm not
sure I can wait for dessert. Here, c'mon in and I'll rustle us up
some drinks.'

Isaac followed them to the kitchen and peered at the bottles
lined up on the counter. 'Whatcha got going tonight?'

'Well, speaking of liliko'i,' she said with a nod toward the
box of rice cake sweets, 'I juiced some passion fruit I got at
the farmers market yesterday, and was going to make liliko'i
Martinis with a hint of cayenne pepper for anyone who cares
for one.'

All three present in the kitchen raised their arms.

'Gin or vodka?'

'Gin,' responded Isaac and Kristen.

'Vodka for me,' said Sachiko. 'But go easy on the pepper, if
you will. I'm kind of a spicy food wimp.'

Isaac grinned. 'Her mom, she nevah serve da spicy kine when
Sachiko was growin' up. It's a Japanese thing. But you can give
me her share – I love da spice.'

'Really, you're not a fan of spicy?' Valerie poured gin into a
metal container filled with ice, then added liliko'i juice sweetened
with sugar and a sprinkling of cayenne, covered it with a bar
glass, and gave it a vigorous shake. 'But I thought your mom

grew up on the Big Island, and I know the locals here tend to love their hot food.'

'Yeah, she did,' said Sachiko, taking a seat at the kitchen table. 'But her mother was very Japanese – culturally, anyway, since she grew up in Shinmachi – so Mom learned to cook in the traditional Japanese way, with lots of fish and rice and fresh vegetables and focused on bringing out the natural flavors of the ingredients rather than adding a lot of seasoning and spices.' She put her hand over her mouth. 'Oh, god, I *so* sound like a restaurant manager.'

Valerie laughed. 'Hey, it goes with the job.'

'I've read about Shinmachi,' said Kristen. 'It was that neighborhood in Hilo that was destroyed in the tsunami of 1960, right? Was your family living there then?'

'The village was actually first wiped out by the '46 tsunami and then rebuilt, only to be destroyed again by the one in 1960. Luckily for my grandparents and mom, they left after the first tsunami and bought a house up in Pi'ihonua. But a lot of their friends weren't so fortunate and lost everything twice, in a span of fourteen years.'

'Ugh.' Kristen shook her head. 'That's awful.'

'Where was the village?' asked Valerie, straining the bright yellow cocktails into three Martini glasses.

'Down where the soccer fields and Waiākea are now,' said Sachiko. 'You've probably seen the clock memorial along the road there that's set permanently at 1:04 a.m., the time the waves hit in 1960? After that second tsunami, they realized they shouldn't rebuild and decided to make the area into a park and flood plain. So all the families who'd lived there ended up scattered all around town.' She let out a slow sigh. 'It's so sad, because Shinmachi was such a special kine place.'

Kristen thanked Valerie for her drink, then took a seat next to Sachiko. 'So what made it so special – you know, other than of course being a close-knit neighborhood of families, an' all?'

'It was how everyone helped everyone else. The village was founded back around 1913 by people who'd completed their contracts with the sugar plantations and decided to create their own community. They all worked together to help everyone else out financially by making loans to each other, even when they were competitors. A lot of those businesses are still around today: the S. Tokunaga Store, HPM builders—'

'Where I bought some deck screws, just today!' put in Kristen.

'And they had their own school, newspaper, a theater, churches and temples, even a baseball team. But now it's all gone.' Sachiko accepted the drink offered to her by Valerie and, after taking a sip, her frown smoothed into a smile. 'Delicious!' she declared. 'Okay, time to talk about something more upbeat.'

They made their way out to the lānai, where Valerie recounted her trip down to Kalapana that morning – leaving out anything to suggest she'd been trying to learn information relevant to the cause of Hank's death. Though she could see Isaac eyeing her with interest as she recounted her story.

'It was interesting,' she said, 'how the three of us were affected differently by the planting of the coconut for Hank. For me, since I never knew the guy, I basically just felt like an impartial observer, but Nalani seemed pretty moved by the whole thing.'

'Really?' Sachiko glanced at Isaac, then shook her head. 'Sorry. I mean, it's not as if that should be super surprising or anything. It's just that . . .'

'Nalani doesn't seem the type to get all emotional over stuff,' filled in Isaac. 'I seen how she is, babe – I get it. Plus, it's not as if Hank was super popular at da Gecko, at least as far as I can tell, anyway . . .'

'Yeah, well, I was a bit surprised, too,' said Valerie. 'Especially 'cause of how matter-of-fact Nalani had been about it beforehand, saying it just seemed like the right thing to do since he used to live down there. And even during the . . . ceremony, I guess you'd call it – since Annie suggested we say a few words for Hank – she seemed pretty unemotional. But then afterwards, as we were walking back to the car, she got quiet all of a sudden and then suggested that the Gecko maybe have some kind of memorial for Hank. You know, that it might be cathartic for the staff.'

Sachiko made no response to this other than to stare out toward the banana grove in the neighbors' yard. A light rain had begun to fall, setting off the chirping of the coquís, and the water dripping from the lānai's corrugated steel roof onto the walkway below was adding a rhythmic percussion to the frogs' song. Isaac gave Valerie an eyebrow shrug, but no one spoke.

'Yeah,' Sachiko finally said with a sad smile, turning back to face the others. 'Maybe it would be a good idea. I know his death has been really difficult for me, so I can imagine it's been hard for the others, too.'

'Though from what I can tell,' said Valerie, 'not too hard on at least some of them.' At Sachiko's quizzical look, she elaborated. 'So, the other thing I was going to tell you about people's reactions to planting that palm for Hank this morning was what Annie said afterwards. While Nalani was over talking to a friend who works at Uncle Robert's, the two of us sat down and had some 'awa – or at least Annie did; I wasn't too keen on the stuff, to tell you the truth, so I didn't drink much of mine. Anyway, we got to talking about Hank, and she told me how he'd been hitting on her – confirming what Jun had told me and what I passed along to you,' she added with a glance Sachiko's way.

'Yeah, I guess I still need to talk to her about that,' Sachiko said with a sigh. 'If she wants to talk, that is . . .'

Valerie nodded. 'So then I asked the obvious question: Why, then, did she want to go down to Kaimū to plant a palm for the guy?'

'And what'd she say?' asked Isaac.

'She said that it wasn't about Hank – that she simply wanted to come down to see the palm grove, which she'd never visited before. But then she added something else: she said, "But now I'm not so sure it was such a good idea."'

Sachiko waved her hand dismissively. 'Oh, it probably just means that having that ceremony – or whatever it was you guys did for Hank – brought back bad memories of how creepy he was to her.'

'But why, then, would *she* be the one to suggest we say something for him? And why would she be the one who ended up actually *saying* it?'

'Huh. Well, yeah, that is weird, I have to say.'

Isaac sought Valerie out in the kitchen after they'd finished eating dinner. 'Hey,' he said as she looked up from rinsing off a salad plate. 'Kristen and Sachiko are talking 'bout a possible remodel of our kitchen, so I figure I got a couple minutes to find out if you've learned anything new about Hank – besides what you said earlier to all of us.'

She shut off the tap and left the stack of plates to soak in the sink. 'You sure they can't hear us?'

'I turned up da stereo as I left the room,' he said with a grin. 'They were too busy discussing tile versus granite to notice I did it, so we should be okay. At least for a couple minutes.'

'Okay, I'll try to be quick.' She recounted what she'd already told Kristen before dinner: about Hank not seeming to have any close friends down in Kalapana – which meant he likely hadn't had any kind of serious relationship while living there; about his moving to Hilo for the paddling; and about his making homophobic slurs about Matt, which made her wonder if there could be a motive there on the part of the cook.

Isaac shook his head as she said this last bit. 'I'd be really surprised if it was Matt. Da guy, he's about the mellowest dude I know. I just can't see him shoving someone over a cliff – even if they had been talkin' trash about him.'

'Yeah, he does seem like a real sweetie. Though the guy's so shy it's hard to know exactly what he's thinking. But speaking of mellow people, what do you think – or know – about Seth?'

'Seth?' Isaac frowned as he thought a moment.

'I only ask 'cause folks have been talking about how Hank having a hot temper was likely related to his being an alcoholic – or a recovering one, as far as anyone knows. Nalani was saying this morning that it's one of the reasons she was able to forgive him for sometimes being a jerk, 'cause of how hard it all must have been for him. And, well, Seth is AA, too, so I was just wondering if you thought he also might be . . .'

'A jerk?' Isaac said with a laugh. 'I dunno. I never seen him be anything but super friendly and nice. But I guess you nevah know . . .'

'No, you don't. And that's the problem. You never know about anyone, do you?'

Isaac gave her a look, as if he were about to say something, then shook his head. Instead, he reached into the pocket of his cargo shorts and pulled out his phone. 'I thought you might want to see the photos I took at the Gecko retreat. They're not that great, 'cause I didn't have my Nikon with me, but maybe there's something there that could be important.'

Valerie leaned over to take a look at the screen. 'Did you show these to the cops?'

'Dey nevah ask if I had any photos, so I nevah told 'um.'

'Okay . . .' *Now why wouldn't he want the police to see any photos he'd taken the day Hank disappeared? Could it be the reason his Pidgin was starting to come out more as they spoke?*

Isaac scrolled through the dozen or so shots he'd taken, pointing out the various people in each photo she may not know. 'Dass Jimmy, Matt's husband,' he said after showing her several photos of the Gecko staff standing around the grassy area at Boiling Pots and seated at the picnic table. The stocky man he indicated had short brown hair and was wearing a tattered Rainbow Warriors T-shirt. 'And dere's Hank, in case you don't know what he looked like.'

'Can you zoom in on his face?' Valerie leaned over to get a better look at the dead man. He had shoulder-length auburn hair and a square jaw with either intentional stubble or severe case of five o'clock shadow. In the photo, he and Nalani were laughing at something – what the other person in the photo had just said? 'Who's this?' she asked, pointing to an arm and back visible on the edge of the screen.

'Looks like Kai, given the shirt he's wearing.'

She squinted to read the print on his tank top: Mahina Canoe Club. 'Ah, yes. Probably right.'

The next shot was of the whole group, throwing shakas for the camera: Matt and Jimmy; Nalani and her husband, George; Sachiko; Hank; Kai; Annie; Jun and his wife, Sherri (who, Valerie couldn't help observing, was much younger than Jun and had the glamorous look of a model); and a couple of dishwashers and a busser she'd only met briefly at the restaurant. Many of them held bottles or cans of beer, answering the question she'd had about whether there'd been drinking going on at the retreat. Though Hank's hands were empty.

'Do you think Hank might have been drinking at the retreat?' Valerie asked. 'I mean, did he seem at all drunk or tipsy that day?'

Isaac shook his head. 'He seemed the same as always to me. But I suppose he coulda fallen off da wagon an' I wouldn't have noticed.'

After scrolling through several photos of people chowing down on bright red hot dogs and Spam musubi, he said, 'An' here's da one I especially wanted you to see. See where they are? Right by the path down to da river? So maybe we need to take a hard look at Kai as a suspect.'

Valerie took the phone from him and studied the shot of Kai and Hank standing at the Boiling Pots overlook with the river in the background. 'What time was this taken?' she asked, then clicked the info button. The timestamp read '5:23 p.m.'

'An' we started packing up to go around five thirty,' said Isaac, 'which means this was taken right before everyone left.'

'Are there any more pictures?' she asked.

Isaac reached out to take the phone back, but not before she'd swiped the screen to see the next photo – this one of Sachiko and Hank, standing under the coco palms next to the ramp up to the overlook. Valerie gazed at the image a moment, then turned to look at Isaac. 'Do you have any idea what's going on here? Hank looks really tense and Sachiko looks super . . . angry.'

'I know.' Isaac let out a long breath. 'Dass why I didn't wanna show the pictures to da cops. But check it out – it's just a weird expression 'cause she's got da sun in her eyes.' He was staring at Valerie with pleading eyes – like a dog begging for its dinner.

Turning once more to the photo, she was unconvinced that this was the reason for the fierce frown and curling lips Sachiko was displaying. And based on the nervous tapping of Isaac's fingers on the kitchen counter, he likely felt the same way.

She went back to the previous picture, in which Hank and Kai appeared happy and relaxed – like two good friends hanging out and shooting the breeze. Not at all like the following photo, where neither person looked the least bit calm.

Returning to the one of Sachiko and Hank, she clicked on its info: 5:46 p.m. She then scrolled forward again, to the next photo on the roll – one of Sachiko down at the Lili'uokalani Gardens, with its distinctive orange bridge in the background – then returned to the previous image. 'So this was the last one you took at the retreat, then.'

The begging expression now vanished, replaced by one akin to a wary dog protecting its bone. 'Never mind,' said Isaac, snatching the phone from her hand. 'Forget I ever brought it all up.' And with that he shoved the device back into his pocket and stalked out of the room.

FIFTEEN

'What was that all about?' asked Kristen once Isaac and Sachiko had taken their leave twenty minutes later. 'One minute we're talking about back-splashes and flooring and the next, Isaac's giving Sachiko an "I can't wait to get the heck outta here" look.'

Valerie collected the wine glasses from the table and carried them into the kitchen, trailed by Kristen bearing a stack of dessert plates dusted with powdered sugar. 'I think he got upset when something I said made him think I might consider Sachiko a suspect in Hank's death.'

'What did you say?'

'Nothing. I was just interested in a picture he showed me of Sachiko and Hank at that Gecko retreat, is all.'

Now Kristen was giving Valerie a look – one that said, 'Uh-huh, and . . .?'

Valerie stopped fussing with the dishes and turned to face her wife, leaning back on the kitchen counter with a sigh. 'Okay, here's the deal. So he had this photo on his phone where Hank looks really on edge—'

'How so?' Kristen cut in.

'I dunno . . . He was frowning and his jaw looked really tight. And Sachiko, she looks super angry. She's glaring at the guy with these hard eyes and flaring nostrils. Kinda scary, actually. Just like Jun and Isaac described how she could sometimes be. Isaac tried to convince me it's just 'cause the sun was in her eyes, but I don't buy it. It didn't even look all that sunny in the picture.'

'And I'm guessing you said as much to Isaac?'

'Yeah. Kinda dumb, I now realize. But at the time, I wasn't thinking about how he'd take it; I was just voicing my thoughts aloud.'

Kristen chewed her lip as she gazed down at Pua, who was returning her gaze with unblinking eyes. Tossing the dog a small piece of chicken left on one of the plates, she turned back to face Valerie. 'And *do* you in fact suspect Sachiko?'

'*No*. I mean . . .' Valerie gave an impatient shake of the head. 'I honestly don't know what I think anymore. But I gotta say the timing of that photo doesn't look good for her – it was the last one Isaac took before everyone packed up to leave. And the fact that he didn't tell the cops that he'd taken pictures at the retreat doesn't help his – or, rather, her – case any, either.'

'Dang,' was all Kristen had to offer.

Valerie retrieved a plastic cottage cheese container from the cupboard and spooned the leftover mashed potatoes from the pot into it. 'But there was also this interesting photo on Isaac's phone of Hank and Kai,' she said, stowing the container in the fridge. 'You know, the Gecko busser who invited us paddling? Isaac was super excited about that one, 'cause they're standing over at the viewpoint, right where the trail goes down to the river.'

'And you're thinking Kai because of his friendship with Craig?'

'Right,' said Valerie. 'As is Isaac, I'm sure, 'cause of what I told him about Craig's being so competitive with Hank.'

'So the theory is that Kai would have knocked off Hank as a favor to his friend, so he could become lead stroker – or whatever it's called?'

Valerie pulled out a chair and plopped down at the kitchen table. 'I know. It sounds pretty far-fetched, I gotta say. And the other problem is that the photo Isaac's so excited about was taken about twenty minutes before the one of Hank and Sachiko where she looks so angry.'

'Do you know what time everyone actually left? Or the last time anyone saw Hank at the retreat?'

Valerie shook her head. 'Huh-uh. Everyone seems pretty vague about both those things.'

'So who knows what could have happened after those two photos were taken.'

'Yup. Back to square one.'

It rained all the next morning, so Valerie and Kristen hung out at home, mostly sitting out on the lānai reading the newspaper, writing emails to friends back in California, and wasting time on social media. A little after noon, it tapered off enough for

Valerie to take Pua for a quick walk, after which she and Kristen drove downtown to shop for paddles.

Walking into the store, Valerie was immediately drawn to a wall of wooden specimens in a variety of styles and colors. Reaching out to touch one with black-and-brown geometric designs worked into its reddish-blond wood, she gasped when she saw the price and drew her hand back as if she'd been burned. 'Yikes! Eight hundred and fifty dollars? What is it made of – gold?'

'It's curly koa,' said the salesman who'd come up behind her. 'And it's actually a pretty good price for that kind of wood.'

'Well, it is beautiful, I have to say. But I think we're looking for something a bit less steep – something appropriate for beginners.'

The young man – who, judging by his broad shoulders and muscular arms, was a serious paddler – led them to another wall, on which hung a row of paddles ranging in price from a hundred and twenty dollars to about three hundred each. Which was still pretty pricey, as far as Valerie was concerned.

'Are you looking for all wood or a hybrid paddle?' he asked.

'Uh, is there a difference – besides in looks?' asked Valerie.

'Well, the ones with carbon blades are lighter, but some folks say that wood feels more alive, more flexible. Also, the heavier wooden paddles are a bit easier to control in the wind and surf. So I guess it depends on your own personal aesthetic.'

Valerie lifted one of the all-wood paddles from the wall and hefted it. 'Doesn't seem that heavy to me,' she said. 'And weren't the ones Tala lent us all wood?'

'Uh-huh.' Kristen studied the array before her for a moment before selecting a paddle with a carbon blade and wood laminate shaft. 'Seems to me that the carbon would slice through the water better than wood, right?'

The young man nodded. 'True. Which is why most folks into racing prefer the hybrids over the wood.'

After a lengthy discussion between Kristen and the salesman about double- versus single-bend paddles, laminate versus all-wood shafts, and the various types of blades, Kristen finally settled on the one she'd first taken off the wall. 'I like this – it feels good in my hands.'

Valerie, however, went with an all-wood model. 'What can I say,' she declared. 'I'm just a traditionalist.'

Which is what she told Kai that night at work. 'I know that carbon paddles may be way better, but when you think about the history of paddling, I just feel like using some modern, man-made composite seems wrong.'

'I hear ya,' he said. 'I use a hybrid for da races, but my favorite is one made by my uncle out of koa. It's a really special kine paddle. I'll try to remember to bring it tomorrow so you can check it out.'

At the clicking of a freewheel, the two looked up to see Seth crossing the room with his bike. After stowing it and his helmet away, he came out to join them. 'Valerie was telling me about the new paddle she bought today,' said Kai.

'Nice. What kind did you get – carbon or wood?'

'I thought you weren't a water person,' Valerie said with a grin.

'I never said I wasn't interested in water sports. When you grow up in a Navy family, you kinda have to learn about boats and paddles and stuff. I'm just not gonna be the one getting in the water, is all.'

'Well, after much fretting and angsting, I finally decided on—'

At the sound of a bell emanating from Seth's black jeans, he held up a finger to stop her. 'Sorry. I gotta see what this is.' Pulling the device from his pocket, he swiped up to unlock the phone, then clicked on the text icon – but not before Valerie got a glimpse of the photo on his home screen of a young girl with pink cheeks and curly blond hair.

He glanced at the message, then swiped away the screen. 'Sorry, again. I'm expecting a text from a . . . friend.'

'A friend?' said Kai with a grin. 'A female friend?'

As Seth's cheeks started to redden, the busboy slapped him on the shoulder. 'Dass great, brah! I hope she comes through. Maybe you should bring her to Hank's memorial.'

'Oh, is that happening?' asked Valerie. 'I hadn't heard.'

'Yah, Nalani told us last night. It's at Richardson's at two o'clock dis Monday. And she said she'd bring some 'ono grindz, so I'm definitely in.' Kai turned back to Seth. 'Brah, you really should bring da wahine. No wayz Nalani would mind, and I'd love to meet her.'

Seth snorted. 'I'm not sure a memorial service makes for a great date. And besides, it's not like we're really "dating" yet.'

'Speaking of females,' Valerie said with a nod toward the phone in Seth's hand, 'I couldn't help but notice the little girl on your screen. She's adorable.'

The embarrassed smile was replaced by one of genuine happiness. 'That's my niece, Emily. And yeah, she's adorable, all right.'

'Is she here on-island?'

'No, she's on the Mainland, alas. Her family lives back east.' Seth shoved the phone back in his pocket. 'So tell me, what's the fabulous Val's drink special for tonight?'

'I'm calling it "Val's Mai Tai." It's like a traditional one – the kind they used to make back in the day at Trader Vic's – but my spin uses amaretto instead of orgeat syrup, and I add a splash of soda water.'

Kai smacked his lips. 'Ho, dat sounds killah! Save me one for aftah work, yah?'

'Agreed,' said Seth. 'Almost makes me wish I could drink again. I always did love me a good Mai Tai.'

'I could try to make you a virgin version if you'd like. Maybe cola with orgeat, orange, and lime? Though it would be awful sweet . . .'

'It would, indeed. My teeth hurt just thinking about it. But thanks for the offer.'

As Seth and Kai headed off to their front-of-the-house duties, Valerie wandered over to the bar. She'd just finished stocking the juices and garnishes when she heard a car door slam outside. Poking her head out the back door, she saw Jun walk around to the driver's side of a convertible Mustang and lean down to give the woman a kiss on the lips.

Valerie recognized the driver as Jun's wife, and she was even more glamorous in person than she'd appeared in Isaac's photo, with a designer scarf about her neck, fine features, and perfectly coifed hair. She also looked to be no older than thirty, which would put her at least twenty years younger than Jun.

'Thanks, babe,' Jun said, then waved goodbye. 'Latahz.'

'That was Sherri, right?' Valerie said as he strode toward her wearing a broad smile. 'You should have introduced us.'

Jun merely chuckled.

'What?' asked Valerie. 'You don't think she'll like me?'

'It's not dat,' he said, waggling his eyebrows. 'But I know you like da ladies, so don' wanna be riskin' anyting wit' you two.'

'You do know I'm a married woman,' she said with a laugh.

'Dat nevah stopped oddah people from hittin' on my Sherri.' He was still smiling, but Valerie got the impression there was a serious side to his banter – that part of him truly was a little nervous about her meeting his wife.

She was tempted to tell him that Sherri wasn't even her type, but managed to refrain herself. That strategy was not likely to gain her any points with the bartender. Instead she merely laughed off his comment and – like Seth had done earlier – changed the subject to the drink special she had planned for the evening.

Which got her thinking: Why had the server been so quick to change the subject when she'd commented on his niece? Was it simply because he didn't want her sticking her nose into his private affairs – a fair response, she had to admit. Or was there something more, something he didn't want her to know?

And for that matter, what was going on with Jun's seemingly excessive jealousy about his wife? If he was worried about Valerie meeting Sherri, she could only imagine how upset he'd be if it were someone of the male persuasion hanging out with her. Someone like Hank . . .

Being a Friday, it was busy that night at the Gecko, and Valerie and Jun had little time for chitchat once the post-work crowd showed up to celebrate the end of the week. But they worked well as a team, Valerie taking most of the table orders and Jun handling the customers at the bar. She was struck by his easy manner with the clientele, bantering in Pidgin with the locals and chatting up the female tourists. *I wonder if the jealousy goes both ways*, she thought, watching the bartender make eyes at a young woman in a form-fitting Denver Broncos tank top. Did Sherri know what a flirt her husband was at work?

But then again, Valerie herself wasn't averse to giving that special smile to a customer when she – or he – seemed to enjoy playing the game. It was part of being a good bartender, she supposed, along with pretending to be interested in the patrons' long stories when the night was slow. And besides, it helped make the hours pass more quickly, and didn't hurt in the tip department, either.

She was interrupted from her musings by Jun sidling up and giving her shoulder a nudge. 'Jus' so you know, dat one, she's a cop,' he said with a nod toward the other side of the room.

Valerie looked up to see Amy crossing the outdoor lānai toward the bar. 'It's okay, she's my neighbor,' she replied in a low voice. 'She's cool.'

'Kay, den. She's all yours.'

'Hey, barkeep,' said Amy, squeezing between two groups who'd already been served and leaning against the bar.

'Hey, you. Nice duds.'

Amy glanced down at the floral-print aloha shirt she wore, as if not aware of what she'd put on before leaving the house. 'Oh, thanks. I got it at the Sally shop last week. Only four bucks.'

'Good find. Thrift stores da bomb. Can I get you an adult beverage of some sort? That is, assuming you're off duty?'

'I am, indeed. And yes, please – one of the adult variety would be great. It's been a long day.'

After shaking up Amy's requested Daiquiri, Valerie handed it over, then flashed a smile. 'Sorry I can't chat, but . . .'

'Yeah, I can see you're just a little busy tonight,' Amy shouted over the din in the bar area. 'You go do your job while I relax and enjoy this luscious cocktail.'

'Ha. Thanks for that.'

As Valerie mashed mint and limes for Mojitos, poured glasses of Chardonnay, and pulled pints of beer for pickup at the servers' area, she kept an eye on her neighbor, who was now chatting with the woman in the Broncos tank top whom Jun had been flirting with earlier. The gal seemed far more interested in Amy than she'd been in Jun, Valerie observed with some amusement.

After about a half hour, she saw Amy finish the last of her drink, then turn Valerie's way. Catching her eye, Amy gave a wave of the hand, and Valerie came over to where she stood.

'Gonna take off. I'm on the second watch and have to be at the station at a quarter to seven tomorrow morning.' Amy hesitated a moment. 'So, I was wondering, are you interested in hanging out on Sunday? It's my day off, and I was thinking we could maybe go for a hike or something, if you were up for it. You and Kristen, that is. The weather report says it's supposed to be nice up in the National Park.'

'Sounds fun, but lemme talk to Kristen and see what she's got going on this weekend. Here, add your contact info, and I'll text you tomorrow.' Valerie swiped open her phone and handed it over the counter.

'Cool,' said Amy. She entered her phone number and email address and returned the device, then flashed Valerie the shaka. 'Hope the rest of the evening goes well.'

Once she'd left, Valerie filled an order of four of her Mai Tai specials for table six, then, noticing they were running low on limes, headed for the walk-in fridge to grab a dozen more. Stopping at the swinging door into the kitchen, she peered through the small window to make sure no one was on their way out the door, and spied Nalani and Matt standing by the stainless steel counter that ran down the middle of the room.

Even out in the wait station, she could hear the owner's strident voice. 'What the hell do you mean you didn't order enough ahi? Our most popular food item and you forget it's a busy Friday night?'

Matt's back was to Valerie and his voice soft, so she didn't hear his answer, but it clearly didn't please Nalani, who stared at the cook a moment, eyes wide with rage.

'And so, what? We're going to have to tell all our customers tonight that we've run out of the ahi tower, the fish 'n' chips, the fish sandwich, and the fish special? And it's not even six o'clock?'

Matt's shoulders hunched in a shrug, and he murmured something else in reply, which only served to enrage Nalani further. Valerie watched in horror as the owner grabbed a metal insert sitting on the counter and hurled it at the cook, who ducked just in time to avoid being hit in the face with the flying container. There was a loud *crash* as it smacked to the floor, sending what looked to be cured lemons skittering all across the hardwood surface.

Nalani glared a moment at Matt, then turned and strode across the kitchen and into the walk-in fridge. As the cook bent to pick up the fallen container, Valerie retreated quickly from the swinging door and into the dining room. *Best wait a bit before fetching those limes*, she thought, and made her way back to the bar.

SIXTEEN

Listening to the rain spatter against the bedroom window, Valerie rolled onto her side and pulled the covers up to her chin. She'd slept poorly and was hoping for a few more minutes' shut-eye this morning. But it was not to be.

'Rise and shine!' Kristen called out in a voice far too cheerful for the hour. A moment later, the curtain next to the bed was swept open, letting in what little light the rainy day had to offer.

Valerie sat up with a groan. 'You really think they'll be going out this morning?'

'I do. Tala said they always paddle unless the weather's really rough. And I wouldn't call this "really rough"; it seems more like your average rainy Hilo day.' At a further groan from her wife, she added: 'And hey, don't you want to try out your new paddle?'

'Okay, okay.' Valerie threw back the covers and climbed out of bed. So much for more sleep. But she was in fact excited to try out her new paddle – and to get a chance to talk to the new lead steersman, Craig, if she could.

On the drive down to the canoe beach, Valerie told Kristen about what she'd witnessed in the Speckled Gecko kitchen the night before. 'It was so weird, 'cause Nalani has always seemed so calm. Bossy and overbearing, yes, but never out of control like that. I mean, to throw a metal container at someone?'

Kristen glanced behind her, then quickly moved to the left to avoid a flood of water collected in the right lane of Kamehameha Avenue. Tapping her finger on the steering wheel in time to the slapping of the windshield wipers, she thought a moment before speaking. 'Yeah, that is bizarre. I've never met the gal, of course, and I know that working in a restaurant kitchen can be super stressful, but throwing a pot or whatever it was at a co-worker seems way beyond the pale. Did you talk to either of them after the incident?'

'Huh-uh. I snuck in a little later to grab the limes I needed but kept my eyes averted and didn't try to make conversation.

They were both really in the weeds, in any case, and wouldn't have been able to talk even if I'd wanted to. They certainly weren't talking to each other. Then after we closed, they both took off right away. I guess neither was much in the mood for chitchat or a beer after what happened.'

'I can see why,' said Kristen, pulling into the Bayfront parking lot. It had started to come down even harder now, so Valerie grabbed the golf umbrella lying on the back seat, which the two shared as they splashed over to where a group of people were huddled around the six-man canoes inside the paddling club's hālau.

'Dere's a high surf warning for da whole morning,' a man Valerie didn't recognize was saying. 'An' check out dis big blob of green and yellow on da weather app headed straight for Hilo Bay.' Several of the paddlers crowded around to stare at the map on his phone screen. 'So our hālau has decided not to go out today. Too dangerous.' He nodded toward the canoe house just down the beach, where a group of men with travel mugs and paddles were fist-bumping each other, then walking back out to the parking lot.

Craig spoke up at this point. 'And that's why we're gonna beat your asses at the Moloka'i Hoe – you're too damn wimpy. A little rain isn't gonna stop us from going out.' He looked about him, no doubt expecting to see a row of nodding heads, but what he got instead were his fellow paddlers staring down at their feet, unwilling to meet his gaze.

All except Tala, who was shaking her head. 'I don't think so, Craig. It's one thing to be determined and gutsy, and another to be stupid. And going out in weather like this would be plain stupid.' She waved a hand toward the bay, where the water was now a muddy brown with spray blowing off the numerous white-caps whipped up by the gusty wind.

Craig glared at her a moment, shoulders rising and falling. Noticing the white knuckles gripping his paddle, Valerie wondered whether he might actually go so far as to strike the woman. But then he merely shrugged and let out a scornful laugh. 'Fine. You wahine can stay here and do whatever you like, but *we're* gonna go out, yah?' he said, turning to face the five men standing around him.

At this point, the guy with the weather app turned away with a snort and a wave of the hand. 'Whatevahz. You braddahs can do as you like. Me, I'm off home for a hot cup of coffee.'

As he headed for his car, Valerie heard Toshi say to Kai in a low voice, 'You know dat guy? Him FBI?'

'Yah,' answered Kai. 'Him fo' real da kine.'

Craig watched the man go with a scowl. 'What a jerk. Like he has any say over what we decide or not. So what is it, you guys? We gonna do us some paddling this morning?'

There was some shuffling of feet before Mike finally cleared his throat and said, 'I don't think so, Craig. It looks pretty damn choppy, and I don't relish doing a huli out past the breakwater in the pouring rain. I'm out.'

This served to embolden the others, who voiced similar thoughts, then picked up their paddles and filed out toward the parking lot. Craig stared after them as they climbed sheepishly into their cars and trucks, then turned toward Tala, who'd been watching him watch the others. 'What are you looking at?' he spat out. 'This is your fault, you know, and I won't forget it.' And with that, he strode from the hālau.

'Wow,' said Kristen. 'Talk about a jerk.'

'Yep.' Tala rolled her eyes and grinned at the five women – Valerie, Kristen, Becca, Sasha, and Leilani – who'd stayed put during the exchange between the men. 'And he's only gotten worse ever since he's taken over as lead steersman – totally bossy toward the rest of the crew. It's like he thinks he's their supreme leader, ever since Hank's been gone. It's so annoying. Thank goodness we don't have to paddle with the guy.'

She picked up her paddle and the canvas bag at her feet. 'So who's up for breakfast at the Kekoa?'

That night at work, Valerie peeked into the kitchen to see if Nalani and Matt were there and, if so, how they seemed to be interacting. But another cook she didn't recognize was at the line in Matt's stead.

Asking Seth about it later, she was told that Matt had the night off, and that the other guy, Jeff, only came in once in a while, when he wasn't working.

'Is Saturday Matt's regular night off?' she asked. 'Or did he take the day off special?'

'No, he usually works Saturdays, but I guess he must have had something going on tonight.'

Interesting, thought Valerie. *Could it be because of what had happened the night before?* Since she hadn't seen the line cook after work last night, she had no idea how the incident with Nalani may have affected him.

But she had little time to worry during her shift about whether Matt had upped and quit, or truly did have an unrelated reason to be off that night. It was a busy Saturday night at the Gecko bar, and her head was far too full of drink orders and talkative customers to spend time thinking about the internal dynamics of the kitchen staff.

After closing, however, she asked Kai about the line cook. 'Did he seem upset last night after work?'

The busser set down his plastic tub and began to fill it with dishes from the last uncleared table in the dining room. 'Uh-uh. Should he a-been?'

Valerie told him what she'd witnessed in the kitchen, and Kai just snorted. 'I'm sure Matt's used to that. Nalani can be pretty intense, but she's okay, and Matt knows dat. He's a big boy.'

'Yeah, you're probably right.' She chewed her lip a moment. 'So, I have another question. Did you agree with what Craig said this morning? That we should have gone paddling? 'Cause you didn't say anything, but it kinda looked like you were willing to go out.'

'I dunno. I tink it was probably a good idea not to go out, given da weather, but I hate to disappoint Craig. He's so . . .'

'Passionate?' Valerie offered.

Kai laughed. 'Yah. I mean, I know he can come off as kinda pushy, but he really does care about da paddling – a lot.'

'I can tell,' said Valerie, doing her best to keep the sarcasm from her voice. 'But to try and push people into going out when there's a high surf warning doesn't seem like such a great idea.'

'I know,' he said with a shrug. 'But dass Craig.'

'Look, Kai. I get that it's probably not my place to judge a guy I barely know, but I have to say it makes me kind of worried to be in a paddling club where one of the leaders might make decisions that are dangerous to the other members of the team. Especially when the others are afraid to question what he says.'

'I'm not afraid of da guy,' said Kai quickly.

'Uh-huh. And that's why you looked so uncomfortable last Tuesday at breakfast when he was dissing Hank yet failed to say anything?'

Valerie was afraid she'd overstepped when the busser gave her a sharp look, then turned quickly away. Using a damp side towel, he began to wipe down the table, concentrating on a sticky spot and studiously avoiding her gaze. She was about to apologize for her sarcastic remark when he tossed the towel into the dish tub and turned back to face her.

'Look,' he said. 'I know I prob'ly shoulda said something – dat it was wussy just letting Craig diss Hank li'dat. But Hank's gone and no can know what guys be sayin' about him, and Craig's still here an' I gotta deal wit' da guy whenevah I go paddling. So I figgah—'

'Let the wookie win.'

Kai looked momentarily confused, then grinned as he got the reference. 'Right. *Star Wars*. Yah, I can see Craig as one wookie. Ha!'

Glad to have taken his mind off her hasty misstep, Valerie changed the subject. 'So, I heard Toshi ask you about that paddler from the other hālau this morning – he said something about him being with the FBI? Is the guy really a federal agent?'

Kai laughed once again, louder this time. 'Ho – dass so funny! FBI, dat mean "from da Big Island." I sure hope we no have any da kine *real* FBI brahs hangin' out down da canoe beach. Not wit' all da pakalolo some of da braddahs like smoke aftah dey paddle.'

He was still chuckling to himself as he picked up his bus tray and headed for the kitchen.

The next morning, Sunday, Amy pulled into the driveway of Valerie's house at a quarter past nine, setting off a series of furious barks from Pua, who at the sound of the car had jumped up onto the couch to peer out the window and see what menace could possibly be invading her territory.

Amy started out of the car but, on seeing Valerie open the door, waved and sat back down. 'Where's Kristen?' she called out as Valerie shouldered her daypack and turned to offer the dog a conciliatory dog biscuit. 'Isn't she coming?'

'No. She got a call last night from Diane, that woman she's helping build a lānai, asking if she could come work on it today. Apparently Diane's going to Oʻahu at the end of next week and wants to get an extra day in so they can hopefully finish the project before she leaves. An extra day of *Kristen's* work, that is,' Valerie added with a snort, locking the door behind her and coming down the stairs.

'Do I detect a tiny bit of resentment there?'

Valerie set her pack in the back, then climbed into the passenger seat. 'I don't begrudge her wanting to help out with the project, but it is kind of annoying to have our plans change at the last minute like that.' She shook her head. 'Whatever . . .'

'Well, I guess I'll just have to be especially entertaining today, to make up for the lack of her company. And, hey, now we have one extra sandwich to share. She'll be sorry to have missed out, 'cause it's one of my specialties: creamy Japanese-style egg salad. It's a recipe my dad picked up when he was stationed over there with the Army. 'Ono-licious!'

'Oh my, that does sound good. Is it lunchtime yet?'

'You'll have to wait. But I may have some stale nuts in the glove compartment, if you're hungry.'

'Gee, thanks. But I think I'll pass.'

On the drive up to Volcanoes National Park, they talked about Amy's job: how her dad had become a cop after retiring from the service and how she'd eventually been inspired to follow in his footsteps after graduating from UH Mānoa in Honolulu, then spending the next eight years back on the Big Island in a variety of unfulfilling jobs.

'So that makes you, what, about thirty years old?' Valerie asked.

'Thirty-four, actually.'

'Such an old lady – more than half my age!'

Amy laughed. 'Yeah, well, to be a new recruit at almost thirty was actually pretty unusual. But having a dad who'd been on the force helped. And it was a big step up from my previous job as a parking lot security guard.'

'I can imagine. So you still like it, being a cop?'

Amy slowed for a pair of black pigs rooting in the dirt along the side of the road, checking the mirror to make sure no one was about to rear-end her. 'I do. Every day is different.'

'Unlike being a security guard.'

'You got that right. And I like the guys I work with – and, yes, they are almost all men. But as I think I told you, I've been thinking of trying to move up to detective, so I've been studying for the exam.'

'Is that all it takes, passing an exam?'

'Well, that's the most important part, but you also have to have been on the force long enough – which I have – and go through an interview after you pass the test. And seniority matters, of course.'

'Of course.'

'So we'll see . . .'

Once at the park, Amy followed the road toward Chain of Craters Road and parked at the Kīlauea Iki trailhead. After swapping out their rubber slippahs for hiking boots and tightening their laces, they took the path skirting the rim of the crater through a dense and primeval rainforest of native hāpu'u ferns and 'ōhi'a trees – as well as an abundance of beautiful, but invasive, kāhili ginger – listening to the distinctive song of 'i'iwi and 'apapane as flashes of red darted above them from tree to tree.

Coming out of the forest, they picked their way carefully down the trail over jagged lava rock onto the floor of the caldera. As they started across the desolate crater, Amy pointed out where some sixty years earlier in 1959, a fissure had opened up, spewing a fountain of lava almost two thousand feet high. 'Back then, this rock we're walking on right now was a roiling lake of molten lava. Check out the steam rising up through the cracks. It's still really hot down below us.'

'Yikes!' said Valerie, jumping back in alarm. 'Is there any chance it could go again . . . soon?'

Amy laughed. 'Well, we are on an active volcano, after all. But there hasn't been much seismic activity of late, so I'd say the chances are extremely low. Here, you want to sit for a bit and eat?'

Valerie had been about to suggest they hurry on with their hike, but at the suggestion of lunch, she put aside her concerns. No way would the volcano pick today to start up again . . . *would it*? With a nervous glance toward the yawning red-and-black fissure looming up behind them, she accepted the sandwich Amy handed her and found a flat rock upon which to perch.

From above, along the crater rim trail, the floor of the caldera had looked completely flat, like smooth clay. But now that they were down on its surface, she could see that it consisted of rough rock fragmented by large cracks, through which not just steam, but hearty plants were sprouting forth: grasses, tiny ferns, and spindly 'ōhelo shrubs with bright red berries.

'It sure is an amazing place,' Valerie said. 'So otherworldly.' Then, taking a bite of her sandwich, she let out a moan. 'Ohmygod, talk about *amazing*! This has to be the best egg salad sandwich I've ever had. What the heck's in it?'

'Hard boiled eggs, obviously – heavy on the yolks – Kewpie mayo, salt and pepper, a tiny bit of sugar, and the secret ingredient: a dash of heavy cream. Oh, and they have to be made with Japanese-style milk bread, which has an incredibly fluffy texture.'

'It sure does, and that filling is incredible, too. Now I'm definitely glad Kristen's not here, 'cause I'm looking forward to eating half of hers, as well.'

They chewed their creamy, eggy sandwiches without speaking, gazing out across the volcanic moonscape. After a bit, Valerie broke the silence. 'So, I've been thinking about what you said about trying for detective, and I was wondering, you wanna practice? You know, being a detective?'

Amy turned to her with a frown.

'Okay, so that came out sounding stupid. I guess what I mean is, would you be willing to listen to what else I've found out about Hank Marino's death and give me your thoughts? Not about any info you might have, of course – which I know you can't tell me – but at least let me know if you think I'm completely delusional?'

Amy thought a moment, then nodded. 'I guess I could do that.'

'Great. Thanks.' Folding up her plastic sandwich bag, Valerie stuffed it into her daypack, then unscrewed her flask and took a sip of water. 'Okay, so I think I've narrowed it down to these suspects.'

'Suspects, eh?' Amy said with a wry smile. 'Now who's trying to make detective?'

'Okay, how about "people of interest" – any better?'

'Even more detective-ish, I'd say.'

Valerie laughed. 'Thank you. I try. Anyway, they're all folks who work at the Speckled Gecko, except for this guy Craig, who paddled with Hank.'

She proceeded to detail what she'd learned about each person: Jun's jealousy issues regarding Hank and Jun's wife; Hank's having hit on Annie and the comments she'd made about him down at Uncle Robert's; Sachiko's having a temper and her argument with Hank, and the carved fox they found in Hank's pocket (though she omitted telling Amy about the photos she'd seen on Isaac's phone); how Hank had made homophobic comments about Matt; the incident of Nalani throwing the metal insert at Matt in the Gecko kitchen and how the line cook hadn't been at work the night afterwards; and Kai's close friendship with Craig, who had made clear his animosity toward Hank.

'And then there's this guy Seth,' she went on, 'who's a server at the restaurant. He doesn't seem to have any apparent motive, but I gotta say, there's just something slightly off about the guy. He's so darn nice and helpful, yet so vague about his past life. And the fact that he doesn't drive seems weird . . .'

'He doesn't drive?' said Amy.

'No, he rides his bicycle everywhere – says there's no need for a car in Hilo, and why add to the carbon emissions, yada yada.'

'Ah. Yeah, I know the type. They can be annoyingly self-righteous.'

'But that's the thing: he's not. He's actually super sweet. But I can't help thinking that there's something he's hiding.' Valerie laughed. 'God, I sound like some TV detective, with my hunches and intuition.'

Amy picked up a rock and examined its fire-red color, then tossed it away. 'Well, if you want my opinion, it doesn't seem like any of the people you describe have a super strong motive to want to actually kill the guy. But then again, sometimes things just happen . . . spur of the moment.'

'True.' Valerie stared out at a group of hikers making their way toward them across the crater floor. Then, turning back to face Amy, she let out a laugh. 'Speaking of famous fictional detectives, I just had a thought: What if they were all in it together?'

'Ha! I saw that movie. Yeah, that must be the answer, for sure.'
With a grunt, Amy stood and brushed the crumbs from her jeans.
'Shall we get a move on?'

'Sure, I'm ready to go,' said Valerie, shouldering her pack. As
she followed Amy back down to the path across the caldera, she
turned for one more look at the fissure, its giant maw reminding
her of an enormous dragon's throat.

Could it have been a joint effort?

SEVENTEEN

The memorial for Hank was the next afternoon at Richardson Beach, and Valerie made sure to get there early so she could check out people's demeanor as they arrived. That, and also get first dibs on any delectable food item anyone might bring. She'd learned soon after moving to the Big Island that whether or not any particular event was labeled a 'potluck,' folks were guaranteed to show up with massive quantities of mouth-watering dishes to share.

The sole picnic table she could spot was taken, so she headed on past the small black sand beach and lifeguard station to a grassy area by the water and spread out her blanket. Setting down the deviled eggs she'd prepared – inspired by those delicious sandwiches Amy had made the day before – Valerie took a seat on the ground, making sure she had a good view of the path from the parking lot down to the beach.

A fair number of people were at the park, some lying on towels atop the coarse black sand, a few kids splashing about in the shallows, and about a dozen swimmers farther out toward the reef, their bobbing snorkel tubes reminding Valerie of a fleet of submarines with their periscopes up.

Across the bay, the green slopes of Maunakea rose up until disappearing into the blanket of clouds that gathered atop the mountain most afternoons. It was warm – in the mid-eighties, Valerie guessed – but a refreshing trade wind breeze kept the temperature pleasant. Pulling on a lightweight, long-sleeved shirt to protect her from the sun, she shaded her eyes and watched the people making their way down to the beach.

The first Gecko employee she spied was Annie, who, in response to Valerie's waving hand, headed their way. 'Good choice of spot,' she said, handing Valerie a paper bag with spots of grease leaking through. 'I'm not a big fan of sand in my food.'

'Oooo . . . I hope this is what I think it is,' said Valerie. 'Yes! Can I have some now?'

'Of course. But I didn't make it; it's courtesy of Sack N Save.'

'Who cares who made it – it's fried chicken!' Valerie extracted a crispy leg and bit into it with relish.

'I brought beer, too, but make sure to keep it hidden from the lifeguards.' Opening the cooler she'd brought, Annie surreptitiously poured a bottle of Humpback Lager into a red Solo cup. 'I guess some might think it's disrespectful to drink beer at the memorial of someone who was AA, but I'm not sure I want to go through this without one.'

'I'm sure he'd just want us all to be happy,' said Valerie, pouring a cup for herself. 'Cheers. Here's to Hank.'

'Ho!' they heard a deep voice call out and looked up to see Kai striding across the sand. 'I see da party's started without me!'

'It's not a party, Kai,' Annie said, but the giggle that accompanied her admonition negated any force it might otherwise have had.

'Sorry. *Memorial.* An' here's some stuffs to help with da occasion.' He set down a plate of Spam musubi and rice balls, along with a six-pack of IPA, which Annie hastily covered with the blanket.

Next came Seth, bouncing down the path astride his bicycle, followed almost immediately by Nalani and Matt, chatting and laughing together as if that incident with the metal insert Friday night had never occurred.

Huh. So Kai must be right that Matt's used to Nalani's temper, was Valerie's thought. Either that, or he was really good at faking it, in order to keep his job.

The three newcomers added their offerings to the quickly growing selection of food and drink atop the blanket: a seaweed salad and bottle of iced green tea from Seth, a baked brie with nuts and cranberries from Matt, and a homemade pear-and-liliko'i pie along with a thermos of coffee from Nalani.

Kai took in the spread. 'Shoots, we should do dis more often,' he said, then smiled sheepishly and looked up at the sky. 'Sorry, Hank. But I know you'd be lovin' all dis food, too, braddah.'

'So who's still missing?' Annie glanced around at the people present. 'Sachiko and Jun are the only others who said they'd be here, right?'

'Dass right,' agreed Nalani. 'Though Jun said he could only stop by for a bit. I guess he and Sherri have plans.'

'Speak of the devil.' Seth bumped fists with the bartender as he came up to join the group. 'Hey, brah, glad you could make it.'

Jun held out the container in his hand. 'I brought homemade lumpia, with pork and cabbage.'

'Yum!' said Valerie. 'Sounds delish!'

'Well . . .' Nalani consulted the time on her phone, then turned toward the parking lot. 'I'm not sure how long we should wait for Sachiko, since Jun's gotta split pretty soon. Oh, wait, dere's a text from her – she says she's on her way.'

Annie picked up the stack of paper plates Nalani had brought and handed them around. 'In that case, I say we start on all this food while we wait.'

Ten minutes later, they were joined by an out-of-breath Sachiko. 'So sorry I'm late,' she said, trotting up to them. 'But my mom called right as I was about to leave and insisted I listen to the report of her latest doctor's visit.'

'Oh, no, I hope she's okay,' said Valerie.

Sachiko waved a dismissive hand. 'She's fine – healthy as an ox. It was just a regular check-up. So, should we get started? How shall we do this?'

Nalani took control. Telling everyone to have a seat and pour themselves a drink of whatever was their beverage of choice, she chanted a few lines in Hawaiian, then provided a translation for those not conversant in the language: 'May his spirit be with the earth, the water, and the sky; may his memory remain in our hearts.'

Glancing around, Valerie studied the group's faces. They appeared serious – Annie, Seth, and Matt with eyes closed, Sachiko and Kai nodding along to Nalani's words. All except Jun, she noticed with interest, who was staring past Nalani out at the sparkling water, wearing a smile that Valerie could only describe as content. Or perhaps even self-satisfied?

With a frown, she refocused on what Nalani was saying. '. . . so I wanted to have this memorial for Hank in order for all of us to have some kind of closure. It's hard enough having someone in your life die, but even harder when that death is so . . .' Nalani paused, searching for the word. 'So *sudden.*'

'And *bizarre*,' added Seth with a shake of the head.

'Yes, bizarre, as well,' agreed Nalani. 'Which makes it even more difficult for us to take in and deal with, emotionally. Especially since it happened on our watch, so to speak.' Looking into the eyes of everyone one by one, she let out a slow breath. 'I know some of you may be feeling some sort of guilt about what happened to Hank – that "if only I'd done X, he might still be here with us." But such thoughts do no good for anyone. Nothing can bring him back, and the best thing we can all do now is be good to each other.' A glance Matt's way accompanied by an apologetic smile. 'And so I wanted us all – the Gecko family – to come together today to share that goodness, along with some 'ono grindz and maybe even a libation or two in celebration of Hank's life.'

Standing up, Nalani raised her glass. 'A hui hou, Hank – until we meet again!'

The other seven followed suit, rising to their feet to drink a toast to the departed bartender.

After a few more toasts to Hank, the group continued with their meal. The local fauna had now discovered the presence of food at their blanket, and they watched with amusement as two black-and-white birds with scarlet heads fought over a scrap of pie crust that had fallen on the ground.

'They're so cute,' Annie said. 'I haven't seen those up at my house. Are they a kind of finch?'

'Nah, I tink dey called da red-headed cardinal,' said Kai, tossing another hunk of crust their way.

Nalani shook a finger at the busser. 'You no should feed 'um,' she said. 'It's not good for da birds, an' not good for us havin' dem get too brazen around people.'

'Yeah, they're one of my favorites, too,' said Seth with a smile. 'And also those over there.' He pointed to a pair of small yellow birds with a tinge of green pecking at tidbits they discovered as they hopped across the black sand.

'Saffron finch,' pronounced Kai, and Seth nodded agreement.

Annie stood and brushed the crumbs off her shorts onto the ground. 'Oops – sorry, Nalani,' she said and then laughed. 'Okay, well, I think I'm gonna go stretch my legs. Be back in a bit.'

'Yeah, good idea,' said Seth, standing as well.

Jun consulted his phone. 'And I bettah hele on. Me an' Sherri are going to her mom's for dinner. Not that I'm gonna be all dat hungry aftah all dis,' he added with a pat to his ample stomach.

Valerie watched Jun head toward the parking lot and Annie walk toward the small inlet where people were entering and exiting the water, then turned to see Seth go the opposite direction, toward the large outcropping of lava rock at the far end of the beach.

'Does the park continue on past those rocks?' she asked. 'I've only ever come out this far the few times I've been here.'

'Uh-uh,' said Nalani. 'It ends dere. But you get a nice view of da ocean from up on top.'

'Oh, yeah? Maybe I'll go check it out.'

Leaving Nalani, Sachiko, and Matt talking about the Gecko specials for the next few days, Valerie wandered over to the promontory, then stopped when she came to a brackish lagoon between where she stood and the rocks beyond. They rose up maybe twenty feet and looked ragged and rough, but still doable in her slippahs.

Looking to her right, she saw that the lagoon narrowed enough to cross via a row of rocks in the water – likely placed there by someone wanting to make the access easier. After clambering up to the top of the outcropping, she saw what Nalani meant. The panorama of ocean and coastline was magnificent, and the aqua color of the water on this side of the outcropping – almost glacial in its hue – was breathtaking.

The rocks were also much flatter up on top, so she took a seat and stretched out her legs to enjoy the view. More clouds had now settled atop the summit of Maunakea, and a line of puffy trade wind clouds had appeared near the horizon far out to the east. But where she sat the sun was out, and its heat felt delicious on her skin.

The water was calm, and a few snorkelers had come around the promontory and were floating lazily about a hundred yards offshore. Out in the distance she could see a pair of six-man canoes making their way down the coast – 'OC-6's, she now knew they were called. But their hulls were dark green, so the paddlers weren't from the Mahina Canoe Club.

At the sound of crunching, she turned to see Seth coming her way. Taking a seat nearby, he dangled his legs over the edge of the rocks and let out a sigh. 'I never get tired of this place. It's so peaceful. So serene.'

'That it is,' Valerie agreed.

Neither spoke, and as she watched Seth, his head back and eyes closed, Valerie's eyes were drawn to the design of the robin on his forearm. 'So, you said you were into birding,' she said with a nod toward the tattoo. 'Are you one of those people who spends all their free days hiking out into the wilds to "get more birds" on their list?'

Seth glanced down at his arm, then chuckled. 'I'm not super hardcore or anything, but I do have a fairly decent list at this point – as well as a nice pair of binoculars.'

'So how come you didn't correct Kai earlier when he called that bird a red-headed cardinal? My wife Kristen – who's a total know-it-all about just about whatever you can imagine – says they're called "yellow-billed cardinals," though they're not really even a cardinal at all.'

'Hey,' Seth replied with a shrug, 'as I said, I'm no expert. If she says that's what it's called, then she's probably right.'

But isn't that a pretty common bird in these parts? was Valerie's thought. *If I know what it's called, wouldn't someone who calls himself a birder – even if he's not 'hardcore' about it – also know?*

Seth returned his gaze to the ocean, allowing Valerie to study his face, which revealed no signs of artifice. Nevertheless, she found the incident slightly disturbing. As far as she was concerned, it was yet another instance of something being slightly 'off' about the mysterious server.

After a bit, Seth stood, startling Valerie from her musings. Pulling his phone from the pocket of his shorts, he took several photos of the vista, then suddenly froze, confusion in his eyes.

'Are you okay?' asked Valerie.

He squatted, dropping his phone onto the rock and setting a hand down as if to regain his balance, then stood back up, wavering like someone who'd had too much to drink. Valerie stood up to step forward, but before she could reach out to grab him by the arm, Seth tottered toward the edge of the promontory and tumbled into the sea.

He immediately began to thrash about, his head floating above water for a few seconds, then quickly sinking under the surface. As he bobbed up once again and gasped for air, she heard him call out feebly, 'Help!'

Right, she remembered, *he can't swim!* Dumping her own phone and car keys onto the rock and kicking off her slippahs, Valerie dove in after the struggling man and swam toward him. 'It's okay, I've got you!' she called out, wrapping her arm about his shoulders.

But rather than calm down, he began to thrash even more.

'No, you have to relax so I can swim with you to shore!' she yelled, but this only served to agitate Seth further. He began to push against Valerie, not only preventing her from holding onto him but also causing her to go under, as well.

It was now Valerie's turn to struggle. Trying desperately to grab onto the frantic man, she did her best to take hold of his flailing arms while at the same time staying afloat herself. Looking back toward the rocks where they'd stood just moments before, she saw that the current had already taken them at least thirty yards from shore. And the snorkelers she'd seen earlier had now disappeared.

What to do? Seth was far stronger than Valerie, and she was rapidly tiring from the effort of trying to save both him and herself. Moreover, at this rate, they'd be swept so far out to sea as they struggled together in the strong current that it would be nigh on impossible to swim back in their exhausted state.

And then, as Seth's movements became ever more violent and powerful, she had a horrible thought: *Is he trying to kill me?*

EIGHTEEN

'No,' Valerie screamed, 'stop pushing, or we're both going to drown!'

But Seth's thrashing only grew stronger, and as Valerie was forced under water once again and then came up gasping for air, she too began to shout for help. But they were now far enough offshore that she was sure that with the sound of the wind and the surf, no one would be able to hear her cries.

Trying in vain to grab hold of Seth's flailing arms, Valerie ceased her yelling, concluding it would be better to conserve what little strength she still had. As she went under one more time, her only thought was, *How could I be so stupid? It was Seth all along.*

But this was followed quickly by a surge of anger. No way was Seth going to win. She needed to save herself, and to hell with him. With renewed strength, she gave a powerful push against his chest and wrested herself away. Once there were several feet separating them, she treaded water as she caught her breath. She expected Seth to swim toward her, but instead he stayed where he was and continued to thrash about.

Could he truly be in distress? she wondered, unsure what to do. But then his body grew quiet, and he stared at her with wide eyes as he started to sink down below the surface.

'No!' she cried out again. Before she could decide whether to go once more to the man's aid, however, she felt a hand on her shoulder, causing her to flinch. 'What the—?'.

The swimmer immediately splashed past Valerie over to Seth and grabbed hold of him, lifting his head above water. 'Seth! Are you okay?'

He nodded numbly and blinked a few times, as if trying to focus on this new arrival. It was Sachiko, Valerie realized with surprise.

'C'mon,' she shouted to Valerie, 'let's get him to shore. But we need to swim out around to the other side – it'll be too hard climbing up onto the rocks from this side.'

Together they slowly made their way out and around the black lava outcropping, Seth's now limp body held between them. Valerie was too exhausted to do anything but swim, and it took quite a while for them to finally make landfall back at the lagoon on the beach side of the promontory.

Fully spent, she collapsed onto the rocky shore under the shade of a spindly ironwood tree as Sachiko tended to the prone form of Seth. His eyes were closed, but from the regular rising and falling of his chest, he appeared to be in no grave danger at the moment.

Sachiko was leaning over him, speaking softly, and Valerie did her best to listen in on what they said. 'What happened?' asked Sachiko. Seth said nothing, merely giving a slight shake of the head. 'Was it a seizure?' A nod in response. 'But you're okay now?' Another nod.

Leaving him, she came over to Valerie. 'And how about you – are you all right?'

Valerie sat up and let out a long breath. 'Yeah, just winded. And a little freaked out, to tell you the truth. That was so weird, what happened.' She lowered her voice. 'Did I hear you ask him about a seizure?'

With a quick glance in Seth's direction – he was still lying on the rock, an arm resting over his eyes – she frowned, then turned back to Valerie. 'Uh-huh. He has epilepsy but doesn't like to talk about it. The only reason I know is 'cause he thought it best if his boss knew – you know, in case he ever had a seizure while he was at work.'

'Ah . . . That explains what happened out there. As he was standing looking out at Maunakea, all of a sudden he froze, then fell into the water and started thrashing about like crazy. It's a good thing you showed up, 'cause I was having a heck of a time trying to save him by myself.'

'Yeah, good thing all right. I'd just climbed up to check out the view when I heard you shouting. And good thing I was on the high school swim team, too,' Sachiko added with a flexing of the bicep and a grin.

At the sound of coughing, Sachiko returned to Seth, who had now also pulled himself into a sitting position. 'How you doing?' she asked.

'Better. Thanks so much. Both of you,' he added, turning to include Valerie in the conversation. 'That could have been real bad. I'm so sorry.'

'Hey.' Sachiko reached out to touch him on the shoulder. 'It's not your fault.'

Seth shook his head. 'It probably is my fault,' he said. 'I think I must have forgotten to take my meds this morning.'

'Well, it's all water under the bridge – or under the lava rock, as it were,' said Sachiko with a gentle smile. 'You think you're able to walk?'

'I think so.' Pushing himself to his feet, he stood a moment, as if making sure his equilibrium was all in order. 'Oh. I dropped my phone up there on the rocks. Any chance you could go get it? It's probably best if I don't climb up there again right now.'

'Sure thing. Are you okay to help him walk back to the others?' she asked Valerie.

'Yeah, no problem. And while you're at it, my phone and keys are also up there if you wouldn't mind grabbing them, as well.'

While Sachiko went in search of their devices, Valerie helped the still somewhat unsteady Seth back to their picnic area.

'What the heck happened?' asked Nalani as they approached. 'You look like two sad dogs who've just been given an unwanted bath.'

Valerie turned to Seth, eyebrows raised, unsure how much he would want the others to know. He smiled sheepishly. 'I . . . uh, kinda tripped and took a tumble into the water and this brave woman jumped in to rescue me.'

'Oh, no!' Annie jumped up to come to his side. 'Are you okay?'

'I'm fine. Just a little wet, is all. And embarrassed.'

'Hey, you did always tell everyone you no like da water,' said Kai with a grin. 'And now we know why. Ho!' This was directed at Sachiko, who was heading across the sand toward them, also dripping water. 'You got in da act too, sistah?'

'I told them how I fell in the water,' Seth called out to her, 'and how thanks to Valerie – and you – I was assisted to the shore.' Then, to Kai, 'It's true; I am so not a water person, and I think this proves why.'

Sachiko handed Seth and Valerie the items they'd left up on the rocks. 'No biggie. The sea can be kind of rough out past the rocks. And besides,' she added with a grin, 'I'm always happy to come to the rescue of whoever needs it.'

There was an awkward silence, this comment serving to remind the Gecko staff of why they were there at Richardson Beach that day – and how Hank had not, in fact, been rescued.

Nalani cleared her throat. 'Okay, well, I think I'm gonna take off. Anyone want to take home the rest of this pie?'

'I'll take it!' piped up Kai. 'I got anoddah potluck to go to tomorrow night, and dis would be perfect.'

'And I need to go home and get out of these wet clothes,' said Sachiko.

Seth wrung water from the bottom of his aloha shirt. 'Ditto,' he said. 'Though I'm guessing I'll be pretty much dry by the time I ride all the way home.'

Sachiko shot Valerie a look of concern and nodded toward Seth as he picked up his bike and started to wheel it across the grass. Taking the hint, she followed as the other ran to catch up to him.

'I'm not so sure it's a good idea that you ride home,' Sachiko said. 'You know, after . . .'

'I'm sure I'll be okay. I feel fine now.'

'Uh-uh.' Sachiko's expression was severe. 'I think it's a really bad idea. Let me drive you home. Oh, wait, I don't think your bike will fit in my car . . .'

'I can do it,' offered Valerie. 'Mine's a hatchback, with plenty of room if we put down the back seat.'

She could tell Seth wasn't happy about this plan, but at another hard look from Sachiko, he shrugged his shoulders in defeat. 'Fine. You're the boss.'

After packing up their food and other possessions, the three-some headed across the beach toward the parking lot, Seth leading the way, as if in a hurry to get the trip home over with as soon as possible. Which made sense, Valerie figured. It had to be pretty embarrassing for the guy, having an epileptic seizure in public and then having to be rescued – by two women, no less.

'So, we haven't really talked since dinner last Thursday,' Valerie said to Sachiko as they followed Seth up past the old Richardson home, now a park building. 'How have you been? And how's Isaac?'

'We're good. Or as good as could be expected, anyway, given all that's been going on. Hey, you and Kristen wanna come over for drinks after you get a chance to shower and get changed? You haven't been to our place in a while, and I know Isaac was planning on making a pot of Japanese curry for dinner. Not that you or I are probably all that hungry after all we ate here . . .'

'But Kristen will be. She's been working on that gal's lānai today and will no doubt have worked up quite the appetite. Though I need to check with her to be sure, in case she's tired and would rather chill out at home tonight.'

'No worries. Just shoot me a text to let me know one way or the other.'

The two parted with kisses to the cheek, and then Valerie unlocked her car and helped Seth get his bike settled into the back.

'So,' she said, once she'd spread towels for them on the seats and they were headed up Kalaniana'ole Street toward town. 'Where are we going?'

'I live past Rainbow Falls, above the hospital,' he said.

'Ah, good – not too far from my place, actually.'

Neither spoke, Seth staring out the window at the ocean to their right as they made their way up the coastline. After a few minutes, Valerie broke the silence, deciding it was best to broach the elephant in the room.

'Look, you don't need to worry,' she said, causing him to turn her way. 'I'm not going to tell anyone about your . . . condition.' *Not anyone at work, anyway*, was her thought, 'cause she sure as hell wasn't going to keep it from Kristen.

'Thanks,' he mumbled. With a frown, he looked back out the window, then immediately turned back to her. 'And I do really appreciate your jumping into the water to save my ass. I'm so sorry about how crazy it was, me thrashing about like that. I'm not sure *I* would have tried to save me at that point,' he added with a wry smile.

There was another pause, followed by a long sigh from Seth. 'That's the reason I stopped drinking,' he said after a bit. 'Since alcohol can trigger a seizure. And it's also why I don't drive, 'cause you never know when you might have another one, even if you're good about taking your meds. I mostly do AA because, believe it or not, it's less embarrassing than telling everyone I have epilepsy. People tend to act weird around me once they know. Though I have to admit I do like to drink, so going to meetings also helps keep me on the wagon.'

'Well, that all sucks,' Valerie offered, and he nodded agreement.

'But I decided I needed to tell Sachiko about my epilepsy, you know, in case something ever happened while I was at work.'

'And I'm guessing that's also one of the reasons you're not a water person?'

'Yup.'

'Which probably didn't go down too well with your Navy dad.'

'You got that right.'

Seth directed Valerie up Waianuenue Avenue and then right, into a neighborhood along Wailuku Drive. 'Here, let me go in with you to make sure you get settled okay,' she said as he pulled his bike from the back of the car.

'You don't need to. I'm fine. Really. You should go home and get changed out of those wet clothes.'

'Just humor me. Sachiko will have my hide if I don't make sure you're all right. And I'm mostly dry already, in any case.'

Seth rolled his eyes. 'Fine, whatever. Come on in. But just know I wasn't expecting company, so who knows what the state of the house might be.'

She followed him up a path along the side of a small bungalow with red-painted siding and a white metal roof. 'I rent the ohana unit,' he said, unlocking the door to what looked to have originally been the garage. 'Voilà. Chez Seth Warner in all its glory.'

The main room contained a small couch and hard-backed chair, a glass coffee table, and a flat-screen TV on the wall. A tile countertop with two stools separated it from a tiny kitchen, and to the right were two doors leading to what she assumed were the bedroom and bathroom.

But contrary to his remark about the state of the place, it was neat and clean. And sparse. There was little artwork save two Hawaiian prints on the wall, one depicting a spray of red ginger and yellow orchids, the other a seascape with a stand of coco palms in the foreground.

'I can't offer you anything hard to drink, but if you'd like a soda or some juice . . .' Seth said, gesturing toward a fridge sporting various magnets with such sayings as 'I lava Hawai'i' and 'Aloha is my mother tongue.'

'No, thanks. I'm not gonna stay long. Oh, wow,' she said, noticing the sliding glass door out to the back yard. 'It looks like you're really near the river. May I?' Valerie reached for the door.

'Be my guest.'

Seth followed her across the lawn to a low rock wall, beyond which a steep incline led down to the Wailuku River.

'It doesn't bother you, having the river this close?' she asked.

'No, it's just being *in* the water that I mind; I love looking at it. It's very meditative. Except when there's been a big rain – now, *that* can be scary. You should have seen when Lane came through. The water came within just a few feet of the back yard.'

As Valerie stared at the water gurgling calmly over the lava rocks as it made its way down to the sea, she couldn't help but think about Hank and wonder once again how he might have met his end in that very same river. 'Can I ask you something?' she said, swiveling around to face Seth.

'Uh, sure. I guess. As long as it's nothing too embarrassing. I've had enough of that for one day.'

'No, nothing about you at all. It's about Jun, actually.'

'Oh, yeah?' Curiosity showed in his blue eyes.

'It's just that he said something kind of weird to me the other night, and since I have to work with the guy, I wanted to run it past you and see what you think.'

'Okay . . .'

She told him what the bartender had said about not wanting her to meet his wife and how agitated he'd seemed when talking about Hank's propensity for hitting on women. 'It just seems like Jun's awful jealous about Sherri. You know, way more than normal . . .' She trailed off, not sure exactly where she was going with this.

But Seth was nodding in agreement. 'You got that right. He's super protective of her. He gave me the evil eye once, and all I'd been doing was talking to her about the weather or some boring thing like that. But Jun's kinda crazy when it comes to his wife.'

'So was Hank in fact hitting on Sherri?'

Seth stared out at the river, a frown creasing his normally boyish brow. 'I'm not sure it's my place to tell you this, but . . . well, since you work with Jun, I guess it's best if you know what's what.' With a sigh, he turned back to Valerie, his eyes now hard.

'The answer is yeah, he was coming on to her, and I'm pretty sure the attraction was mutual. I don't know if they ever did anything more than flirt, but one day Jun walked in on them making googly eyes at each other and he went completely ballistic. They were in the street behind the bar, and I'd just ridden up on my bike and saw it all go down. Jun starts screaming at Hank and picks up a bottle from the recycling bin, and I thought for sure he was gonna smack the guy over the head with it. But then Sherri started yelling at him to stop, and when I ran over to help out, he smashed the bottle down onto the street instead.'

'Whoa,' was all Valerie had to say.

'I know. It was pretty intense. Jun told Hank in no uncertain terms that he better stay away from Sherri – or else.'

'Or else,' Valerie repeated. 'That's not good for Jun, given what eventually happened to Hank. Did you tell all this to the cops?'

'More or less. Maybe not with as much detail as I just told you. I mean, it's not as if I think Jun actually went so far as to kill Hank, so . . .'

'So you're protecting the guy.'

Seth shrugged. 'I guess if you put it like that, then yeah, I am.'

NINETEEN

'You think Isaac will be glad to see you?' Kristen asked as she and Valerie crossed the lawn toward his and Sachiko's house later that afternoon.

'I'm really hoping he's had time to get over his annoyance with me,' Valerie answered in a low voice. They climbed the front steps, and she rapped on the screen door. 'But I guess we'll see soon enough.'

Sachiko popped her head out of the kitchen. 'Come on in! I'm just finishing up the prep for our drinks.' After kicking off their slippahs, the two headed indoors and found Sachiko working through a bowl of mandarin oranges with a sturdy manual press juicer. 'A neighbor just gave us all this citrus, so I thought I'd make a batch of screwdrivers for everyone.'

'Sounds good to me,' said Kristen. 'Nice and refreshing after a hard day's work out in the sun. And speaking of working stiffs, where's Isaac?'

'I think he went to take a shower after finishing up his curry.'

Valerie crossed the room to peer into the large pot simmering on the stove. 'Yum. That smells heavenly.'

'It's super simple, since you use those store-bought curry cubes, but something my mom used to make for us growing up.'

'Comfort food,' said Valerie.

'You got it. Ah, here's Isaac now.'

Valerie turned to him with a bright smile, hoping to smooth out any tension remaining from their last meeting.

But Isaac's face was impassive. 'Howzit?' he said. It was more of a growl than a real question.

Okay, so he hasn't gotten over it.

'Good to see ya, brah,' said Kristen, striding over to give him a hug. He graced her with a lackluster grin, then – ignoring Valerie – headed for the stove and gave the pot a quick stir.

Sachiko, watching Valerie watch Isaac, frowned. 'So what's going on with you two, anyway?'

'Nothing,' Isaac responded, now avoiding her eye as well.

'It sure doesn't seem like "nothing" to me,' she said, then turned toward Valerie. 'What the heck's up? You're both acting really weird.'

Isaac shrugged and finally gave Valerie a look as if to say, 'It's on you, girl. Go ahead and explain.'

Which she most definitely did *not* want to do. But Sachiko was now staring the both of them down, her bare foot tapping out an impatient cadence on the linoleum floor.

'Really?' she asked Isaac. 'You actually want me to tell her what's going on?'

He shook his head impatiently. 'I dunno . . .'

'Okay, now you're starting to scare me. You *really* need to explain what the hell's going on, or I swear I'm gonna scream.' Sachiko's foot had stopped its tapping, but her face was so tense that Valerie was afraid she might indeed lose it right then and there.

'You want to, or shall I?' she asked Isaac, who merely shrugged once more. 'Right, I guess it's on me. Why don't we get our drinks and go sit down while I explain. We might need the medication.'

'Great,' said Sachiko. 'I can't wait.' Nevertheless, she mixed their cocktails and handed them around, and the four of them went outside and settled down on the lānai, Valerie and Kristen on the hibiscus-print couch, Sachiko and Isaac on the two rattan chairs.

'Okay, here's the deal,' said Valerie once they'd clinked glasses in a cursory, half-hearted toast. 'After Hank's body was found and it seemed from their questions that the police were considering you as a suspect regarding his death, Isaac asked if I'd do a little poking around to see if I could find out anything about what really happened to him. But he didn't want me to tell you, 'cause he was worried it would only upset you more, to know . . .'

'To know he was so scared the cops might come haul me off to jail for Hank's murder that he asked you to investigate?' Sachiko swiveled around to face Isaac, her eyes full of . . . anger? Fear? Despair? Valerie couldn't tell. Probably a mix of all three.

'I just wanted to help you, babe,' he said in a pleading voice.

'An' since she was so good 'bout figuring out what happened with dat body in da lava last spring, I just figured maybe she might be able to help out here, too. I didn't know what else to do.' Isaac lay his head in his hands and let loose a deep sigh.

Sachiko followed this with a sigh of her own, after which the group was silent. Finally she shook her head, then took a sip of her drink. 'Okay, I guess I get why you did that. Though I can't say I'm happy that no one ever thought I should be in on what was going on. I suppose you knew, too?' she asked Kristen, who nodded sheepishly.

'Great. Nothing like being the one everyone's afraid to tell the truth to. But this all still doesn't explain why Isaac and Valerie have been acting so weird around each other. What else aren't you telling me?'

Valerie shot a glance at Isaac, who was studying his highball glass intently, as if it were some kind of holy relic. 'Okay, me again,' she said, then cleared her throat. 'It's because I, uh . . . Well, I think Isaac might have gotten the impression that *I* suspected you, too. But I don't!' she quickly added. 'Not in the slightest. I was just worried there was evidence about you that the *cops* might take the wrong way.'

'Which was?' Sachiko asked, her voice cold.

'It was a picture Isaac took at the retreat of you and Hank – the last photo on that roll, taken at around a quarter to six. And, well, you looked pretty darn angry at the guy.'

'Ah.' With a nod, she turned to gaze out at the tall plumeria in the middle of their back yard, its bright yellow blossoms vibrant against the tree's skeletal limbs, now bare of leaves.

'Do you remember what you two were talking about when the photo was taken?' Valerie asked.

'Not exactly. But I do know I was still pretty ticked about what happened with that customer a few days earlier. Or, rather, more about how he refused to own up to it and take responsibility than the actual incident itself. With Hank it was always the other person's fault.' She shook her head. 'I know that doesn't sound good for me, given what happened to him after the retreat, but it's the truth.'

'Sounds like what everyone else says about the guy,' Valerie said, a trace of disgust slipping into her voice. The more she heard about Hank, the more she was sure she wouldn't have much liked the guy. 'So do you think he stole your carved fox?'

Sachiko blinked a few times. 'How do you know about that?'

'I told her,' said Isaac. 'I figured it was best if she knew all da facts.'

'Right. Well, I wouldn't be surprised if he did. He was pretty angry at me, and it did go missing sometime that day before the retreat. And I also know they found it in his pocket when . . .' Even though she didn't finish the sentence, Valerie couldn't help but envision that orange helicopter hovering over the Wailuku River, searching for the dead man's drowned body.

'Why don't you tell Sachiko all you've learned,' said Kristen. 'You know, now that the cat's out of the bag.'

'Yes, do tell me. Hopefully it's good news?'

'Well, I haven't solved the mystery, if that's what you mean. And if anything, I've actually moved back a few squares today. But I have discovered possible motives for several people to want Hank out of the way, shall we say.'

Valerie proceeded to lay out her theories and suspects, ticking them off on her fingers as she went. First there was Annie, whom Hank had come on to, and who'd made that comment about not being sure it was a 'good idea' to come down to Kaimū to plant the coconut for him. 'Whatever that means,' Valerie said.

Second was Matt, about whom Hank had apparently made homophobic comments. 'But not that strong of a motive there,' she added. 'And I'm not even sure Matt knew what Hank had been saying.'

And then, third, the incident of Nalani demonstrating her violent temper in the Gecko kitchen the previous Friday night. 'And she did feel the need to go down to Kaimū to plant a palm for Hank, so maybe she's feeling guilty?' Though Valerie conceded she had yet to come up with any possible reason for the restaurant owner to want her bartender dead.

Fourth, she went on, was the paddler, Craig, whose fierce competition with Hank gave him reason to want him out of commission, and his close friendship with Kai, who seemed to treat Craig as a sort of mentor.

'So the theory is Kai could have done it on Craig's behalf,' explained Kristen.

Sachiko was shaking her head. 'I can't believe Kai would do something like that. He doesn't have a violent bone in his body.'

'Agreed,' said Isaac. 'I'd love to pin Hank's death on someone besides Sachiko, but Kai seems like an awful big stretch. You got any other suspects?'

'Well, there's Seth,' Valerie said. 'And up until today, my pet theory was that it might very well be him. I didn't have any particular motive for the guy, but he just seemed somehow . . . suspicious.'

'In what way?' asked Sachiko.

'I dunno . . . He's always so vague about his past life on the Mainland. And he's so damn *nice*.'

Sachiko laughed. 'Well, if that's cause for suspicion, then I can think of a lot of folks who should also be under consideration.'

'Yeah, I know,' said Valerie. 'But there were other things, too. Like, he professes to be a birder, yet he didn't know the name of the yellow-billed cardinal – a super common bird around here. And then when he fell in the water today and I jumped in to help him – 'cause, you know, he always talks about how he can't swim – and he kept grabbing on to me and pulling me under water, all of a sudden I had this horrible thought that he'd fallen in on purpose and was trying to kill me. At that point, I was *sure* he'd killed Hank.'

At Sachiko's look of disbelief, Valerie shrugged. 'I know, it sounds pretty far-fetched. Especially now that I know he fell in the water and was freaking out because he was having an epileptic seizure. So it's actually kind of embarrassing on my part, I gotta say. And I now also realize that's why he's seemed so secretive about stuff – 'cause of his epilepsy – and why he doesn't drive. So my Seth theory now seems to have flown out the window. Except . . .'

'Except what?' the others said in unison.

'Well, first of all, the place where he lives is right on the Wailuku River. And second, it was super neat and clean – not at all like your usual straight guy's house.'

Kristen raised her eyebrows skeptically. 'And this is relevant because . . .?'

'Okay, so what if Seth and Hank were both gay, and Seth had Hank drive him home after the retreat. Or I guess it doesn't really matter if they were gay or not; he could have just asked Hank for the ride. And then once they were at Seth's house, he takes Hank out to show him the river like we did this afternoon, picks up a rock, and *wham*! All he has to do is roll the guy down the embankment, and—'

'Time out,' Isaac said, making a T with his hands. 'That's not possible, because Sachiko and I drove him home from the retreat.'

'You did?'

'Uh-huh. He was about to ride home but then saw that his bike had a flat, so we put it in my Suburu and took him down da hill.'

'Dang,' said Valerie. 'Oh, well. It was just a thought. And anyway, I'm thinking our best bet now in any case is Jun.' She explained about his jealousy – what he'd said to her about not wanting her to meet his wife, and how angry he looked when telling her about Hank hitting on women at the bar. 'And then today when I was at Seth's house, he told me this pretty scary story about the guy.' After recounting what Seth witnessed behind the Speckled Gecko, the others drew in their breath.

'Whoa,' said Kristen, 'that's pretty intense.'

Valerie nodded. 'Agreed. And it doesn't sound like Seth told the cops the whole truth about what happened, either. I think he wanted to protect Jun for some reason.'

Standing up, Isaac started to pace across the lānai. 'Sounds like he's gotta be da guy,' he said. 'But how do we prove it?'

'We don't know it's Jun,' said Sachiko. 'Though I'm damn well gonna have a serious talk with him about his controlling temper. No way is that behavior acceptable for one of my employees.'

'You think that's safe, babe?' Isaac stopped his pacing and turned to Sachiko with a frown. 'I mean, if it *was* him who killed Hank, who knows what he might do if you start gettin' on his case.'

'He's got a point,' said Valerie. 'Which isn't to say you shouldn't talk to Jun, but maybe hold off a bit. Give it a while to see if the cops end up figuring out how Hank did in fact die. And who knows, maybe Jun'll say something incriminating at work that we can take to the cops to prove he did it.'

Sachiko snorted. 'I'm not counting on that happening anytime soon. But fine. I'll wait to talk to him. Let's just hope he doesn't bash anyone over the head with a bottle – or a rock – between now and then.'

Much as Valerie was eager to get Jun talking about Hank and see if he slipped up in any way, it wasn't going to happen for several days, as they weren't scheduled to work together until the coming Friday night.

It was now Wednesday, and as she prepped the bar for lunch service, she considered where she really stood with her investigation. She'd talked the big talk on Monday at Sachiko and Isaac's house, suggesting all those people as suspects in Hank's murder, but the truth was, she didn't feel much enthusiasm for any of the theories she'd proposed. None of the Gecko workers seemed to have any good reason to go so far as to actually kill Hank.

And then yesterday at their paddling practice, she'd learned that Craig – her sole non-Gecko suspect – hadn't even been on-island the day of the retreat: he'd been on Moloka'i, paddling with friends who were helping put on the upcoming Hoe race. So unless Kai had killed Hank at Craig's behest, the stroker couldn't have been involved in Hank's death. And why would Kai do such a thing?

Which prompted an ugly thought: *Could Craig have some kind of hold over the Gecko busser? Something serious enough to be able to blackmail him into committing murder?*

But Kai sure didn't *act* as if he had anything horrible hanging over his head. The guy came across as totally laid back, with little cares in the world other than paddling and hanging out with his brahs. *No*, she decided. *It couldn't have been Kai.*

So that left Jun, Nalani, Matt, and Annie as her remaining suspects.

And Sachiko, she amended. Much as Valerie couldn't fathom her friend having killed Hank, she realized she had no tangible proof that she hadn't done so.

She was startled from her musings by a voice calling out her name. 'Oh, hi,' she said, looking up to see the dining room manager waving a hand at her. 'Sorry, I was thinking about . . . you know . . .' Hoping the flush she felt spreading to her cheeks wasn't obvious, Valerie smiled. No way could Sachiko have any idea she'd been thinking about *her* right then as she'd come up to the bar, right?

Apparently not, as Sachiko merely returned her smile with a friendly, conspiratorial look. 'And?'

'And nothing,' said Valerie with a sigh. 'Sorry.'

'Oh, well. But that's not actually why I came over. I wanted to see if you could possibly work tomorrow night. I know it's your night off, but we have a big party coming in – and I mean an actual "party." It's an anniversary celebration with about sixty covers, and they've reserved the entire lānai for the event. We're doing a buffet for them out here, but it would be great to have a second bartender, since they'll be having a no-host bar and the indoor dining room will also be open as usual.'

'Oh . . .'

'I know,' Sachiko went on. 'It's super late notice, but we only got the booking this morning. I gather the place they were supposed to have it at fell through at the last minute, and they were scrambling to find an alternate location. And not only is the money great, but they're also friends of Nalani's, so, well, she said yes.'

Valerie had been hoping to have a quiet night alone with Kristen on Thursday, but from the pleading expression in Sachiko's eyes, she could tell there was no Plan B for a second bartender. If Valerie didn't come in, they'd be in a world of hurt. 'Sure, I can do it,' she said. 'No worries.'

'Ohmygod, thank you!' Sachiko dashed around to the back of the bar to give Valerie a tight hug. 'I so owe you, girl.'

'Nah, it's all good. I get how restaurants work.' *And besides*, she thought as Sachiko headed back to the front of the house, *it'll give me a chance to work with Jun a day earlier and see if I can get him to cough up anything about Hank's death.*

But how exactly she might do that, she had no idea.

TWENTY

Kristen was in the back yard pulling weeds when Valerie finally emerged from her slumber Thursday morning. Tropical gardens in East Hawai'i are wonderfully lush and vibrant from all that warm trade wind rain, but along with the ferns, ginger, heliconia, and hibiscus come invasive grasses, vines, and baby 'junk' trees that seem to sprout up overnight. And if you don't keep after those interlopers, your garden can soon turn into an unmanageable jungle.

'Hey, sleepy head,' called out Kristen, setting down her trowel and wiping her brow with a muddy gloved hand. 'I thought I'd get in a little gardening before it got too hot.'

Valerie took in the circle of red dirt around their bottle palm, now a pristine and weed-free area. 'Looks great. You want me to bring you a cup of coffee?'

'Nah.' Kristen stood and brushed the dirt from her knees. 'I'll get it myself and come take a break with you.' She headed to the kitchen and returned a few minutes later bearing a steaming mug and a plate of toast, followed closely by Pua, her slender nose raised high to track the heady scent of butter.

'You're not working on the lānai today?' Valerie asked.

'I am, but not till noon. Diane has a doctor's appointment this morning, and we need two people for most of the roof work.'

'Sounds like you're pretty close to done.'

Kristen nodded as she swallowed a bite of toast. 'Very close. We finished the purlins yesterday – you know, the things you screw the roofing panels into – so all that's left now is to put up the roofing. We should have it all finished by tomorrow afternoon, assuming this weather holds up.'

'Cheers!' said Valerie, raising her mug in salute. 'That's gotta feel good.'

'It does, indeed. Hey. I know you work tomorrow and Saturday night, but how 'bout we celebrate my finishing up – and thereby having more time to spend with my lovely wife – by going somewhere nice to eat tonight. Maybe the Hilo Bay Cafe for some of their amazing Hāmākua mushroom pot pie?'

'Uh . . . I kinda agreed to work tonight.'

'Kinda?'

'Okay, not "kinda." I am in fact working tonight. They had a last-minute private party booking and desperately need a second bartender.'

Kristen held Valerie's eyes for a moment, then turned with a shake of the head to look out at the garden.

'I'm so sorry, hon. But I felt like I couldn't say no to Sachiko.'

'I know,' said Kristen. 'I get it. It's the restaurant biz. It just sucks, is all, 'cause now – since I'll be gone during the day today and tomorrow – I won't hardly see you until what . . . Saturday?'

'Right. Saturday day, anyway, since I work that night.'

'Right.' Kristen took a sip of coffee, then handed Pua a morsel of bread. 'Okay, how about Sunday night, then, for our celebratory dinner?'

'It's a date,' said Valerie. 'Pinkie swear.' The two linked fingers, then giggled like schoolgirls.

'So you have any plans for this afternoon while I'm at Diane's?' Kristen asked.

'It's such a nice day I think I'll take Pua for a walk down to the water and then maybe do a little work in the garden myself.'

Three hours later, Valerie was wrestling with a vine that had wound its way tightly around the trunk of their yellow hibiscus tree when her cell phone rang out from the lānai. Pulling off her gloves, she darted across the lawn to answer it.

'Isaac,' she said. 'What's up?'

'What's up is that da cops just came to the Gecko again to ask Sachiko more questions, and she's totally freaking out.'

As are you, was Valerie's thought, listening to the frantic tone in his voice. 'What exactly did they want to know?' she asked.

'I think dey finally got Hank's phone unlocked and dere was something bad about her on it. I dunno what, but dey were real interested in dat argument she an' Hank had da night before da retreat.'

'But they already knew about that, right?'

'Yah. But I guess dey wanted more details. Or maybe just to intimidate her. I dunno. I'm wondering if maybe she should refuse to talk to them again without a lawyer present.'

'They didn't say they were going to arrest her or anything, did they?'

'No. But she said dey weren't particularly friendly, either. Oh, and dey asked about dat carved fox – like how much it's worth and exactly when it went missing, and if she suspected dat Hank had stolen it.'

'Did they talk to any of the other Gecko staff?'

'I don't think so,' said Isaac. 'Sachiko says it seemed like dey just wanted to talk to her.'

'Huh,' was all Valerie could muster. The police were clearly as stymied as she was, with not enough evidence to arrest anyone for the crime. But the fact that they were focusing on Sachiko was disturbing.

'So I was wondering,' Isaac went on, 'if you'd come up with any more ideas about who might-a killed Hank. You know, anything to absolve Sachiko?'

'I'm afraid not,' she said. 'But I'm hoping to get Jun talking tonight, so maybe I'll learn something relevant from him?'

'I wouldn't count on it. If he did kill Hank, he's sure not gonna say anything to you 'bout it. Anyway, I gotta get back to the classroom; lunch is almost over. But let me know if you have any new thoughts about da case.'

'Will do.' Valerie ended the call and returned to her gardening with a renewed vengeance. She couldn't do anything to control how the cops handled the mystery of Hank's death, but at least she could tame the invasive weeds attempting to take over her garden.

Valerie headed straight for Sachiko's office when she arrived at work at four that afternoon, but the front-of-the-house manager wasn't at her desk. Turning from the door, she heard Sachiko's voice coming from the lānai, where she found her instructing Annie and Seth on how to set up for the private party, which was due to arrive at six.

'Go ahead and set all the tables as usual,' Sachiko was saying. 'We'll have plates over by the buffet, and you can place pitchers of ice water on all the tables a little before six. Seth, you'll be handling the regular diners indoors, and Annie will help you in there as needed, but she'll also be taking care of the folks out here on the lānai. Getting their drink orders and doing anything else that comes up – which shouldn't be too much, as they'll be serving themselves all the food. And they can also get their own drinks at the bar,' she added, spotting Valerie. 'So you and Jun might want to divvy up your jobs between helping bar customers and filling table orders from Seth and Annie. Okay, everyone good?'

Valerie, Seth, and Annie all nodded.

'Good. I gotta go confer with Nalani about the buffet,' said Sachiko, who strode off toward the kitchen.

Valerie clearly wasn't going to get to talk to her any time soon about what had happened with the cops earlier that day. Instead she made her way to the bar and began checking and refilling juice bottles, slicing garnishes, and making sure there was plenty of wine in the cooler. At the sound of a car engine outside the back door, she poked her head out to see Sherri pull up in her cherry-red Mustang. Jun gave his wife a kiss on the lips, then climbed out of the passenger seat and slammed the door shut.

Not wanting him to see her looking, Valerie retreated back into the bar and was filling a plastic squeeze bottle with cranberry juice when Jun came inside.

'Ready to rock 'n' roll?' he asked. ''Cause it's gonna be ca-*ray*-zee here tonight. Thanks for agreeing to come in, by the way.'

'No worries. And hopefully the tips will be good.'

'They will be,' said Jun with a grin. 'Sachiko told me she's adding a twenty percent service charge to the bill for the happy couple – on top of whatever people tip on their own. So, you got a drink special for the night?'

'Not really. I was thinking of just doing a variation on a Margarita – maybe with liliko'i in addition to lime? Sachiko told me a lot of the guests tonight for the anniversary party will be from the Mainland, so that'll seem exotic to them, but it'll also go with the menu they're serving, which I gather is mostly Mexican.'

'Works for me,' said Jun. 'I'll make up a big batch of the mixer in advance.'

He seemed to be in a good mood, so as they prepped for the big evening, Valerie took the opportunity to get Jun talking. 'So, how'd you and Sherri meet?' she asked.

He stopped squeezing limes and gave her a questioning look, and Valerie was afraid she'd crossed a line. But then he leaned back against the bar with a smile. 'It was at the Flores de Mayo festival five years back here in Hilo – you know, the big Filipino celebration that happens every spring? She was selling lumpia at one of the booths, and I couldn't take my eyes off her. Problem was, she already had a boyfriend.' He laughed. 'But after meeting me, she let him go pretty easy. And then a year later, we were married.'

And lemme guess: now you're worried that some other guy will do the same thing, was Valerie's thought. *That he'll steal Sherri away from you, like you did to her previous boyfriend.* Because if she let that guy go so easily for Jun, what was to keep her from doing the same thing again?

Which went a long way in explaining his issue with jealousy.

'Does Sherri work?' Valerie asked.

'No, I don't need her to work,' Jun said with a frown, as if the question offended him. 'I can take care of her just fine. But she still makes some amazing lumpia, I gotta say. That was hers that I brought to the thing for Hank on Monday.'

'Oh, wow. It was delicious – so gingery. You think she'd give me the recipe?'

'No wayz. It's a family secret. But she makes 'um for our church sales sometimes. I'll let you know next time one happens.'

As Jun went back to squeezing his limes, Valerie pondered this new information she'd learned. He certainly kept his wife on a tight leash. *Or at least he thinks he does.*

Which prompted another thought: *What if Sherri had in fact been messing around with Hank – not just flirting – and then Jun had discovered what was going on?*

What followed would not have been pretty, Valerie was quite sure.

By six thirty, Valerie and Jun were totally in the weeds. They had a thirsty full house indoors, and the anniversary party guests out on the lānai were in the mood to do just that – party down. Which translated into a lot of bar traffic.

Luckily, their pre-mixed Margarita special was a big hit, which made life a little easier for the two bartenders, but there were still enough orders for more labor-intensive drinks such as Mojitos and Piña Coladas that they never had a moment's respite.

'Two more specials – rocks, no salt!' Valerie called out to Jun, who nodded and grabbed a pair of Margarita glasses from the overhead shelf. While he was filling that order, she dumped strawberries, ice, lime juice, and rum into the blender for a frozen Daiquiri, then started filling the undercounter dishwasher rack with dirty glasses from the bus tray.

A middle-aged man in a peach polo shirt stretched tight over his biceps caught her eye from the end of the bar and she held up a finger to let him know she'd be right there. Once she'd poured the Daiquiri into a glass and garnished it with a sprig of mint, she set it on the service area with the two Margaritas to await Annie's pickup, then headed over to take the new customer's order.

Yup, definitely a body builder, she concluded, reading the 'Ocean Beach Fitness' logo on his shirt.

'Howdy. What can I get ya?'

'A dirty Martini, please. Up. With gin.'

'Of course,' agreed Valerie. 'It's not really a Martini if it's made with vodka, right?'

'Truth.' His smile was warm and friendly, making her rethink her first impression of the guy as just another self-centered jock.

'So, how do you know the happy couple?' Valerie asked as she poured gin, vermouth, and a splash of olive juice into a metal shaker.

'Jack and I were college roommates, but we don't get the chance to see each other much anymore, now that he's moved here to Hilo. So I'm super happy to have the excuse to come hang out with the guy for a few days. And I gotta say, the Big Island is pretty awesome. Who knew?'

'Those of us who live here,' said Valerie with a grin as she served up his chilled drink and took his credit card in exchange. Ringing up the sale, she returned with the card and receipt. 'Enjoy your stay.'

On to the next customer. She pulled two IPAs and poured a glass of Chardonnay, then shoved the now-full rack of dirty glasses into the dishwasher and switched it on. Spying Seth start across the lānai toward the bar, she headed to the service area to await his table's order. But before he made it halfway across the room, the server suddenly stopped, and then – as if he'd just remembered something – turned and walked quickly back into the indoor dining room.

A minute later Annie appeared with an order from one of her tables and waited while Valerie mixed the two drinks. 'Did you see the cops when they came by at lunch?' Valerie asked as she shook up a Cosmopolitan.

'No, but I heard they spent a while talking to Sachiko in her office. I wonder why they only wanted to talk to her and nobody else.'

'Who knows?' said Valerie, feigning ignorance. 'Did she seem upset after they left?'

'More pissed off than anything, I'd say. But that could have been because of the timing – you know, right when we're scrambling to get ready for sixty-plus extra covers tonight?'

Valerie set down the Cosmo, then poured a gin and tonic and garnished it with a slice of lime. 'Well, she seemed okay when she was giving you and Seth the lay of the land earlier. But I can only imagine what she's been going through of late.'

'Me too. I'd never want to be a restaurant manager. Much better to be a lowly server. Her stress level has gotta be cray cray right about now.' Annie lifted the tray from the bar top. 'Thanks!'

And you don't know the half of it, thought Valerie as she watched the server deftly thread her way between tables and customers in the crowded lānai.

Once the food service began for the anniversary party and the guests were helping themselves to kālua pork tacos, shrimp a la diabla, and cheese enchiladas from the buffet, the bar traffic finally slowed down, and Valerie and Jun were able to catch their breath – as well as restock garnishes, well bottles, and mixers that had run low during the rush.

'We're almost out of lemons,' said Jun, holding up a small stainless steel insert. 'Wanna go grab some?'

'You got it.' Valerie made her way across the lānai, through the indoor dining room – which was still full of customers – and into the kitchen. Nalani was at the stove tending several sauté pans, and Matt had just pulled a hotel pan full of enchiladas from the oven. After holding the door open so the cook could take the hot pan out to the buffet table, she fetched a bag of lemons from the walk-in fridge.

'How's it going?' she asked Nalani on her way out of the kitchen.

'Don't ask,' growled the chef, not looking up from the stove.

Okay, then. Valerie walked back through the dining room, where she was surprised to see Sachiko taking the order at one of the tables. Seth must have been overwhelmed by handling the room all on his own, she figured. *But then who was at the host stand?*

Ah, Kai was there, greeting customers with a broad smile. And the dishwasher, Mano, she saw, was busy clearing the empty tables.

Returning to the bar, she commenced slicing lemons, only to be interrupted by Annie with a drink order. 'It's completely nuts out there,' the server said, using a damp side towel to wipe her brow.

'I know – I saw Sachiko waiting tables and Kai at the host stand. It must be super busy right now.'

'That's not the reason it's so crazy,' said Annie. 'Seth left us in the lurch.'

'What?'

'I guess there was some sort of emergency – he didn't say exactly what – and he just split. Said he had to take off right then.'

'Whoa.' Valerie poured two Margarita specials, then reached for the vodka to make a Moscow Mule. 'That's all Sachiko needed tonight.'

'No kidding. She's about as angry as I've ever seen her – said she was gonna fire Seth on the spot. But I convinced her to wait and see what was going on with the guy. Who knows, maybe his dad had a stroke or something.'

'Well, let's hope that's not the case. But for his sake, I hope it's something important enough to warrant putting his fellow employees through such hell.'

Now, even more than before, Valerie wanted the chance to talk to Sachiko. Or at least see what this 'scary' Sachiko looked like.

She didn't have to wait long, as just a few minutes later the dining room manager came striding up to the bar with a drink order for an eight-top whose table she'd taken over during the rush.

'Did you hear about Seth?' Sachiko asked, eyes blazing.

'Yeah, I did,' said Valerie. 'That so sucks.'

'I mean, tonight of all nights? I don't care what the hell's going on in his life – you don't just walk out on people and leave them *hanging* like that.' Smacking her hand upon the bar top for emphasis, Sachiko came close to knocking over a lilikoʻi Martini Valerie had just set down. 'At this point, he better *not* come back in to work tonight, because I swear I could *kill* the little—'

Noticing Valerie's widening eyes, Sachiko didn't finish the sentence, and instead turned to glare out over the crowded lānai, shoulders rising and falling as she took a series of deep breaths.

Now that she'd seen the 'scary' Sachiko, Valerie wasn't sure she'd be able to un-see it.

TWENTY-ONE

B y the time the private party crowd had cleared out at around nine thirty, the indoor dining area was down to only a few tables, all of whom had been served their mains. The restaurant was a mess, littered with dirty glasses, crumpled-up napkins, and plates of half-eaten anniversary cake. As Annie helped Kai bus the tables, Sachiko came behind the bar and poured herself a shot of tequila.

'That was not fun,' she said, then downed the drink in one gulp. Sachiko watched Jun at the other end of the bar as he loaded glasses into the dishwasher, then turned to Valerie. 'But what I said earlier – about Seth . . .?'

'No worries.' Valerie gave a dismissive wave of the hand. 'I get it. You were super stressed – with good reason.'

'Yeah, but I really should try to have a little more empathy for the guy. 'Cause you're right. Who knows what horrible thing might have happened to him tonight?'

'About that . . .' Valerie glanced over at Jun, then picked up a bus tub and motioned for Sachiko to follow her from behind the bar to one of the tables at the far side of the lānai.

'What?' asked Sachiko.

'It's just that I'm thinking there may not have been any "emergency" at all,' Valerie said in a low voice as she loaded water glasses and dessert plates into the tub.

'What do you mean?'

'Okay, so earlier tonight – it must have been around six thirty or seven? – I saw Seth crossing the lānai to come place a bar order, when all of a sudden he stops, then walks quickly back into the dining room. That was the last time I saw him tonight.'

'Uh-huh . . .' said Sachiko.

'And right before that happened, I was talking to a customer and noticed he was wearing a shirt that said 'Ocean Beach Fitness' on it.' At Sachiko's blank look, she explained. 'Ocean Beach is in San Diego – where Seth is from.'

Sachiko still looked confused.

'So I'm thinking maybe Seth recognized that guy – or maybe someone else at the party. Chances are there were other people here tonight from San Diego if that guy was. And maybe Seth didn't want to be recognized. That would explain his sudden need to get the hell out of the restaurant.'

Sachiko's frown suggested skepticism at this idea, but she nodded nevertheless. 'Maybe.'

'What's Seth's last name?' asked Valerie. 'Warner? I think that's what he said when we were at his house. 'Cause I wanna look him up online to see if I can find out anything about his family or history or whatever.'

'Right, it's Warner. But I can't imagine what you'd find online that would tell us anything.'

'You never know. It's worth a shot, anyway.'

Once the last customers had left and the tables had all been cleared and the bar closed up for the night, Valerie joined Kai, Annie, and Matt for a much-needed post-work beer. Jun, as usual, didn't stay, and Nalani and Sachiko were in the kitchen discussing something.

While the other three debriefed about the hectic night, Valerie did an online search for Seth Warner on her phone. There were quite a few people with that name – the most prominent of which was a Revolutionary War soldier – but none were the Seth she knew. He seemed to have no social media presence at all.

'Is Seth on Instagram or Twitter?' Valerie asked the table. 'Or does he maybe have a Facebook page?'

Kai shook his head. 'He doesn't seem da Facebook type. Why you ask?'

'I'm just curious about him, is all. He's so private about his life outside work. And after what happened tonight . . .' She trailed off, not sure exactly what to say.

'Ho!' Kai slapped his knee. 'Da guy, he nevah talk story 'bout himself. But he sure does seem like some kinda goody-goody. No, dass not da word. More like . . .'

'Sanctimonious?' put in Annie, causing Matt to laugh.

'Yeah, he can be a bit righteous about his beliefs,' said the cook. 'But it all seems to come from a good place, so hey, who am I to judge?'

'Like what?' asked Valerie. 'Can you give an example?'

'I got one,' said Kai. 'Da guy, he no get one credit card, 'cause he says dey bad for da poor.'

Matt was nodding. 'That's actually true. Merchants pass on the processing costs they're charged for each credit card use to their customers, which means higher prices all around. Which is fine for folks who have cards, since they get all the benefits of their rewards programs. But for those who can't get a credit card, they end up screwed, essentially paying a tax to support those rewards everyone else benefits from.'

'So what's the answer?' asked Annie, and Matt shrugged.

'Who knows? I don't see us going back to a cash culture any time soon. People love to charge stuff.'

The others continued to discuss the morals and economics of a credit-based society, but Valerie's mind was elsewhere: Really? Seth didn't have a credit card? The not driving thing made sense with his epilepsy, as did his being private about his life. But not having a credit card?

His lifestyle was starting to seem more and more fishy. *There has to be something else going on with the guy*, Valerie mused. *Could he in fact be someone other than who he claims to be?*

The next morning when she emerged from the bedroom, Kristen was surprised to find her wife sitting at the kitchen table frowning at her laptop. 'You're up early. Couldn't sleep?'

'Check this out,' said Valerie, ignoring her question. 'It says that people who take on new identities tend to use the same initials as their real names.'

'Huh?' Kristen poured herself a cup of coffee and joined Valerie at the table. 'What, are you thinking of going under cover?'

'Not me. Seth. I think he may be someone other than who he says he is.' She told Kristen what had happened the night before, and how hearing that Seth didn't have a credit card had got her thinking that there was something really strange going on with the guy. 'So I've been researching fake identities. It's apparently not all that hard to get ID cards and stuff if you have the money. You know, the dark web an' all. But what's interesting is that apparently people who take on new personas tend to use names with the same initials as their real ones. I guess so they don't get tripped up as easily? So Seth Warner could really be . . .'

'Steve Wilson!' shouted Kristen, causing Pua to look up expectantly from her dog bed. 'Or, no, Steph Walker! Oooo . . . I like this game.'

Valerie closed her laptop. 'Yeah, that's the idea. Not that it helps a whole lot. There's gotta be a zillion possible combos. If my theory is even true. For all I know, Seth could in fact simply be a guy with epilepsy who prefers his privacy and wants to crush the capitalist state, just like he says he is.'

'Well, I think we should run with it,' said Kristen, a gleam in her eye. 'Is he working tonight?'

'I'm pretty sure he's scheduled to come in, but after last night, who knows? He may never show up again. Or if he does, Sachiko may just send him on his way. She was pretty upset with him last night.'

'Well, if he does end up working tonight, shoot me a text to let me know. I can come down and sit at the bar, and every time he comes to place an order, I can say an S name loud enough for him to hear, and then see if he reacts to any of them.'

'Right,' said Valerie with a laugh.

'Hey, it'll be fun. And after finishing up the roof on Diane's lānai today – which looks like is gonna happen – I'll be ready for a celebratory drink with my wife. Even if she is on the other side of the bar from me.' Kristen stood up and grabbed a pen and a piece of scratch paper from the junk drawer under the kitchen counter. 'Here, I'll start compiling possibilities: Stuart, Shelby, Steve, Sean . . .'

As she scribbled down names, Valerie walked over to plant a kiss on her cheek. 'Thanks, hon. And hey, don't forget Sylvester. And Seymour!'

Seth did show up for work that night, full of apologies. He'd felt another epileptic seizure coming on, he said – dizziness and a metallic taste in his mouth – so he went to a friend's house who lives nearby to lie down.

'I don't know why I'd have two episodes in the same week,' he told Sachiko, frowning at the handle bars of his mountain bike. Other than Valerie, they were the only ones in the front of the restaurant at that moment, but Seth was nevertheless talking in low tones. 'I made an appointment with my doctor and am gonna see him on Monday, so we'll see what he says. Though I'm thinking he'll probably tell me I need to tweak my meds.'

Valerie, who was taking her time stowing her bag and umbrella in the wait station in order to listen in to the conversation, rolled her eyes. She didn't buy any of it.

But Sachiko apparently did. Or at least she was pretending to. 'Dang, Seth,' she said. 'That sucks. So are you feeling okay today?'

'Yeah, yeah, I'm fine. And again, I'm *so* sorry to have left you all hangin' last night. I'm happy to cover for someone who wants an extra shift off this weekend, to try to make up for it.'

Having heard enough, Valerie headed for the bar, where she pulled out her phone. 'HE'S HERE,' she texted Kristen. 'SEE YOU AROUND SIX?' On receiving a thumbs-up emoji in response – followed by a dancing woman and a Martini glass – Valerie chuckled, then set to work setting up the bar for the Friday-night rush.

At ten to six, Kristen strode across the Speckled Gecko lānai. All the barstools were currently occupied, but there was a duo waiting to be seated in the dining room, so Valerie motioned for her to hold tight. Five minutes later the couple's table was ready, and Kristen snagged the empty spot next to the service area.

'Perfect,' she said. 'I'll be right next to him when he comes to place his orders.'

As if on cue, Seth walked up to the bar and asked for two Mai Tais, a Longboard Lager, and a Chardonnay. While he waited for Valerie to prepare the drinks, Kristen lifted her phone to her ear and said, 'Oh, hi, Steve! How's it going?'

No reaction whatsoever from Seth, who was staring out at the diners on the lānai, seemingly paying her no mind.

'Is that *Sam* with you?' she went on.

Still nothing.

'Oh, look, it's *Sebastian*!' she tried, paying close attention to Seth's eyes.

Nada. She might as well not have even been there, as far as she could tell.

Valerie set the last drink down on the tray, and Seth thanked her and carried it off. 'Anything?' she asked Kristen.

'Nope. He's either a good actor, or none of those are his name.' Unfolding the sheet she'd compiled, Kristen grabbed a pen from the bar top and crossed off the three names she'd tried, then studied the list for a moment before returning it to her pocket. 'But hey, I wouldn't mind something to drink. What's your special this evening?'

'Same as last night – a Margarita with liliko'i. I didn't have the chance to come up with anything else for tonight.'

As she sipped her cocktail and chowed down on a plate of kalbi ribs, Kristen watched for Seth, and any time he came to the bar to order drinks for one of his tables, she tried out more names as she pretended to talk on the phone.

An hour later, after Seth once more left with his tray full of drinks, Kristen shook her head at Valerie, who'd been monitoring both her wife and the server's comings and goings. 'None of them have produced any reaction,' she told Valerie when she came over for a report. She flicked her finger at her list: 'Not Stuart, Sean, Scott, Sal, Sage, Shane, Spencer, or even Seymour or Sylvester made him so much as blink. And now I've gone through all my names,' Kristen said, folding the paper back up. 'I guess I should just pack it in.'

A lull in the bar's crowd noise allowed them to hear the song playing over the Gecko's music system, and as Kristen scraped up the last of her rice soaked with sweetened shoyu, garlic, ginger, and sesame oil, she hummed along with 'Slip Slidin' Away.' And then she smiled. 'Ah-*ha*!' she said aloud. 'A name I neglected to add to my list.'

Valerie was too busy mixing drinks for a trio who'd just sat down at the bar to ask her what new name she'd come up with, but the next time Seth came over with an order for one of his tables, she watched him closely as Kristen raised her phone to her ear once more.

'Simon!' she said to her imaginary friend.

It wasn't much, but Valerie saw the server momentarily freeze, then glance Kristen's way. Seeing her seemingly chatting away to someone else on her phone, he exhaled, then shook his head as if in relief.

Once Valerie had filled his cocktail order and he'd retreated back to the dining room, she leaned over the bar and said to Kristen, 'Did you see what I did?'

'Yup. Though it was only out of the corner of my eye. But I'd say he definitely seemed to react to that name.'

'Agreed. But now the question is, what do we do with the information?'

Kristen shrugged. 'It's not much to go on, but at least it's a start. In any case, I think I'm gonna head on home. My job here is done, and it's been a long day.'

'Oh, shoot,' said Valerie. 'I was so focused on our name game that I didn't even ask you about Diane's lānai. Did you two get it done?'

'We did, and it looks great, if I do say so myself.' Kristen raised her empty glass in a toast.

'Hey, that's bad luck, toasting with an empty glass,' said Valerie. 'Let me get you a drink on the house so we can do a legit "cheers." What's your pleasure?'

'Got any bubbly?'

Valerie filled a flute with Prosecco for Kristen, then poured a small serving for herself and toasted her wife's finished project. Setting down her glass, she glanced down the bar, which had now emptied out save for a pair chatting with Jun. 'I was kind of surprised you didn't bring Diane with you here tonight,' she said.

'She had a hot date – some guy she met at the Yacht Club. But I'm actually glad, 'cause it would have been hard doing my sleuthing with her along. Oh, and she said she wants to take us both out to a fancy dinner at the club as a thank you after she gets back from Honolulu next week.'

Ah, so she's straight, after all. Not that Valerie had been truly jealous of the woman, but it was a bit of a relief not to have it as a potential issue.

'Sounds fun,' she said. 'I've always wanted to go there. Do they have actual yachts?'

'I think not. But I hear tell they have noodles for their swimming pool.' Draining her glass, Kristen stood. 'And now I really am gonna get out of here. See you tonight – if not in person, since I'll likely be dead to the world when you come home, then in my dreams.'

'Not. I know what you'll really be dreaming about tonight: roof posts or joists or purlins or some such thing.'

Kristen laughed. 'You know me too well, girl.'

'Knock, knock.' Three hours later, Valerie tapped a finger on the restaurant office, where Sachiko was standing at the desk going through a stack of papers.

'Oh, hi,' Sachiko said. 'I'm trying to find the schedules I drew up for next week. Annie's taking Tuesday and Wednesday off, and I need to see if Seth can work a couple extra shifts.' She waved Valerie into the room. 'What's up?'

'May I?' Valerie asked, pulling the door shut. 'It's kind of . . . private.'

'Sure. Nothing bad, I hope.'

'It's not about me; it's actually about Seth. Remember how I was wondering if he might have recognized someone last night that he didn't want to see him?'

Sachiko nodded. 'Uh-huh.'

'So then after we closed last night, Kai told me that Seth doesn't have a credit card.'

'Yeah, I know,' said Sachiko. 'For ethical reasons – he doesn't believe in them.'

'Right. I get that that's the *excuse* he gives for it. And that he's got reasons for all the other odd things about him, too. You know, not driving and being super private because of his epilepsy.' Valerie came closer to Sachiko and lowered her voice. 'But what if that's all those things really are: excuses.'

'What do you mean?'

'I mean, what if it's all a ruse? What if he doesn't even have epilepsy – that he just made it up as a cover for all the weird things about him? What if he isn't really who he says he is?'

'That seems hard to believe,' said Sachiko, taking a seat at the desk.

'Maybe. But it would explain a lot about the guy. Kristen and I were talking about it this morning and came up with a plan to test the theory.'

'A plan?'

Valerie told Sachiko how she'd read that people with aliases tended to choose names with the same letters as their real names, and how they'd decided to have Kristen come in and try out different names around Seth that night.

'And guess what. He totally reacted to the name Simon.'

'He did? Are you sure?'

'Well, we can't be *sure*,' said Valerie. 'But he definitely froze for a second on hearing the name and then turned to look at Kristen. Whereas he had no reaction whatsoever to any of the other S names she used when he was around. So here's my question for you: What kind of ID does someone need to get a job at a restaurant here in Hawai'i?'

Sachiko didn't answer, instead turning with a frown toward the filing cabinet in the corner of the room. 'All you need is two pieces of proof,' she said after a bit. 'I think Seth had a driver's license and a birth certificate. I didn't check them out, but they seemed legit, so I just made copies for our files and then sent in the Form I-9 to the feds.' She thought a moment, then stood up. 'I technically shouldn't do this, but here. I'll show you.'

Pulling a manila folder from the filing cabinet, she flipped through the pages and handed Valerie two sheets of paper. As Sachiko had said, one was a California driver's license for Seth Warner and the other a birth certificate for a person of the same name, showing his birth year as 1983 and place of birth as Norfolk, Virginia.

'But wait; I thought he didn't drive,' said Valerie.

'Just 'cause he doesn't drive now doesn't mean he never did. Maybe he only stopped driving once his seizures became worse. Plus, lots of people have licenses who don't actually drive.'

Valerie handed the papers back with a shrug. 'Well, I'm certainly no expert on forged documents, so who knows if these are real or not. The feds don't check them out to make sure they're authentic?'

'Not as far as I know, and I can't imagine they'd have the resources to do so. In any case, no one's ever contacted us about any of our employees in the eight years I've been working here.'

'Okay, well, thanks. I'll let you know if I find out anything else.' Valerie opened the door, then quickly closed it again.

'What?' asked Sachiko.

'It was Seth, walking down the hall away from the office really fast. You think he could have been listening at the door?'

TWENTY-TWO

It was with some trepidation that Valerie pulled up a chair a few minutes later at the table with the other Gecko staff, a post-work beverage in her hand. Seth sat between Kai and Matt, regaling the group with a story about one of his customers that night – a woman from Germany who'd had a hard time understanding that no, the kālua pork was not made with Kahlua, the liqueur.

Annie barked out a laugh. 'Hey, at least she sounds like she was genuinely confused. I can't tell you how many times I've had someone from the Mainland make a stupid joke about ordering pūpūs. Like I've never heard *that* one before.'

As Valerie listened to the others' tales of quirky patrons they'd served over the years, she kept an eye on Seth. He seemed to be acting completely normal – not a bit like someone worried that a deep-dark secret concerning him was about to be revealed. But then again, she mused, if it was all a ruse and he was in fact someone other than Seth Warner, then he had to be a pretty darn good actor to have pulled it off for this long.

After a few minutes, Matt consulted his phone. 'Gotta jam,' he said. 'Jimmy and I are going to the Mauna Kea for lunch tomorrow and want to get an early start over to Kona-side.'

This prompted movement from everyone else at the table. 'Yeah, me too,' said Annie. 'Not that I'm going to a fancy restaurant tomorrow like you, but I should hit the hay.'

'And I got paddling in da morning,' Kai said, downing his IPA and tossing the bottle into the recycling bin. He turned to Valerie. 'You gonna be dere?'

'I am, indeed. And it looks like the weather should be good, which is nice.'

Seth stood as well, dropped his bottle on top of Kai's, and headed to the storage room for his bike. Waiting till he'd rounded the corner, Valerie picked up her purse, her empty bottle, and the paper cocktail napkin she'd been using and walked over to the recycling bin. Making sure no one was watching, she leaned down to deposit her own bottle inside, then quickly used the napkin to grab the ginger beer bottle Seth had been drinking from, and slid it into her bag.

'Okay, see you all tomorrow,' she said in a cheery voice and headed out the restaurant's front door.

The sidewalk was wet from an earlier rain, but the sky was clear now, and a refreshing trade wind breeze was blowing in off the ocean. Walking down Kamehameha Avenue, Valerie turned left onto Haili and headed toward home. A cluster of people were hanging around the entrance to the Palace Theater and chatting in animated voices, the last of the movie crowd, no doubt.

She waited at the signal, admiring the slashes of red and green reflected in the puddles from the theater's iconic neon sign, then crossed Keawe Street and continued on past the church and McDonald's. The rain had set off the chirping of the coquí frogs, whose chorus grew louder as she headed uphill.

Taking a deep breath, Valerie enjoyed the heady scent of pua kenikeni mixed with damp soil and smiled as she thought how very different this was from Los Angeles. Yes, she was glad to have moved here with Kristen. How marvelous to have left the traffic and smog and hustle and bustle of a city of over three million souls for quaint, rainy Hilo Town.

She'd just passed the Sack N Save grocery store and was gazing up at the stars splashed across the night sky when the squeak of a bicycle brake made her turn.

'Hey,' said Seth, rolling up onto the sidewalk behind her and dismounting. 'I thought that was you.'

'Oh, hi,' Valerie replied, trying to mask the trepidation that had come over her at his sudden appearance.

'Do you live far from here?'

'Not far. It's just a few blocks away.'

'How 'bout I keep you company? I know Hilo's considered a safe town an' all, but I'm not sure it's such a good idea for you to be walking home alone late at night.'

Not with you, *it isn't*, was her thought, which she of course kept to herself. 'Oh, that's very sweet,' she said instead, 'but I'll be fine. It's really not far, and I know you probably want to be getting home yourself.'

'No, no, I'm happy to do it.'

Damn. The last thing she wanted was to be alone with Seth right now.

Once past the next street, the neighborhood became more residential, their having now left the downtown area. Which meant less light and far fewer people about.

No one at all, in fact, she realized, glancing up and down the street.

As they walked on, Valerie saw Seth glance about him, too, as if he were also checking to see if there was anybody in the vicinity.

Huh-uh. No way.

Valerie stopped and patted her pants pockets. 'Shoot,' she said. 'I left my phone back at the restaurant. Gotta go back and get it.'

And with that, she strode off downhill, back toward the lights and the cars pulling out of the McDonald's parking lot. When she turned to look back, she saw Seth stand there a moment, then mount his bike and pedal off uphill.

On their way down to paddling the next morning, Valerie filled Kristen in on all that had happened after Kristen had left the Speckled Gecko the night before. 'Luckily, Sachiko was still at the restaurant when I got back there,' Valerie concluded, 'and she gave me a ride home, so I didn't have to worry about running into Seth again.'

Kristen pursed her lips as they pulled into the Bayfront parking lot. 'I dunno, Val . . . maybe he's right. Maybe it's not such a great idea for you to be walking home late at night after work.'

'What? You're defending *Seth*?'

'I'm not defending *him* – just that he does raise a valid point. It's not like there aren't some sketchy people who hang out downtown after dark. And if you were to take the car, I could always get a ride if I wanted to go out and do something while you were at work.'

Valerie stared at her wife a moment, then shook her head as she opened the passenger door. 'Fine. I can take the car from now on. But I think you're missing the point of this conversation – that Seth may be the one I need to be afraid of, more than any so-called "sketchy people" in Hilo.'

'No, I get that. And I'm really glad you decided to ditch the guy last night, and that Sachiko was still at the restaurant.' Kristen grabbed her paddle and followed Valerie across the parking lot to the Mahina Canoe Club's hālau. 'So what are you going to do now?'

'Give that bottle to Amy, in the hopes that the cops can run his fingerprints. Maybe they can figure out if he's really who he says he is.'

They joined Tala and Becca at the canoe house, putting an end to their discussion about Seth.

'Are we it for today?' asked Kristen, looking around for any other paddlers.

'No, Leilani and Sasha should be here soon. Ah, there they are.' Tala waved as a green Honda pulled up next to the hālau. 'But Mara's still out with that cut on her leg. You up for being steersperson again?' she asked Kristen.

'Absolutely; it was super fun last time.'

'How about the guys?' Valerie shaded her eyes from the sun and stared out at the bay, searching for any of the club's blue-and-green canoes. 'Did they already head out?'

'I think they left about an hour ago,' said Becca. 'They were going to do a long paddle today, is what I heard.'

Darn, thought Valerie, who'd been hoping for another chance to see Kai and Craig interact. Although she'd relegated both of them to pretty much the bottom of her list of suspects, she wasn't *positive* they'd had nothing to do with Hank's death, and she was still curious about the relationship between the two men.

Paddling that day was strenuous but invigorating. Tala had apparently decided that Valerie and Kristen had now passed the newbie stage, and the stroker set a vigorous pace from the get-go. By the time they'd made it past the breakwater, Valerie was breathing hard and her arms were starting to ache, but at the same time, she realized how much she needed this: the hard exercise and the camaraderie of the paddling crew. Not to mention the salt-sea tang in the air, the early morning sun sparkling off the blue-green sea, and the call of the petrels soaring above. It was the perfect way to momentarily banish from her mind thoughts of Seth and Hank and all the other stressors in her life.

Back on land, Valerie turned to Kristen, her face shining. 'That was amazing!' she said as they dragged the heavy canoe up onto the black sand beach.

'Totally. And, not that I wish Mara any ill luck with her recovery, but it sure is fun being steersperson.'

Tala slapped Kristen on her back. 'Hey, it looks like we might have enough women for a second canoe by next season. If so, I'll vote for you in that position.'

'Awesome!' said Kristen. 'I'm your gal!'

Once she'd showered and poured herself a much-needed cup of coffee, Valerie sat down after their paddling workout with her laptop to do some research. Typing 'Form I-9' into the search box, she clicked on the link that came up, which took her to the Department of Homeland Security's Employment Eligibility Verification form. As Sachiko had said, the form required only two forms of ID, including a driver's license and a birth certificate, and the employer was merely required to attest that they 'examined' the documents presented by the employee and that the documentation 'appears to be genuine and to relate to the employee named.'

More importantly, she saw, the I-9 form was not to be filed with any governmental body. All the employer was required to do was retain the form on file 'in case of an inspection' by a federal agency.

Valerie closed her computer and stared out the window at Kristen, who was tossing a tennis ball for Pua in the back yard. IDs could easily be forged, she knew, and it was doubtful that Sachiko would be able to identify a good fake. But the question was, if Seth had in fact used fake IDs to get his job at the Gecko, could that be related to Hank's death?

If Hank found out Seth's secret, it sure could. And if that were the case, and Seth had ended up killing Hank to keep him quiet, then he'd likely be willing to do the same thing again.

How much did Seth know about Valerie's sleuthing? Had he overheard her talking to Sachiko the other night? Is that why he'd followed her home last night?

I really need to watch my back, was Valerie's conclusion. *And I need to talk to Amy, pronto.*

Standing up, she grabbed a napkin and paper bag, fetched her purse, and used the napkin to transfer the bottle into the bag. Then, calling out the window to Kristen that she'd be back in a few minutes, she headed down the street to Amy's house.

The cop's gray SUV was in the driveway. *Good.* Valerie took the front steps two at a time and knocked loudly on the door.

'Hey.' Amy peered through the screen. 'C'mon in.'

'Thanks.' Valerie stepped inside and took in the room, furnished with a couch, two comfy chairs, and a coffee table covered with open books and sheets of paper.

Seeing her look, Amy picked up one of the books and showed it to Valerie: the Hawai'i *Penal Code*, annotated. 'Riveting reading,' she said with a laugh, tossing it back onto the table.

'Ah, studying for your detective's exam. Sorry to disturb you.'

'No worries. I was ready for a break. Can I get you a cup of coffee or something?'

'No, thanks. I won't stay long. I just have a question . . . or really more of a favor, to ask you. Remember that guy Seth I told you about who works at the Speckled Gecko?'

'The super sweet waiter who doesn't drive, and who you got the feeling might be hiding something?'

Valerie grinned. 'You've got a good memory. I'm guessing that test will be a breeze for ya. Anyway, yeah, that's the one. So, long story short, I think he may not be who he says he is.'

She explained what she'd seen and learned that week regarding the server: about his almost drowning her at Richardson Beach and his supposed epilepsy; his turning tail and retreating from the room where the anniversary party was going on and then suddenly leaving work; his not having a credit card; his possibly overhearing her talk to Sachiko about the paperwork he used to get the job; his reacting to the name Simon; and then, finally, his following her home from work the night before.

'Okay . . .' said Amy. 'All a bit fishy, I admit, but there's no real evidence of any wrongdoing there – just conjecture.'

'Yeah, I know.' Valerie handed her the paper bag. 'Which is why I took the bottle he was drinking from last night – so you guys could maybe see if his fingerprints match someone on the list of . . .' She stopped, not sure what the correct word was.

'Convicted felons? Warrants for arrest?' Amy filled in.

'Right. One of those.'

Amy smiled, but it seemed more a polite smile you'd give someone out of courtesy than one of actual agreement or accord. 'Look,' she said, setting the bag on the coffee table. 'I appreciate your investment in all this, but the department isn't going to do a CJIS search for prints based solely on your hunch about the guy. They'd need some actual evidence that he's committed some sort of crime.'

'Yeah, I was afraid you might say that. But I figured it was worth a shot.' Valerie bit her lip, then gestured at the paper bag. 'I'm gonna leave that with you, in any case. 'Cause you never know . . .'

'Sure, I can hold on to it, if you like.'

Valerie thanked her and then headed back home. So how could she get some actual proof?

That night at work, Seth once again seemed totally normal. He greeted Valerie with a cheery grin and asked if she'd found her phone.

'Oh . . . yeah. It was here behind the bar,' she said. 'Glad I realized when I did and was able to get back here before Sachiko shut up shop. And by the way, my wife convinced me that you were right, so you'll be glad to know I drove to work this evening.'

Flashing a boyish grin and a thumbs up, Seth headed to the pass where Valerie could hear him ask Nalani about the night's specials. She made her own way through the restaurant to the bar, where she found Jun stocking the wine fridge.

'You're here early,' she said. 'I thought you weren't coming in till five.'

'Yah, well, my wife had to be someplace at four thirty, so she dropped me off early.'

'You have your own car, though, right?'

Jun laughed. 'Course I do – a cherry Mazda CX-5. But I like her to drive me 'cause then she gotta pick me up aftah my shift. I tell her it's 'cause I don't want my car sitting on the street while I work, but you know, it keeps her outta trouble at night, yah?'

'Uh-huh,' was all Valerie could manage in response. She was

so glad she wasn't the one married to the crazy-possessive Jun. But she did very much wonder how the mysterious Sherri spent her evenings while the cat was away tending bar . . .

Being a Saturday, the Gecko did good business that night, and Valerie and Jun had their hands full mixing drinks and pulling beers for the diners in the restaurant as well as the bar patrons. By eight thirty, however – this being Hilo – the crowds had dwindled, and they were able to catch their breath. Valerie figured that was it for any new customers, but at a little before nine, she saw Seth approaching the bar.

'Got a late table,' he said with a shake of the head. 'Two Margaritas up, no salt; one draft Longboard; one Chardonnay.'

'No worries,' said Valerie, grabbing two glasses from the overhead shelf. As she mixed the drinks, Seth leaned on the bar and watched her pour tequila, lime juice, and triple sec into a metal canister over ice and shake it vigorously, then pour it into the glasses. As he reached out to place the drinks onto his bar tray, her eye was caught by the robin inked onto his forearm.

He sure didn't seem to be the birder he claimed to be, she mused as she turned to pull the Longboard Lager. So why a robin tattoo? Placing the pint glass next to the Margaritas, she glanced again at his forearm. *Could it be someone's name?*

She must have blinked or frowned or done something with her face, because at that moment, Seth, too, looked down at his forearm, and then back up at Valerie. With what she hoped was a bright smile, she said, 'Just let me get that Chard,' and fetched the bottle from the bar fridge. But when she returned with the wine glass, he was still staring at her.

Now she was truly glad she'd opted to drive that night.

Skipping the post-work drinks with the Gecko staff, Valerie headed straight home as soon as the bar was closed down for the night. Once inside, she grabbed her laptop and took it to the kitchen table. Kristen was already in bed, but Pua had rousted herself at the sound of the back door opening and, after giving Valerie a series of happy kisses, curled up at her feet and went promptly back to sleep.

Valerie opened her browser. So what did she know – or at least suspect – about Seth's 'real' identity. That his first name was 'Simon' and his last name likely started with a W. Clearly not enough to narrow down a search online. But what if she added the name 'Robin' into the mix? As well as 'San Diego'?

She typed all those things into the search bar, then hit return.

The top of the list that came up was a series of paid ads by real estate brokers. Scrolling down, she scanned the articles that followed, mostly variations on the names she'd entered – Simon Robins, Robin Simon, Robin Williams, Carly Simon . . .

But then she saw one that piqued her interest: 'San Diego Teacher Found Strangled in Pacific Beach.' Clicking the link, she read the text of the article, a piece from a San Diego newspaper dating from three years earlier, in 2015:

> Marilyn Watson, a popular local elementary school teacher, was found strangled to death in her home on Tuesday evening. Ten-year-old Robin, daughter of the deceased, discovered her mother when she was dropped off at home after soccer practice and immediately called 9-1-1, but when emergency crews arrived, Ms. Watson was declared dead at the scene. Anyone with knowledge of the whereabouts of Simon Watson, husband of the deceased, is asked to contact the San Diego Police Department.

The photo with the article included a grainy headshot of a clean-cut man with short blond hair and a baby face. Squinting, she stared at the picture, trying to envision the guy with Seth's long, dark hair and full beard and mustache. She wasn't positive, but the eyes could well be those of the Gecko server.

Whoa. Valerie sat back in her chair and took a deep breath, then saved the link from the article and texted it to Amy with the message: 'I bet this is Seth. He's from SD and has a tattoo of a robin on his arm. You think it's enough to warrant running the prints?'

TWENTY-THREE

Valerie was far too amped up to go to sleep, so she watched a couple episodes of *The Good Place* while sipping a nightcap of hot milk with brandy to try to take her mind off what she'd just learned. But it didn't work, and she found herself checking her phone every ten minutes to see if Amy had written back. *She must either be asleep or working the night shift*, Valerie concluded as midnight rolled around with still no word from the cop. *Best try to get some rest.*

Lying in bed listening to the rain drum on the metal roof, she took a series of slow breaths and willed her body to relax. But it was not to be, and the lone coquí right outside her window – which let out a resounding chirp every time she found herself finally dozing off – didn't help. Valerie was considering just getting up once again when Pua jumped up onto the bed next to her and snuggled down. *Can't disturb the dog.* So instead, she continued to lie still, thinking about Seth and his robin tattoo as both Kristen and the dog slept soundly beside her.

The next thing she knew it was morning, with the sun streaming through the window right into her eyes. Checking the clock on the bedside table, Valerie saw that it was past ten thirty. She climbed out of bed and made her way to the kitchen, where she helped herself to a cup of the coffee Kristen had brewed and then headed outside.

'Ah, there's the sleepy head!' Kristen chimed out, causing Pua to look up and thump her tail. 'Late night?'

'Uh-huh.' Valerie plopped down onto the other director's chair and took a drink from her mug. 'But it wasn't 'cause of work. Or at least not related to *my* work.' She told Kristen about her revelation about Seth's tattoo and how he'd reacted upon seeing her staring at it. 'And so I came home and did an online search and here, check out what I found.' Fetching her computer from inside, she pulled up the article she'd discovered the night before.

'Yikes,' Kristen said once she read it. 'You think this Simon Watson could be Seth?'

'I'm not positive, since the photo's kind of blurry and it's hard to tell with all that hair he has now, but I think it's probably him. Anyway, I sent the article to Amy, and I'm hoping it'll be enough for them to run the fingerprints that are on that ginger beer bottle.'

At the ringing of her cell phone, Valerie glanced at the screen and accepted the call. 'Sachiko. I was just about to phone you. What's up?'

'It's Seth—'

'Oh, no. What's he done?'

'It's what he's *not* done that's the problem,' Sachiko spat out. 'He was supposed to be here a half hour ago for his lunch shift, but he seems to have gone AWOL again. I've tried contacting him several times, but he doesn't answer his texts, and his phone just goes straight to voicemail.'

'Oh, boy . . .'

'What does that mean?'

'It's something I found out last night, which could be the reason he's a no-show.'

'Well, whatever the reason, we're now down a server and we open in fifteen minutes.' Sachiko's voice had an edge of panic to it. 'Any chance you could—'

'No worries; I'll be right down,' Valerie said. Ending the call, she looked up at Kristen with a shrug. 'Sorry, but I really think I need to get down there. Not just to help out with lunch, but also to warn Sachiko about what the heck is going on.'

Kristen was shaking her head. 'No, it's okay. I heard her end of the conversation. Go do what ya gotta do. And take the car; I don't have any plans other than lazing about here today.'

'Thank you.' Valerie stood to give her wife a kiss on the cheek, then headed indoors to change clothes.

When she got to the Gecko, Sachiko was at the hostess stand greeting customers. Valerie would have liked to fill her in right away on what she'd learned about Simon Watson, but the dining room manager was clearly far too busy to talk at that time. After seating a table of six, she gave Valerie a hurried run-down on the day's sandwich special – a Cuban sandwich made with kālua pork and mango-infused ham – and handed her a pad of guest checks. 'You'll be in the lānai, and Annie will take the dining room,' she said. 'Any questions?'

'No, I think I'll be fine. But I should warn you that I've never actually waited tables before.'

Sachiko waved a hand. 'You've been in the biz long enough that I'm sure you'll do fine. And thanks. I owe you big time. Now I gotta go deal with a clogged sink. It never rains but it pours.'

Valerie did do fine. In some ways, she found being a server easier than tending bar. There were no bottles and mixers to restock, no garnishes to slice, and nothing to prepare yourself. All you had to do was bring the already cooked and plated food to the tables. And the clientele tended to be more sober, which was a nice change from the usual bar crowd.

On the other hand, there was far more running around involved: taking orders; entering them into the POS; fetching customers' bar orders from Jun; refilling their water glasses; serving all the appetizers, mains, and desserts; clearing tables and resetting them. It was pretty exhausting, and after three hours of work she'd acquired a new respect for waitstaff the world over.

By two thirty, the place had mostly cleared out and Valerie gratefully plopped down onto a chair to drink a much-needed glass of ice water.

'I wonder if Seth will be here for his shift tonight,' said Annie, taking a seat next to her.

'I doubt it,' Valerie replied.

Sachiko joined them at the table as she made this pronouncement, raising her brows in a questioning manner. 'Why do you say that?'

'Because I'm guessing he figured out that I'm finally in on his big secret, and so he made a run for it.' She explained to Annie and Sachiko what she'd guessed about Seth and then pulled out her phone to show them the article she'd discovered.

'Ohmygod,' said Annie. 'You think we've been working the past two years with a *murderer*?' She glanced about her. 'Do you think it's safe being here at the restaurant?'

'I can't imagine him coming back at this point,' said Valerie. 'I think his noticing me checking out his tattoo last night must have spooked him. The last straw, or whatever – especially if he did in fact hear you and me talking about him the other night – and so he took off. I'm betting he's somewhere down in Puna – or maybe even in Honolulu by now.'

'Do you think we should tell the police?' Sachiko said, handing Valerie's phone back to her.

'I already did. I sent that article last night to my friend Amy who's a cop. And I also gave her a bottle Seth had been drinking from, so hopefully they can run it for fingerprints and we can settle this once and for all. What?' asked Valerie, seeing Sachiko let out a sigh. 'Really, I don't think we need to worry about his coming back at this point.'

'And that's the problem,' said Sachiko. 'I know this whole thing is far bigger than the Speckled Gecko, but the bottom line – for me, at least – is that it looks like we're gonna be down a server again for dinner.' She turned to Valerie with a pleading look. 'Any chance you could come in tonight?'

'Sure. In for a dime, in for a dollar.'

Valerie had just enough time to shower, take Pua for a quick walk, and then spend a few minutes off her feet doing the Sunday crossword puzzle before having to return to work. She'd written Amy a follow-up text after her lunch shift at the Gecko, but there'd still been no answer, and her car had been gone when Valerie and Pua had passed by her house on their walk.

Back at work at four thirty, she was surprised to see Jun tying on the short apron that the Gecko servers wore. 'I thought I was on the floor tonight,' she said to the bartender.

'Nah, I got this. I used to wait tables back in the day, so I'm happy to fill in tonight. You go ahead and take bar duty.'

'Thanks, I appreciate it. Though I wouldn't be surprised if it was Sachiko who put you up to this after my stint as a server at lunch today.'

Jun didn't respond to Valerie's implied question, but the grin he shot back suggested she might indeed be right.

The bar traffic that Sunday night was mercifully light – though Jun still razzed her about taking too long to get his table orders filled. In turn, she gave him grief for not doing enough to push her drink special for the night: a Broke da Mouth cocktail of spiced rum, lemon juice, and ginger ale, with a pineapple garnish.

At a little after eight o'clock, seeing that the bar customers all had drinks and the dining room had mostly thinned out, Valerie took the opportunity to empty the overflowing trash. Swinging the black plastic bag over her shoulder, she opened the back door and carried the garbage outside. It was now dark, the sun setting quickly in the tropics, but a dim outdoor light lit up the dumpster which abutted the building, casting Valerie's shadow out into the street.

She set down the garbage to heft open the dumpster's heavy lid, then reached down for the bag's strings. But as she leaned forward, she saw a second shadow rise up in front of her. *What the—?*

Before she could react or call out, something was thrown around her neck. Reaching up, she managed to get two fingers under what felt like a necktie or thin scarf as it was tightened from behind.

'You think you're so smart,' a voice hissed into her ear. 'But all you've done is cause even more grief.' The tightening had now lessened, though Valerie was still unable to speak or turn around. But she knew who it was.

There was a pause, and then Seth went on in a shaky voice. 'All I wanted was to live out the rest of my life doing good. To atone for my sins and do my best to help other people. But no, then Hank had to ruin it all by blackmailing me. And then *you* came along. What business was it even for you?'

Was he *crying*?

Valerie wriggled her fingers, trying to turn her hand sideways to make more room between the scarf and her throat, but at her movement, Seth tightened the cord once again.

'And now I have to decide what to do with you. Which really pisses me off, 'cause the last thing I wanted was to hurt anyone else.'

'Ahggghhh . . .' was all she managed in response.

Seth grew quiet, and Valerie could feel his body shaking, as if he were trying to hold back sobs. 'I actually liked you,' he said after a bit. 'You seemed like a nice lady.'

Not good, his using the past tense.

'But I guess you don't really leave me with much choice . . .'

A light suddenly switching on at the end of the block made

Seth look up and loosen his grip, at which point Valerie managed to swing around and give him a hard knee to the groin.

As he dropped to the ground with a low moan, the light came closer. A flashlight beam, she now saw.

'Police! Don't move!'

Valerie raised her arms in the air and turned slowly toward the voice.

'Not you. Him!'

But Seth wasn't going anywhere any time soon. As he rolled onto his back, hands over his crotch, the cop came running up to Valerie. 'Are you okay?'

'Yeah, I think so,' she coughed out, gingerly touching her neck. 'Thank god you happened to come by just now.'

'It wasn't just happenstance. We were staking out the restaurant.'

At his glance toward the other end of the block, Valerie looked up to see Amy striding her way. 'The fingerprints,' Valerie said. 'You must have run them.'

'We did indeed. What a surprise to discover the guy's wanted for murder in San Diego. Or maybe not so much of a surprise,' she added with a wry smile in Valerie's direction. 'And when we didn't find him at home, we figured this was the next most likely place he'd show up.'

'Only 'cause he wanted to silence me,' said Valerie. She turned to the still prone Seth. 'You could've been all the way to the Mainland by now if you hadn't come back for me. So much for your wanting to do no harm.'

The next morning, there was a knock on Valerie and Kristen's screen door. 'Hey, Amy,' said Valerie. 'Come on in. Want some coffee?'

'Yes, please. I was worried you might still be in bed, after all that happened last night.'

Valerie led Amy into the kitchen and poured her a mug of coffee. 'Well, I am a bit groggy this morning. Staying up late giving a statement to the police isn't particularly conducive to a good night's sleep, but I was actually up pretty early.'

The two joined Kristen out on the lānai, Amy taking the second director's chair, Valerie stretched out in the sun next to Pua on the wood planks. 'So,' said Valerie, 'are you at liberty to tell me what, if anything, Seth – I mean, Simon – said last night?'

'I don't see why not, since he blurted it out for the whole world to hear. I think he realized the jig was up and he might as well come clean. Or maybe his conscience just finally kicked in. In any case, long story short, he apparently was blotto drunk when he killed his wife and, after fleeing to Hawai'i with a new identity, vowed to live a so-called "good" life. He joined AA, started volunteering for charities, riding his bike instead of driving . . .'

'But I thought that was all just a ruse because of his saying he had epilepsy,' said Valerie. 'Did he actually have it?'

'No, I don't think so. That was the excuse he came up with for not driving, since he couldn't get a valid driver's license – and for being super private about his life.'

So he had *been trying to drown me, after all*, thought Valerie with a shudder.

Amy continued on: 'But from what he said last night, the guy does seem to truly care about all that stuff. Maybe not being able to drive or have a credit card made him become more concerned about the world at large? Or maybe he truly did want redemption. Who knows?

'But then Hank found out who he really was. I'm not sure exactly how, but since you figured it out, he could have, too. But Hank's mistake was that he tried blackmailing the guy. And then at that retreat up at Boiling Pots, Hank told him that he'd decided to tell the police what he knew. I guess he'd just had some kind of argument with Sachiko and took out his anger on Seth. Bad timing that.'

'Yep,' said Valerie. 'And so let me guess: he knocks Hank over the head with a rock.'

'Right you are. They were up by the overlook all alone, so once Seth – or, rather, Simon – realized that he'd killed Hank, he shoved his body into the vegetation on the other side of the railing where no one could see him, then came back after dark and dragged the body down the hill and pushed it into the river.'

'Did you ask about that carved fox they found in Hank's pocket?'

'It wasn't me asking the questions, but yeah, the lead investigator did. He said he found the fox the night before on the sidewalk as he was leaving work and had been planning on returning it to Sachiko at the retreat but forgot to do so. But then he gets the idea of planting it on Hank's body to place suspicion for his death on Sachiko.'

'Yep, a real "good" guy, all right,' said Kristen with a sneer.

Amy took a sip of coffee and set the mug down on the table. 'So, anyway,' she went on, 'it turns out you were right, Valerie – about pretty much everything.' And then she laughed. 'Maybe it should be you who takes the detective examination instead of me. You seem to be pretty good at this investigation stuff.'

'Thanks but no thanks. I'm plenty busy as it is without taking on a new job. Speaking of which.' She turned to Kristen. 'I'm gonna tell Sachiko that as soon as she finds people to replace Hank and Seth, I'm cutting back to just two nights a week, max. If she still wants me after they get a new bartender, that is. I definitely need some more time with my wife, now that we're living the retired life here in Hilo.'

'Oh, she'll still want you, I'm sure,' said Kristen with a grin. 'Not only did you just save her from a possible murder rap, but I happen to know you make one mean Hawai'i Island Iced Tea.'

RECIPES

HILO SUNSET
(makes one cocktail)

This is Valerie's local riff on the Tequila Sunrise, substituting gin for the tequila, tangerine for the orange juice, and Campari and triple sec for the grenadine syrup. Tangerines are grown in many yards in East Hawai'i and are thus easy to find there, but feel free to substitute orange juice if you like.

Ingredients

6–8 ice cubes
2 oz gin
½ oz (1 tablespoon) triple sec
1 oz (2 tablespoons) tangerine juice
2 teaspoons Campari
1 slice tangerine
1 Maraschino cherry

Directions

Place the ice in a metal cocktail shaker, add the gin, triple sec, and tangerine juice, and shake until well-chilled. Pour everything (including ice) into a highball glass, then top with the Campari (don't stir; let the Campari float down on its own to create the 'sunset' effect). Garnish with the tangerine slice and cherry.

JAPANESE-STYLE EGG 'SANDO'
(makes 2 sandwiches)

This creamy egg salad sandwich (tamago sando) is hugely popular in Japan, where it's commonly sold as a grab-and-go item at convenience stores such as 7-Eleven. What differentiates the egg 'sando' from your typical American egg salad sandwich is its yolk-to-white ratio (heavy on the yolks), the use of Kewpie Japanese mayonnaise (made with yolks only, as well as a special blend of vinegar and spices, which makes for a flavor high in umami), the hit of cream or milk, and the use of fluffy white milk bread.

Can you say heaven?

Kewpie mayonnaise can be found in the Asian food aisle of most supermarkets, or online. (Note that there are two varieties of Kewpie mayo – the Japanese one with a hugging baby on the label, and an American version depicting a sandwich. Make sure to buy the Japanese version.)

If you can't locate any Japanese milk bread (sometimes called by its Japanese name, Shokupan), your two best options are either brioche-style sandwich bread (which, like milk bread, contains dairy for added richness but is sweeter than milk bread), or plain old American-style white bread (which isn't as sweet as brioche but lacks the fluffy-mouth feel of milk bread and brioche).

Ingredients

5 large eggs, at room temperature
¼ cup Kewpie mayonnaise
¼ teaspoon salt
½ teaspoon white sugar
⅛ teaspoon black pepper
2 teaspoons cream or milk
1 tablespoon butter, softened (optional)
4 slices Japanese milk bread (Shokupan bread)

Directions

Bring a large saucepan of water to a boil over medium-high heat, then gently lower the eggs into the water. Cook for 11 minutes. While the eggs are cooking, prepare a bowl of ice water. Remove the eggs from the pan into the water bath and let them sit until they are cool, about 15 minutes. Dry and peel the eggs.

Break open the eggs with your hands and separate the whites and yolks. Mash the yolks in a bowl with a fork until only a few chunks remain. Finely chop the egg whites.

Add the mayonnaise, salt, sugar, and pepper to the yolks and stir, allowing some chunks to remain (you don't want it to be a paste).

Add half of the chopped egg whites to the yolk mixture and gently stir in. (Save other half of whites for another use.) Chill for about an hour.

Stir the cream or milk into the egg mixture, then season with more salt, if necessary, to taste.

Trim the crust off the bread and, if using butter, spread it evenly on all four slices. Top two of the buttered slices with the egg mixture, then place the other slices of bread (butter side down) on top. Cut sandwiches in half diagonally and serve.

CELERY SALAD WITH WALNUTS, DATES, AND PECORINO
(serves 6–8)

This is one of Valerie's go-to potluck dishes, as it can sit for a fair amount of time without losing its crunch, and the unusual combination of ingredients makes for a distinctive and flavorful salad. Be prepared to give out the recipe to all the people who will surely ask for it!

Ingredients

1 cup raw walnuts
1 small shallot, minced (about 1 tablespoon)
2 tablespoons sherry vinegar
2 tablespoons walnut oil
2 tablespoons extra-virgin olive oil
salt and black pepper
1 bunch celery, sliced thinly on the bias
½ cup dried pitted dates, thinly sliced
3 oz Pecorino cheese, shaved with a vegetable peeler

Directions

Preheat oven to 350°F.

Spread walnuts out in a single layer on a rimmed baking sheet and toast until browned and fragrant, about 7–10 minutes. *Watch carefully, as they can burn quickly*. Remove nuts from oven and, once cooled, coarsely chop.

Combine the shallot, vinegar, and oils in a bowl and whisk well. Season with salt and pepper to taste.

In a large bowl, toss the celery, dates, and walnuts together. Whisk the dressing one more time, then add to the salad and toss. If you're making composed salads, plate up the individual dishes and then top with the shaved cheese. If you're serving it family-style in a large bowl, add the cheese along with the dates and walnuts.

KALBI RIBS
(serves 4)

Kalbi (also known as 'galbi') ribs are Korean-style barbecued ribs, made with flanken-cut short ribs. Because flanken ribs are sliced across the bone using a band saw, it's a thin cut of meat which efficiently absorbs the tasty marinade and cooks up quickly on the grill.

This sweet and savory dish is hugely popular in Hawai'i, and often served as part of the traditional 'plate lunch,' which generally consists of a meat (such as kālua pork, Korean chicken, or kalbi ribs), two scoops of white rice, and a scoop of Hawaiian-style mac or potato salad.

Note that mirin, a sweetened Japanese rice wine, is readily available in the Asian food aisle of most supermarkets.

Ingredients

3 pounds flanken-cut beef short ribs
¾ cup soy sauce
½ cup brown sugar
3 tablespoons mirin
1 tablespoon toasted sesame oil
1 tablespoon sesame seeds
3-inch piece ginger, finely chopped (about 3 tablespoons)
4 cloves garlic, finely chopped
1 small yellow onion, finely grated or chopped
6 green onions, coarsely chopped
½ teaspoon black pepper

Directions

Combine in a large baking dish all the ingredients except the ribs and three of the green onions. Add the ribs, pressing down to ensure they are completely submerged in the marinade. If necessary, add enough water so the liquid covers the meat. (Alternatively, place ribs in a large freezer bag with the marinade, pressing out all the air before sealing.) Cover and marinate in the refrigerator at least 12 hours and up to 3 days.

Remove from the fridge at least a half hour before cooking, to allow the ribs to come to room temperature.

Shake excess marinade off the ribs (discard remaining marinade) and grill on a medium-hot gas or charcoal barbecue (or broil on high in the oven, if you prefer), turning once, until desired doneness – about 3 to 4 minutes per side.

Serve with steamed white rice, garnished with the remaining 3 chopped green onions.

UBE BLONDIES
(makes one 9x13-inch pan)

Ube is the Filipino word for purple yam, and when made into a jam (ube halaya) or mashed with sweetened condensed milk, the tuber is used in a variety of delicious desserts such as cake, ice cream, cookies, cheesecake, and flan. Ube was first brought to Hawai'i by sugarcane workers from the Philippines, and has now become an integral part of the local cuisine on the islands.

These purple blondies are sweet and chewy, and because of how rich they are, one small piece goes a long way. (Note: the bright purple ube extract is liable to stain, so have care when using it.)

Both ube halaya and ube extract can be purchased at Filipino/ Asian markets, as well as online.

Ingredients

butter or vegetable oil for greasing pan
½ pound (2 sticks) unsalted butter, melted
1 cup white sugar
¼ cup brown sugar, packed
1 large egg
12 oz (1½ cups) ube jam (ube halaya)
2 tablespoons ube extract
2½ cups all-purpose flour
1 teaspoon baking powder
1 teaspoon salt
1 cup white chocolate chips

Directions

Preheat oven to 350°F.

Grease a 9x13-inch baking pan with butter or vegetable oil.

In a large bowl, combine the melted butter, white sugar, and brown sugar until the sugars have dissolved.

Add the egg, ube jam, and ube extract to the butter/sugar mixture and stir until well-combined. Add the flour, baking powder, and salt and stir until no significant streaks of flour remain. (The batter will be thick.) Fold in the white chocolate chips until evenly distributed.

Dump the batter into the greased baking pan and spread it out evenly with a spatula. Bake for 30–40 minutes, until a toothpick inserted into the middle comes out clean.

Cool for 20 minutes, then cut into squares.

GLOSSARY OF HAWAIIAN AND PIDGIN WORDS AND PHRASES

(Hawaiian words are in italics)

'ae?	right?, you know?
aftah	afterwards
a hui hou	until we meet again
'āina	land
ama	outrigger
anoddah	another
'apapane	Hawaiian honeycreeper (*Himatione sanguinea*)
auright	all right
'awa	kava
brah, braddah	pal, friend, brother
broke da mout'	used to describe delicious food
cuz	endearing term for buddy, friend
da	the
da kine	the thing, person, place, event – something you can't think of the word for
dass	that's
dat	that
dere	there
den	then

dey	they
dis	this
e hele kākou	let's get going
e'ry	every
get	have
grindz	food
hālau	school, group, canoe club house
hāpu'u	tree fern native to Hawai'i
haole	foreigner, usually of European descent
hele on	let's get moving, get out of here
howzit	how's it going?
huli	turn, rotate, overturn
'iako	boom of an outrigger canoe
'i'iwi	scarlet honeycreeper (*Drepanis coccinea*) native to Hawai'i
jam	get going
kāhili	ceremonial pole decorated with feathers, kind of ginger plant
kālua pork	traditional Hawaiian dish of pork steamed in *ti* leaves
kama'āina	Hawaiian resident, local (lit., 'of the land')
kay	okay
killah, killahz	killer, great
kine	kind, sort
kukui	candlenut plant, whose nut is eaten and also burned to provide light

kumiai	neighborhood association
lānai	porch, veranda
latahz	see you later
lauhala	leaves of the *hala* (*Pandanus tectorius*) tree, used for weaving
lau lau	steamed pork and fish wrapped in *ti* leaves
li' dat	like that
liliko‘i	passion fruit
loco moco	white rice topped with hamburger patty, gravy, and fried egg
lomi lomi salmon	raw, marinated salmon dish (from *lomi lomi* – a kind of Hawaiian massage)
lumpia	Filipino fried spring roll
mahina	moon
māhū	gay, third gender (lit., 'in the middle')
mālama ‘āina	care for the land
malihini	newcomer
manjū	Japanese confection of pastry and filling
mochi	Japanese sweet made from glutinous rice, sugar, and corn starch
musubi	rice ball with vegetables or meat (often Spam), wrapped in nori seaweed
noni	plant whose stinky fruit is used for medicinal purposes
no worry, beef curry	don't sweat it

no wayz	no way
oddah	other
'ohana	family
'ōhelo	shrub (*Vaccinium calycinum*) endemic to Hawai'i with edible berries
'ōhi'a	flowering tree in the myrtle family, important in Hawaiian culture
one	a
'ono	delicious
pakalolo	marihuana, pot, grass
pali	cliff
Pele	the Hawaiian volcano goddess
pilau	dirty
poi	Polynesian staple food made from pounding and fermenting taro root
poke	diced raw fish, often made with ahi tuna
primo	the best
pua kenikeni	tropical tree (*Fagraea berteroana*) with highly perfumed blossoms
pua	flower
pūpū	appetizer
saimin	Hawaiian noodle soup, similar to ramen
shaka	friendly hand gesture meaning 'hang loose,' 'thank you,' 'cheers'
shoots	darn, dang
shoyu	soy sauce

sistah	sister, female friend, pal
slippahs	flip-flops, rubber slippers
stuffs	things
talk story	chat
ti	tropical plant (*Cordyline fruticosa*) of great cultural significance to Hawaiians
tink	think
uku	a lot
'um	him, it, them
wahine	woman
wen'	used to form past tense of verbs (e.g., he wen' eat – he ate)

Acknowledgments

Many people assisted in the process that led to this book finally being in print. Thanks, first, to my beta readers, Robin McDuff, Nancy Lundblad, and Māhealani Jones, who were the first to see the manuscript and provide their thoughtful feedback. Thanks also to my fellow Hawai'i crime writers, Jane Hoff and Frankie Bow, for helping me brainstorm plot ideas way back in the early stages of the process, and to Shirley Tessler for once again acting as my recipe editor.

Several folks were kind enough to share with me their specialized knowledge: Christine Reed, owner of Basically Books (employment laws in Hawai'i); Robin McDuff (construction); and Norbert Furumo and Michael Shintaku (paddling). In addition, a big mahalo to Officer Ali'i Kuamo'o of the Hawai'i Police Department for giving me a tour of the Hilo Police Station, and to both him and Officer Darryl Castillo, for patiently answering my questions about the workings of the department. (Any remaining errors regarding any of these matters, however, are entirely mine.)

My heartfelt thanks also go out to my amazing agent, Erin Niumata of Folio Literary, and to everyone at Severn House, including editors Rachel Slatter, Tina Pietron, Lianne Slavin, and Eleanor Smith, senior brand manager Martin Brown, and cover designer Piers Tilbury. I can't tell you how much it means to know you all believe in me.

Finally, I'm sending big love to my fellow bloggers at Chicks on the Case (Ellen Byron, Jennifer Chow, Becky Clark, Vickie Fee, Cynthia Kuhn, Lisa Q. Mathews, and Kathleen Valenti) and at Mystery Lovers' Kitchen (Leslie Budewitz, Lucy Burdette, Valerie Burns, Peg Cochran, Maya Corrigan, Cleo Coyle, Vicki Delany, Libby Klein, Molly MacRae, Edith Maxwell, and Korina Moss). It's wonderful to know you always have my back.

About the author

The daughter of a law professor and a potter, **Leslie Karst** is the author of *Molten Death* and the Lefty Award-nominated Sally Solari culinary mysteries, as well as the IBPA Ben Franklin and IPPY silver award-winning memoir, *Justice is Served: A Tale of Scallops, the Law, and Cooking for RBG.*

Leslie waited tables and sang in a new wave rock band before deciding she was ready for a "real" job and ending up at Stanford Law School. It was during her career as a research and appellate attorney in Santa Cruz, California that she rediscovered her youthful passion for food and cooking, at which point she once again returned to school – this time to earn a degree in culinary arts.

Now retired from the law, in addition to writing, Leslie spends her days cooking (and eating!), gardening, cycling, and observing cocktail hour promptly at five o'clock. She and her wife and their Jack Russell mix split their time between Hilo, Hawai'i and Santa Cruz, California.

www.lesliekarstauthor.com